ROYAL BOROUGH OF GREENWICH

ELTHAM
CENTRE
LIBRARY
0203 915 43

KT-493-715

Please return by the last date shown

'It's breath-taking stuff, handled with the daring and pace demanded by the risks of such storytelling. Things don't get much more original than this.'
BOOKS FOR KEEPS

'A celebration of all forms of diversity, a joyful call to inclusion [and] Yaba Badoe's love-song.'
BORDERS LITERATURE

'A memorable, haunting young adult tale.'
THE BOOKBAG

'Issues like the migrant crisis exist side by side with magic to create something unique.'
THE ROARING BOOKWORM

'A rich and vibrant YA novel...
definitely one to watch.'
ASKEWS CHILDREN'S NEWSLETTER

GREENWICH LIBRARIES

3 8028 02383562 9

'Yaba Badoe's novel deftly entwines some of the tropes of the fairy-tale tradition with the tragic realities of Europe's contemporary migrant situation... one of the most interesting and unusual debuts I've read for a while. Badoe throws you straight into the action and yet manages to also infuse the story with magical qualities.'
CHILDTASTIC BOOKS

'One of the best pieces of storytelling I have read in a long while. Our protagonist Sante is phenomenal and amazing.'
JUDITH MOORE, CHAIN INTERACTION

'A book that is haunting, seamless and a rare kind of brilliance. Once I started reading I couldn't put it down.'
MEGAN CONLAN, MOO MOO BOOKS

'A wonderful book, rich with magic and folklore while successfully tackling the subject of human trafficking.'
JO BOYLES, WATERSTONES SALISBURY

'An ambitious, diverse and challenging novel, the like of which I'm really pleased to see in YA. It's vastly different to anything else being marketed at teens and also features plenty to engage an adult reader.'
KATY GOODWIN-BATES, FOURTH AND SYCAMORE

A JIGSAW of
FIRE and STARS

YABA BADOE
is an award-winning, Ghanaian-British
documentary film-maker and writer.
In 2014 Yaba was nominated for the
Distinguished Woman of African
Cinema award.

A JIGSAW
of
FIRE
and
STARS

YABA BADOE

ZEPHYR
An imprint of Head of Zeus

First published in the UK in 2017 by Zephyr,
an imprint of Head of Zeus, Ltd. This paperback
edition first published in the UK in 2018 by Zephyr.

Text copyright © Yaba Badoe, 2017
Artwork copyright © Leo Nickolls, 2017

The moral right of Yaba Badoe to be identified as the author
and Leo Nickolls to be indentified as the artist of
this work has been asserted in accordance with the
Copyright, Designs and Patents Act of 1988.

All rights reserved. No part of this publication may be
reproduced, stored in a retrieval system, or transmitted in any form
or by any means, electronic, mechanical, photocopying, recording, or
otherwise, without the prior permission of both the copyright owner
and the above publisher of this book.

This is a work of fiction. All characters, organisations,
and events portrayed in this novel are either products of
the author's imagination or are used fictitiously.

9 7 5 3 1 2 4 6 8

A catalogue record for this book is available from
the British Library.

ISBN (PB): 9781786695499
ISBN (E): 9781786695475

Typeset by Adrian McLaughlin
Designed by Louise Millar

Printed and bound in Great Britain by
CPI Group (UK) Ltd, Croydon CR0 4YY

Head of Zeus Ltd
First Floor East,
5–8 Hardwick Street,
London EC1R 4RG

WWW.HEADOFZEUS.COM

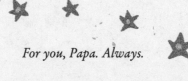

For you, Papa. Always.

GREENWICH LIBRARIES	
WO	
3 8028 02383562 9	
Askews & Holts	23-Nov-2018
JF B BLUE	£7.99
5900408	

I

There's only one thing makes any sense when I wake from my dream. I'm a stranger and shouldn't be here. Should my luck run out, a black-booted someone could step on me and crush me, as if I'm worth less than an ant. This I know for a fact. And yet once or twice a week, the dream seizes me and shakes me about:

'*Kill 'em! Kill 'em! Take their treasure!*' *The order goes out and a dilapidated trawler in a stormy sea shudders. An iron-grey vessel, lights blazing, rams it a second time. The iron monster backs away, then with engines at full throttle, lunges again.*

Faces contort. Old ones, young ones, men and women, brown and black faces. Screams punch through the air. Fishing nets tangle, spill over. A fuel tank explodes and the sea glows, roiling with blood and oil.

Below deck, a stench like an over-ripe mango oozes

from a crouched woman. She shrieks: 'My baby! My baby! Save my baby!'

A tall man responds with a command: 'The sea-chest. Fetch our treasure. Quickly. For the child's sake. Move.'

A figure tumbles into the sea. Then an old man, a girl in his arms, leaps. A deafening jumble of sound and sea swallows the cries of the drowning. The slip-slip-patter of bare feet on galley stairs ascend. Anxious eyes flit in faces bright with fear in the flame-light.

The hand of the tall man pummels a pillow of yellow dust, then a footrest filled with glittering stones for the baby's feet. Someone folds a cloth, a fine tapestry of blue and green, into a blanket.

'Give her this,' says a burly, bald-headed man. 'My dagger to help her in battle. May the child be a princess, a true warrior, valiant in the face of danger yet merciful to those she defeats.'

'May your spear arm be strong, my daughter,' the tall man adds. 'Your legs swift as a gazelle's, and your heart the mighty heart of a lioness protecting her cubs.'

The petrified woman scribbles a note and hides it beneath the pillow, whispering a prayer. 'May our ancestors watch over you, my child. May the creator of all life guide you and make you wily in the ways of the world we are sending you to.'

The grey vessel, a trail of carnage in its wake, surges forwards with a splutter of gunfire. Bullets splinter the deck, tearing it open, and the trawler erupts in flames.

The tall man grabs the baby and bundles her into the chest. He holds it aloft and flings it into the sea. It lurches and almost capsizes. The baby gurgles, entranced by the rough play of water as a wave steadies her boat. She smiles, a jigsaw of fire and stars reflected in her eyes, and she stretches a dimpled hand to touch the moon.

Burning timber from the trawler's bow crashes down and splashes the baby's face. Enchanted by flying embers, she coos. But when the sobs of the dying reach her, and waves stifle their gasps, she begins to whimper.

And, flung to and fro, bobs up and down, crying in the night.

2

It took me a while to realise the baby was me. Even now, when I wake in a sweat, chest heaving, hands clammy, and Cobra tells me to relax – I'm just having another nightmare – I still can't quite believe it's me in the water.

What I know to be true is that, for as long as I can remember, we've been on the move: Cat, Cobra and me. We roam from place to place, spending more time in the spaces in between than in the cities. Yet when I wake up frightened and confused, all it takes is Priss to hiss in my ear, to twist my hair around and make a nest of it, to calm me.

It's thanks to Priss that I've figured out as much as I have. The first time I tore myself out of that dream and found enough words on my tongue to tell her about it, she suspected who I was straightaway, because she knows what happened next.

She found me in the water. There was a mist next morning. One of those whirling sea-fog days that makes it hard to tell where shoreline begins and sea ends. A sort of blurring where time seems to stop. It was like that when Priss, flying beneath a cloud, sees this big chest. She sees it, then hears a baby crying. Swoops to take a closer look. Lands on me, almost tipping me over, so tries again.

Second time round, she steadies herself, and settles just below my feet. Talons scratch me and I squeal. She could tell I needed feeding, 'cause after I squeal, I start shrieking louder than a banshee. Priss doesn't know what do. She's a bird, a bright golden eagle. Eats rabbits and rats, and, when she's lucky, small flying creatures on the wing. There's a whole heap of things she can eat. Could have eaten a baby, I suppose. Fact remains she liked the look of me: black face, big eyes. Just couldn't figure out how to feed me. So she brushes a golden wing over my face. The musty scent of her feathers, the soft swish and tickle of their kiss, quieten me.

There are two of us now, Priss and me in the chest, as it drifts to the shore. The tide recedes, wedging us on a slipstream of seaweed. Priss watches over me while, rattled by hunger, I cry myself to sleep.

A little later, a spaniel scampers up the beach and starts sniffing around the chest. Priss squawks, flapping her wings. She's so fierce the dog cringes and scrambles away. I wake up and begin to howl.

The owner of the dog hears me, a fat giant of a woman. Black hair, rosy cheeks, hands as wide as a bat's wing. The dog leaps ahead of her and she follows, flipper feet pounding the shore.

Priss won't let anyone touch me. She just won't let 'em. Scraps with the dog, screeches at the woman. But the woman inches closer: 'Easy, my pretty. What have you got there? Easy, girl…'

By now I'm busting a gut with my howling, and because she's beginning to understand just how hungry I am, Priss yields. Hopping from one foot to the other, she stays close. Says she would have pecked out their eyes, the woman and the dog's, plucked them out and eaten 'em just like that, if they'd hurt me.

The woman lifts me up: 'Little one,' she says. 'My precious…'

Her dark, pebbled eyes loom over me. Sticky-out ears, stringy hair. She's no beauty, but Priss can see she cares. I stop crying as she holds me tight to her chest, the way mothers are supposed to. And when I snuffle up against her and dive down, rummaging for breast, something to suck on to take away the ache in my belly, Priss can see she was right to let her come near. I need to feed.

Not yet. The woman wants to know more.

'Quiet now,' she says. And slinging me over her shoulder, patting me all the while, stoops to inspect my sea-chest cradle.

She fingers the blue-green blanket, savours the silky-smooth waft and weft of its weave. Finds a dagger, a leopard-skin drum. Beside the drum, a thin bamboo flute. Then she lifts the pillow and sees the note. Reads it. Looks inside the pillow and her mouth opens wide. 'Buttercups and daisies,' she says. 'Well, I never! Who would have thought it, Mama Rose? Who would believe it?'

She drags the chest into a patch of tall grass and hides it. Takes me home and Priss follows. Won't let me out of her sight, not for a moment. It's been like that ever since.

Before I had memory, I had Priss.

She was with me before my dreams began.

And before I landed on the seashore and Mama Rose took me in, there was Cobra and Cat.

3

They don't look like me. None of 'em do. Cat and Cobra are brown skins. Brown, the colour of wheat burning in the midday sun, green eyes vivid as beech leaves in water. Long-limbed, they walk tall, black hair cut short, slicked up in spikes. Twins, Mama Rose calls them. 'Found them in the forest,' she says. 'Would have turned out wilder than polecats if I hadn't fed and clothed them. Same goes for you, Sante,' she tells me.

Today, soon as we wake, Mama Rose says: 'Clean up, you three. We hit the road in an hour. Should reach the city in two. And by evening, if we're lucky, we'll be back in clover.'

'Back in clover' is her way of saying we need money. A lot of it: *dinero*, *pasta*, *rupees*. I know the slang for money in fifteen different languages, the word for police in twenty. Just as well, 'cause getting back in clover usually means trouble.

I sigh. Guzzle a hunk of bread, boil water for the Old Ones to drink, and use what's left over to splash my face clean. Then I lure Taj Mahal, our horse, into his trailer and we pack up. Put the cast-iron pot in the back of the truck with Mama Rose's silver spoons, tin plates for us, a bone china one for Mama; the very last one.

I stamp out the embers of the fire and jump in the front of the truck with Cat. Mama Rose is at the wheel, Cobra behind. Redwood and Bizzie Lizzie, Midget Man and Mimi – the rest of our crew – bring up the rear, while straight ahead Priss blazes a trail on a hot current of wind.

The way I am with her, I can almost feel the wind whistling through her feathers. What she sees she tells me with tremors of her wing, an upward jerk of her beak, a dip of her head. Beyond the fir trees are rolling hills of olive groves, silver leaves whispering to the breeze. And in the far distance, fields of sunflowers clamour at the sun. We're in the foothills of southern Spain, on our way to the city of Cádiz to ply our trade.

We're travellers. Not your usual kind of travellers. I mean, we're not tourists or hippy-dippy types or anything. Nothing like that. We're travellers with an itch to camp in out of the way places. We live off the grid as much as possible, 'cause the Old Ones and Priss like to breathe clean country air and do things their way. No interference from black-boots. No electricity, no gas bills. No tax to pay. No computers, television or phones. Hand-me-down clothes when we need 'em from thrift shops. Makes us hardy. Survivors. 'Prepared for every eventuality,' Redwood says.

Redwood, our teacher, is a Harvard man. The son of a preacher, he knows the ins and outs and contradictions of the Bible and other holy books better than the back of his hand. Took to the road on principle: 'The way the world's going, kid, best to be roving with the sun on our faces, a fair wind behind us.'

Mama Rose is the same. Used to be rich but gave away a fortune to travel. 'Best keep to ourselves,' is her mantra as well. 'Live free, forever free!'

Fine words when there's a warm wind behind us. But on cold days when my bones are rattling, I'm like a bird that's hurt its wing. How can I fly free and know where I'm heading when I haven't a clue where I come from?

We tend to stay out of sight until we need to stock up on food and diesel, then we become circus folk: freaks with a mission to entertain. Mama Rose has webbed hands and mermaid feet. Redwood swears he's the Tallest Man on Earth, Midget Man the smallest. Claim their wives are the tallest and smallest too.

Cobra, Cat and me weren't born different like they were: eight fingers, two thumbs, ten toes. We're the regular shape and height for youngsters our age. I may be a bit on the scrawny side, but even though Cobra and Cat are bigger than me, I'm catching up fast.

Spain's hot. Hotter than France where we travelled last summer, but cooler than Greece. Had to get out of Greece fast.

I look at Priss in the sky to shake off the memory, but before I can blink it away, it has me in its claws and I hear them yelling: 'Parasites! Gypsies! Scroungers!'

Black-booted men, mouths twisted in fury, pursue us: 'Go back where you came from! Get away from here!'

I shiver, remembering their blurred faces, the venom in their eyes.

Mama Rose shoved me in the back of the truck while Midget Man bellowed: 'We work for our living, we do! We work hard, just like you!'

Didn't stop 'em hating us. Didn't stop 'em chasing us out of town.

Ignorance, Mama Rose calls it. Redwood puts it down to fear and superstition, human tendencies that flourish in the worst of times when folk have to rummage for food in the rubbish.

Maybe so. Didn't stop my ribs hurting or ease the pain in my heart one little bit.

I keep my eyes on Priss as she swoops through a patch of cloud, then lingers, slip-sliding between shafts of air spiked with pine.

'Wish we lived in one place all the time,' I say. 'Wish we didn't have to keep travelling.'

'Me too!' Cat puts her arm around me and opens a side window to let in the fragrance.

It's early morning, the sky clear and blue. Already hot inside and out, the secret scent of forest soothes me. Soothes Cat as well. In a twinkling she's dreaming of running water and lights, clean clothes and bread. I can tell, for I hear the splash of water on her skin, feel her teeth and taste buds craving a bite of fresh bread. Would give anything for a few days of easy living. She knows I know what she's thinking 'cause she smiles her special smile: a twitch at the edge of her mouth, eyes squeezed almost shut.

I grin and Cobra grunts: 'Want to stay in the city, do you?'

'Not necessarily. Countryside would be as good. I just want to stay put.'

'Me too,' says Cat. I nod the same time she does.

'And what would you do if those black-boots come after us again? If the police take a shine to us and find us out?'

'Thank you, Cobra,' says Mama Rose, smiling at him in the mirror.

Cobra's the good one. Cautious, looks out for me. Holds my hand when I'm freaked out. Lets me snuggle up against him at night, then folds me in his arms. While Cat likes to hiss and spit and scratch.

'We should be fine,' I tell Cobra. 'We've got proper passports now. The best. And since Mama Rose adopted us on paper, we don't have to keep running. Could stay in one place. Be a proper family. A *real* family.'

'After what happened in Greece?' he says. 'Count me out, Sante.'

'Thank you again, Cobra.' Mama Rose smiles at him a second time.

I ignore 'em and so does Cat.

We travel in convoy down a mountain road, through pine and cork oak forests, over hills covered with olive groves. Once we've seen the last of the olives, Mama Rose accelerates and heads south with Priss still ahead of us.

Two hours later, her foot slams on the brake and the truck comes to a halt. 'Remember the drill?' Mama Rose says.

Priss flies to settle on my gauntlet-covered hand. Licks the lobe of my ear with the tip of a feather and blinks at what I'm staring at. Way down on the coast is a silver city of white-washed houses and a gold-domed cathedral. In the late afternoon haze it looks like an ornate bowl of candied fruit rising from the sea. A dazzling bowl that whispers: 'Come closer. Taste me. Take a bite out of me.' A spasm of fear sizzles the tips of my fingers.

'The drill,' Mama Rose says again.

I tear my eyes away from where we're heading.

'Stay close,' Cobra mumbles.

'Don't stare,' Cat.

'What else, Sante?' Mama Rose turns, peering at me, as if I'm still a baby and can't remember a thing.

'Stay alert and if anyone's rude, never chat back, especially to a policeman.'

'And?'

'Never listen to their thoughts. Never delve deep. Never. Ever.'

'Good. We don't want a repeat of what happened in Greece, do we?' she says.

I try to laugh but can't. None of us can.

I answered a question too soon; answered before a black-boot asked it.

He was thinking it through, about to place words on his tongue, when I jumped in first. Caused a riot. Men ran after us, thumped Redwood and Mama Rose, smashed the truck windows. Almost got us trampled on because of the way I am.

Mama Rose is forever saying, 'Everyone has a special talent.' Cobra's good with snakes. Can charm them out of trees, make 'em slither around him, then glide over his body. Cat can do just about anything with knives – knives, spears and arrows, bits of flint, even needles. She's a thrower. I'm a juggler. I know how to sing and dance, walk on wire, turn somersaults, do back-flips on Taj Mahal. But I'm a mind-whisperer as well. Seems tuning in to people's thoughts and catching the fizz and whirl of what's deep inside 'em is what I do best. Problem is, last time I was caught using my talent they called me a witch, and Cobra and Cat devil's spawn. I'm not sure which is more insulting. Shouldn't care really. But clear as the day is bright and stars shine at night, I know for a fact: if I mess up again, those black-boots will be on to us.

4

Arm in arm with Cat, I peek at townies ambling on the ramparts of the old city. A sea breeze whispers in my ears and kisses my cheeks. Hovering above the waves of the wild Atlantic, Priss is fishing. No one sees her today but me, and no one feels her thrill as keenly as I do. Irises widening, she glimpses a fleck of silver and dives. Feeding time for Priss, while Cat and I begin the task of sowing a field of clover.

First off, we stalk a family and imitate 'em. They pat a toddler on the head. Cat and I pat each other. They kiss, so do we. It's a game we play called Blending In. We may look different, but we figured out long ago that if we walk like other people walk, pretend to talk and be as much at ease as they seem to be, they're less likely to notice that we're working. Playing 'em.

We follow our family into the park. Gravel crunches

underfoot. Pigeons fly away. We trail them past palm trees and pink oleander, past restaurants in the market square. They don't seem to realise that they're moving in the direction of Midget Man's accordion.

We smile at everyone we see. That's our job: to look excited. So excited that families follow us and come to see our show. It's easy when you know how to be friendly but not too friendly. Look convincing, and no one can tell who's following and who's leading; who's the piper and who's dancing to his tune.

The accordion picks up pace, Cat claps her hands, and we add a hop and a skip to our walk, a lilt to our hips. We wave the crowd on and begin to run as they follow us into the cathedral square. Midget Man's music always attracts an audience. Even more so when he opens his mouth and begins to sing in a ragged Romany voice, the voice of a born traveller.

Half in the shadow of the cathedral lights, cheeks flushed, curly hair thick and wild, he looks like a gargoyle dislodged from above the cathedral doors to a stool in the middle of the square. Goosebumps freckle my arms as his tenor voice rips through the night.

'"*Dos Gardenias*,"' a young woman in a restaurant calls out. 'Sing *"Dos Gardenias"*.'

Midget Man strokes his goatee. Hooded eyes twinkle, then, with a courtly flourish to the woman, he obliges and the crowd swells – the cue for Cobra and me to mark out our territory. We spread a sprinkling of sawdust to create a magic circle around Midget Man in which anything can happen. Not too big, not too small, but snug and intimate. Mama Rose's Circus is flexible, portable. Quick as a flick of the wrist, shiny as a shower of glitter.

Soon as we're done, I slip in the back of the truck to get ready. Mama Rose is almost dressed: red jacket above a striped red-and-white circular skirt, underneath the skirt, a trillion petticoats. Pulls on a pair of black riding boots. Puts on grease paint: rouge on her cheeks, ruby-red lipstick. Smudges thick lines of kohl around her eyes and then, her face dusted with powder, says: 'What sort of house have we got tonight, Sante?'

'Pretty full,' I reply.

'Good girl. We'll be on for an hour and a half at the most.' She taps a top hat on her head and peps herself up by saying: 'Let's give 'em what they want!'

'Sure we won't get busted halfway through?'

'Where's your spirit, Sante?'

I want to say, 'Left me in Greece,' but don't. No point in raking over the past when talking about it brings back the certain knowledge that there are people in this world who'd like to see us dead.

'Don't worry, Sante.' She pulls on her lucky white gloves.

Mama Rose is forever claiming that the best performances are achieved through daily application of strength, discipline and persistence. Luck has little to do with it. But the fact remains: most people in our game are mighty superstitious. Entertainers. Can't help it. Once it's in you, there's no way you can get it out again: those rituals that help us give our best. Before any performance Midget Man rolls his head around one hundred times, wiggles his tongue to the count of forty. Redwood lies flat on his back and burps. Fifty times, last I counted. Bizzie Lizzie kisses her mirror, while Mimi stands on tiptoe and spins twice. What I do is kiss Priss and touch her feathers for luck. Bird smells of fish tonight.

'Eat well, did you?' She blinks as I smooth her down and sit her on her perch in the truck the way I always do. Finish by rubbing sawdust on my hands. Then I watch Mama Rose taking in the crowd.

The cathedral square's almost full, just as I said. Mama Rose looks at the faces of children, their eyes bright with curiosity, fingers itching to clap. Then, like an old diesel engine revving up, she begins shaking her large behind to the beat of the music box Midget Man's left playing. She shakes herself about and steels her muscles so hard, beads of sweat gather on her brow. Finally, she looks at me and says, 'Ready, Sante?'

She dashes into the circle we've made, whip in hand. Bows and simpers, salutes the crowd with her top hat. 'Ladies and gentleman,' she roars in broken Spanish, 'girls and boys. Welcome to Mama Rose's Family Circus for an evening of magical entertainment.

An evening of incredible tricks and daring feats created for your delectation alone.' She brings down her whip, a dash of sawdust mixed with gravel leaps into the air, and I'm on.

Since before I could walk, she's been training me. Bareback riding. Me and Taj in the ring together. Me in a turquoise tutu studded with luminous stones. Taj's mane a shower of silver ribbons. Drew the crowds when I was younger, still got the crowd where I want 'em today. A shining black girl on a white stallion, his flanks rippling and gleaming like seashells in moonlight.

I'm bigger than I used to be, but Taj's back remains broad and strong. I stand on his rump and, as he trots, flip forwards and land on his back, arms outstretched, a smile on my face. I execute a whole heap of flips in quick succession, then a handstand. I steady myself and slowly bend over backwards.

Taj begins to canter, calm as you please, his rhythm steady, sure of every beat. Slows down as I straighten up, and then using his body as I would a wooden bar, slip under and over him. Legs straight, toes pointed, hips flexed, moving this way and that. After a final somersault, I'm on the ground again, arms open wide, embracing applause. 'Bravo! Encore!'

I strut around the circle, back arched, Taj nodding and bowing with me. I wrap my hand around his ear and he snuffles my cheek. 'Good boy, Taj,' I say, and the crowd yells for more.

We're the opener and for now we're done. After the fifth roar of, 'More! More!' we step back and Midget Man and Redwood, Mimi and Bizzie Lizzie, dressed in gaudy clothes, their clown faces on, stumble into the ring. Tumble on the ground, miming with hands, faces and eyes. Hunger. Anger. Love. Despair. Bizzie Lizzie chasing Redwood bumps into Mimi. Mimi falls down. Lizzie trips over her, then Redwood careers over 'em and Midget Man's on top. The Smallest Man in the World is King of the Castle. A king who bursts into song, Midget Man's favourite aria, a throbbing song of love. Mimi, Redwood and Bizzie Lizzie join in.

The audience laughs and cries at the same time. They laugh loudest at Lizzie 'cause she's all arms and legs, long, elastic face topped with a mop of crazy, cherry-pink hair. Lizzie swoons. Makes eyes at Midget Man. Skips around him. Embraces him. Would have him too, but Mimi leaps on Lizzie's back and now they're all fighting again.

From where I'm standing in Mama Rose's shadow, Priss swinging above me in the truck, I see children cackling. When the Old Ones begin to catch fire as well, the cathedral square crackles with belly-bursting laughter. Can't hear for the thunder in my ears, so I don't notice it at first. Not a glimmer. Don't see anything suspicious, not even when I feel them staring at me, probing my insides: a sure sign something's not right.

Deep within me I sense a quiet patting sensation. Gentle, like I'm a kitten and fingers are running through my fur, tickling my belly.

'Who are you?' says whoever's poking about. 'Are you who I think you are?'

Someone I don't know is asking questions about me and I don't like it one little bit. Don't answer, not even in my thoughts. I don't say: 'What business is it of yours, scumbag?' Not me. Not this time. My eyes flit over the audience searching for whoever's asking, whoever's interested.

Old Ones stroke their youngsters. Lovers link fingers. City folk, arm in arm, smile. Have to look hard to track 'em down. I search faces old and young, tourists, locals, before I find 'em. A bald-headed man, an African, same colour as me. Shiny, coral-black. And beside him a middle-aged white man, grey hair spruced in a crew cut. The African's not much taller than I am, but both of 'em are bulky, jowly. And both sets of eyes are fastened on me.

My fingertips tingle. I step deeper into the shadows but those eyes follow, magnets drawn to iron. The white man's gaze is as ravenous as a lone wolf on a winter morning: a wolf with grey eyes. Fear spikes my innards and before I can blink, I'm shivering.

'Are you all right, Sante?' asks Mama Rose, touching me. Feels a slick of sweat on my forearm, sees my eyes glazing over. 'Sante, are you OK?'

I should tell her someone's on to me. Should ask for time out. But it's been bred into me: *no matter the circumstances, the show must go on!* So I nod and I'm on again. This time with Cobra, who's in a costume that sparkles like the scales of a fish as it slips through water.

Cobra carries a huge basket on his head. While he shows the audience the tangle of slithering snakes in it, I play my bamboo flute. Long and slim with an ivory mouthpiece. It fits my mouth perfectly. Mama Rose gave the flute to me when I was twelve years old. Told me it was in the chest I pitched up in, along with a leopard-skin drum. Told me that's all I arrived with, and where I'm from is as much a mystery to her as it is to me.

I purse my mouth, as if I'm kissing the cheek of an old friend, and blow. My fingers move down the bamboo ridge of the flute as youngsters shriek at the snakes. Cobra closes the lid and sits in the middle of the circle. Within moments snakes push the lid off and slide out. A few jump, leaping on to sawdust and gravel. Children shriek louder. I would too if I were them, but I'm playing. The tone of the bamboo's warm, the music coming out of it mellow and slow.

Should be concentrating, but with those men's eyes on me, I can't. Can't stop myself delving, can't block my talent. They may be in the shadows out of earshot, but their muffled voices come directly to me.

'It's her,' the African hisses. 'I recognise Mamadou's flute. I would know that sound anywhere in the world.'

'Impossible!' says Grey Eyes.

'I would think so too, if I hadn't been there. Believe me, it's the flute we put in the chest. I know it is. I helped Mamadou make it.'

'You're deceiving yourself. Every flute sounds the same.'

'They may to you, Wolf, but not to me. I made the mouthpiece myself with ivory from the Guinea coast.'

'Well, if it is the instrument you think it is, the girl may know where the rest of the haul is.'

'Don't you see the stones on her dress?'

'Those?'

I should be poised, precise, intent on charming snakes with Cobra. Should be, but I'm thinking: *What's wrong with my tutu? And Mamadou? Who's Mamadou?* All I do is say the name to myself, and the music I'm playing changes. The flute seems to sigh: 'At last! At last!' Then, as the weight of invisible fingers presses down on mine, a golden thread of sound reels me into a different world. A world before Priss, before memory.

I hear the roar of a leopard, screech of a vulture. I see the claws of a lion on the back of a gazelle, hear it yelp in pain, and then all at once I'm drifting through savannah. Fingertips graze over grass. Stubble underfoot. My fingers on the bamboo flute move faster and faster, notes reach higher and the snakes, jiving with those high notes, leap in the air.

They should be heading in Cobra's direction, but the music's got them as rattled as I am, and all of 'em, every single one of those thirty-one snakes, turn away from Cobra and head out of the ring to the audience.

Children scream while the Old Ones, backing away, say: 'Don't worry, this is all part of the act.' Everyone cringes and wails, about to turn tail and run. Even Priss on her perch joins in, screeching and flapping her wings. She snaps and hisses as Cobra gets up from the ground and touches me. Cobra reaches into my heart and stops the riot there. A single touch and the music stops. He claps his hands and whistles. Then he sits down and closes his eyes.

The snakes, as if drawn to him by invisible yarn, turn and slither back. They glide around his hands and knees, slide over his shoulders, up his neck until all thirty-one of them are coiled, a writhing turban on his head.

Relieved, the audience claps loudly. They shout, 'More! More!' Roar and laugh like it's Christmas tomorrow, while Cobra takes my hand and we bow. My legs about to buckle, I lean on him as he follows my eyes to catch a glimpse of what's got me so twitchy, my hands clammy and cold.

The African and Grey Eyes are clapping hard, as pleased as Cat is when she gets a hunk of fresh bread and bites down on it. They're delighted to have met me. They want more of me. Much more, I can tell, for the African says: 'It's her, all right. She plays just like Mamadou used to.' He nods at me. Gives me a knowing smile, while Grey Eyes snorts in disbelief and laughs. He laughs, yet his withered eyes, old as the hills, scare me.

5

Before I can make sense of what's going on, everyone's talking.

'What happened, Sante?' Cat.

'Are you all right, darling?' Mimi.

'She's having one of her turns,' says Mama Rose.

She rubs my arms, wraps a red shawl around my shoulders. When she hugs me, I realise that I'm shaking like a terrified pup.

Mama Rose turns to Cobra, questions him with a dark glow of those pebbled eyes.

'Two men in the audience,' he says. 'Must have got to her somehow. If something's not right, Sante usually feels it first.'

Cobra's saying what I want to, but can't. Tongue's sluggish.

Mama Rose touches my forehead, places the palms

27

of her hands on my cheeks and strokes 'em. Looks me in the eye.

'Perhaps we should pack up and go,' says Cobra. 'Might be heading for trouble.'

Can't talk, but I shake my head. There's money to be made here. Money we need if we're going to survive winter. Doesn't make sense to leave before summer's over, before the last tourist returns home. There's trouble in the air for sure, but there's something else turning me inside out, back to front. It's frozen my tongue, left me dazed. Don't know him, don't much care for his smile but Mamadou's friend, that African, of all the people in the world, may help me answer questions no one else can. Questions Mama Rose doesn't like me asking.

Can't talk, can't breathe. I bend over, push my head between my knees. Then, when I'm able, I go to Priss. Slip on my gauntlet and she hops on my hand, blinks at me and straightaway I sense her strength flowing into me. The pulse and heat of her body warm me, until gradually my breath settles.

'I'm OK,' I say to Mama Rose. 'I'll be ready for Cat's act.'

I try hard to stay calm, even though tears well up in my eyes. Redwood sees 'em. Wipes my face clean with the long nub of his finger. 'We've got your back, Sante,' he says. 'Take your time. We'll improvise.'

He runs into the circle with Midget Man and

they start fighting. After the clowns have fallen over themselves again and again and the crowd's still laughing, Mama Rose says: 'Are you sure, Sante? There's no need to risk it if you're not.'

Taking calculated risks is what we do every time we step in the ring. It's what we train for. I take a deep breath, kiss Priss, rub sawdust on my palms, and then run into the circle hand in hand with Cat. She's in her throwing clothes, a glittering steel sheath of a dress that makes her every move sizzle.

She places me against a white wheel, straps me on to it, and sets the wheel spinning. It picks up speed. Cat smiles and settles down to throw knives at me.

Flashes of silver whizz past drawing the outline of my body. Knives around my torso, arms and legs. Cat's fast, good. Knows exactly what's she's doing. Just as well, 'cause I'm trembling.

Those men are back in the audience again and they're talking to Redwood.

My hands start to quiver, face sweats. Trick is to stay calm, keep as still as a sloth. 'Breathe, Sante, breathe,' I tell myself.

The wheel spins faster. *Whoosh*. Knives slice through the air carving out the shape of my hair; the left side of my neck. Only the right side to go, when Cat pauses.

I sense a flicker of uncertainty in her, a moment of distraction. She steadies herself, then throws. I shiver, and the last of her knives nicks me.

The audience gasps. Blood trickles from a nip on my neck. First the snakes; now this.

The wheel stops turning. Cat mouths, 'I'm sorry,' and spins around. Her eyes pounce on a ginger-haired boy with a begging bowl, clothes mended in patches. Close by are a husband and wife who look just like him. Hungry. Woman's skinny as a river reed, husband's even skinner. Scrawny, hollow-eyed. And in the shadows, a girl with a mane of red hair, who belongs to them, head downcast in shame.

'Hey, you!' Cat shouts at the boy. 'And you and you,' she says as the couple tries to disappear into the crowd. 'Yes, you two! If you want to see another sunrise this side of heaven, don't mess with my hustle! And don't make your boy do your dirty work. We've worked hard for our dues tonight.'

Cat's the fiercest creature in the world I know. Got a streak of meanness running through her too. Comes at you suddenly, could kill you. But underneath the swill and bilge of emotion, there's something glorious bursting to come out. Her brightness doesn't show itself tonight and the family scuttles away.

We finish the show, and once the back-patting and applause is over, once we've passed a hat around and the audience shows their appreciation, we sit down and count our takings.

We don't count 'em in the café we eat in that night –
a cheap place by the seashore where we feast on fried
squid and shrimp soup, pork chops and rice. Eat our
fill of meat and fish for the first time in weeks. Eat and
jubilate. I even pat the plaster Mama Rose puts on my
neck. Pat it as though it's a badge of honour, and laugh.

We don't count our money among strangers. No,
sir! We wait till we get outside the city, back to our
camping ground. Bring out chairs, a foldaway table and
watch as Mama Rose hauls pouches from an enormous
black handbag. Carries our loot in a handbag, she does,
never a rucksack. Easy as anything to steal money from
your back.

Mama Rose gives one of the pouches to Redwood
and they pour everything out. Coins clatter on the
table, notes scatter, as the two of 'em arrange silver in
piles, notes in rows of ascending value.

We've done well, much better than usual. And with
the prospect of a week or two of entertaining in store: a
few weeks of juggling and acrobatics, tomfoolery and
busking, evenings of improvised spectacles with Taj
on the beach, the Old Ones whoop with joy. Cobra,
Cat and me sitting at the table smile, confident in the
knowledge that if the rest of our time here is as good
as today, we'll be warm over winter. Have enough to
eat. Might even buy new clothes, if we're lucky.

'I think it's time to have a drink,' says Mama Rose.
'Don't you? We've certainly earned it tonight.'

Doesn't take much to set the Old Ones drinking: good times, bad times, they reach for a tumbler and fill it to the brim with Redwood's home brew. Whisky, wine, beer, he makes it and stores it in kegs in his truck.

Mama Rose, still in her circus clothes, fumbles in her bra and brings out a key. Totters into the back of our truck and returns with a tray. On the tray are five crystal glasses. Must be feeling good, 'cause those glasses only appear on her birthday, when she remembers her 'provenance': her way of talking about where she comes from and everything she gave up.

Mama Rose puts the glasses on the table.

'What's it to be tonight, Rosie?' asks Redwood.

I sneak a peek at Priss on her perch. Opens an eyelid. Spreads out her mighty talons, fluffs her feathers.

'On a glorious evening like this, my dearest dear,' says Mama Rose, 'some of your cherry wine would go down a treat.'

The Tallest Man in the World disappears. Returns with a jug of wine for Mama Rose, a flask of whisky for the others.

Cat, sitting next to me, says: 'What about us?'

Midget Man brings out three beakers. Red plastic.

Don't like the taste of liquor in my mouth, so I ask for a Cola. Cat fills her cup with wine, Cobra a tot of whisky. He claims wine's a drink for girls, though I know for a fact he can't stand the taste of whisky on his tongue any more than I can.

'Here's to us!' Mama Rose says.

Glasses sparkle in lamplight. Crystal flashes and sings as Midget Man tapping, finds the pitch of his hooch and hums it.

'Well done, all of you,' says Mama Rose. 'Apart from a wobble here and there we excelled tonight!'

The Old Ones laugh. Laugh louder than a pack of hounds baying at a hunt. Yet underneath the hullabaloo, the hooting and whooping and noisy chatter, so small I scarcely feel it at first, there's a worm. And if my hunch is right, the worm's beginning to turn.

Burrowing up from deep down takes time. Liquor has to loosen their tongues for the worm to show itself. The first drink makes 'em jolly. Cheeks flushed, eyes bright, Mimi takes pins out of her hair and flings her curls about. Hair's almost as long as she is: black-peppered, grey-frizzy, soft to touch. Midget Man rubs Mimi's back. Bizzie Lizzie and Redwood exchange glances, then Redwood looks at me. He's feeling it too: that worm of anxiety that's growing plump with each passing minute.

Cat waves her beaker for more booze, and Redwood obliges, while Cobra on the other side of me shakes his head. Hasn't finished what's inside his cup yet. Cobra puts his hand on my lap and my fingers curl over his. I catch his eye, and my face brightens with a smile for him alone.

By the time the wound on my neck is starting to

throb, the Old Ones are on their third drink and the fattened worm, the one no one wants to talk about, slithers into the open with a question from Midget Man. 'Your playing's getting better and better, Sante,' he says. 'You played like a dream tonight, like someone possessed.'

He says that 'P' word and it stops their shouting and laughing. Stops 'em dead in their tracks. Don't rightly know what 'possessed' means, if I'm honest. But if it's anything to do with that Mamadou fellow taking hold of my wits and playing his flute through me, it's got 'em as spooked as I am.

Mama Rose swills wine in her glass, holds it up to the lamp and asks: 'What do you think happened tonight, Sante?' She doesn't look at me. Doesn't want to, I reckon. 'I'm waiting, Sante.'

I shrug and search the Old Ones' faces for clues as to what they're thinking. They know how to block my prying, so I don't even try. Stare instead. Redwood, tracing the slope of his nose with his forefinger, flinches as Bizzie Lizzie places a hand on his arm. Redwood smiles at me: a long, loping grin that lightens the amber of his eyes. 'Yeah, what happened out there, kid?'

Midget Man and Mimi nod, encouraging me to talk, while Mama Rose holds her breath. Turns to me at last, her eyes so scared, I taste her fear. The longer I gaze at her, the more a trace of sour milk furs my tongue and trickles, bitter as bile, down my throat.

'Two men in the audience got to me.' I tell 'em. 'Lost my concentration. One of the men's as black as I am. Don't know where the other's from, but the African seems to know something about me. Claims to have helped make the mouthpiece of my flute.'

Cobra squeezes my hand beneath the table. His smile bolsters me and I look at the Old Ones again. Redwood's still stroking his nose, Midget Man's still nodding. Only thing different is Mama Rose's eyes are glued to me now. Her fingers on the wine glass tremble. She pushes the glass aside, then looks up at the stars.

'Those men want to talk to me,' I say to her. 'Seems they think I might have something they want.'

Redwood starts tapping the table. Gaunt cheeks pucker and he says: 'Too right they want to talk to you, Sante. They came up to me after the show. Gave me this.'

He takes a folded note out of his shirt pocket. Shoves it over. I reach, but before I can touch it, Mama Rose covers it with a large, webbed hand. Gathers the note, tucking it deep in her bosom.

Priss reacts before I do. Hisses, flaps her wings, while I struggle to find words strong enough to take the taste of sour milk away. 'Mama Rose,' I say at last. 'That note's mine. The man gave it to Redwood to give to me.'

'And what do you know about these men, Sante? Do you know what their intentions are?

'I only want to speak to 'em,' I say. 'Ask a few questions.'

'What if they want to harm you?'

'You can come with me if you want. Redwood can come too.'

The woman I call Mama isn't listening, for she says: 'Buttercups and daisies! You haven't a clue what they want. Might even give you up to the police for all we know, and what would happen to you then? You could end up in a camp for illegals.'

'Rubbish,' Cat jeers. 'We've got our papers now and so's Sante. We've worked hard and saved up to make everything right.'

'It may sound harsh, child,' Mama Rose says to me, 'but for as long as you remain in my care, I'll decide who you see, what you do.'

Trouble's been brewing between us Young Ones and Mama Rose ever since the twins turned fourteen. Now that I'm fourteen as well and the twins are two years ahead of me, Cat snarls: 'You have no right to talk to Sante like that, Mama Rose. Not when we all have a stake in this outfit. We three work our butts off for you.'

Cool as can be, Mama Rose replies: 'And who took you in, Cat? Who gave you food and drink and went hungry for you? Who adopted you, raised you? Taught you right from wrong? Trained you for the circus?'

Cat screams. Holds her head in her hands and bangs it on the table.

Old Ones grab hold of their glasses. Hold 'em tight to ward off Cat's fury, as red plastic leaps in the air.

I hush Cat, tell her to stay cool as she reels off a list of all the things we do. Cobra too. Shouldn't boast but Cobra's snakes, Cat's knives and Taj and me are the star turns of Mama Rose's show.

Cobra thinks so too, for he says with a slinky, snake-man smile: 'Last time I reckoned everything up, seemed to me the three of us here have more than paid off our dues. Been working for you for as long as we can remember, Mama Rose, and we're grown now.'

'So, you're willing to take full responsibility for Sante, are you?' Mama Rose replies.

'I look out for her, always have done,' says Cobra.

'I said *take full responsibility*, Cobra. I thought not. Tell me who's the adult here?'

I want to say that I can look after myself just fine. Can draw a fire out of damp wood, build a shelter to live in, hunt rabbit and pheasant with Priss for food. I can look after myself for sure, but the truth is, the Old Ones and Cobra and Cat are the only family I have. And with the exception of Priss, Mama Rose is the closest creature to a mother I know.

Take that time Cat and I went thieving. Brought back skin-tight jeans and slinky tops. Soon as she saw 'em, Mama Rose took us back to the shop. Made us apologise and give everything back, 'cause she didn't save our lives, she said, didn't drag us out of the sea and forest, to raise a pair of lowlife criminals. Not her! True as the day is bright, she saved us so we could make something of our lives. Could be. But last I heard, being our saviour doesn't mean she's always right.

So I say, when Cat's calmer and Cobra's silent again, what I'm going to keep on saying until she hears me: 'Mama Rose, that note's mine. The man gave it to Redwood to give to me.'

I say the words like I mean 'em. And if she doesn't hear me by this time tomorrow, I swear on Priss's feathers, the storm I'm going to call up will blow her clean away.

Mama Rose refuses to hear me. Ears blocked, mind's set. Redwood says: 'Rosie, don't you think it's time you told her? She's old enough to know now. Tell her.'

Mama Rose shakes her head.

'Rosie, we owe it to her,' Redwood insists.

'Tell me what?' I ask

The Old Ones stare at each other: wives glance at husbands and then all eyes fix on Mama Rose. And somehow, all of it – is about me. Something I don't know yet, that Mama Rose doesn't want to talk about.

'Tell her,' Redwood urges.

'In my own sweet time and not a moment before,' says Mama Rose.

I look from one to the other, Redwood to Mama Rose. The night thickens with secrets as each of 'em – Midget Man, Mimi and Bizzie Lizzie – murmur in agreement with Redwood. I tear the plaster off my neck, fling it to the ground. A summer breeze licks my wound and then takes up the Old Ones' plea as shrubs and leaves, flowers and trees, every living thing about us, it seems, whispers: 'Tell her. Tell her.'

Cobra and Cat don't know what the Old Ones are talking about any more than I do. 'Tell her what?' says Cat.

Silence.

I'm tight as a wire about to snap, when Priss flies down from her perch and sits beside me. Polishes her beak on my jeans and I cry. '*What?*'

The air's fat with secrets now, so fat Cat could slice it in pieces and not reach the bone. She's as twitchy as I am, so it's Cobra who says. 'Someone, anyone, please tell us what's going on.'

Mama Rose gathers her precious glasses and places 'em on the tray. Face glowing white in the Spanish night, she stands up and says: 'I shall tell Sante everything when she's good and ready. I know her better than if she were my own flesh and blood and she's not ready yet.'

'You're not talking about me,' I reply. 'You're talking about yourself! Seems to me the older I get, Mama Rose, the tighter you try to hold on to me.

And the tighter you hold on, the more I want to break free.'

She sits down again, exhausted. Shakes her head as if she's in a bad dream and can't snap out of it. I recognise the feeling, but the urge to find out more, to gather every morsel that will help me understand who I am and where I come from, is powerful indeed. 'Tell me what you're keeping from me!'

'When you're older,' she says and gets up, the note still tucked deep in her bosom.

6

That night I try not to sleep, 'cause chances are I'm going to dream that dream. And if it grabs me and shakes me about, it'll turn my up-side down, drag my insides out, twist me around, till I'm more snarled up than I am already. Don't want to dream, so when I'm laid out on my bunk, I go over every word of my conversation with Mama Rose and what Cobra, Cat and me plotted afterwards.

'*You're not old enough. You haven't a clue what they want of you, Sante. So who's the adult here?*' Mama Rose's words rankle. Most of all what she says when she's backed in a corner: '*Who took you in? Gave you food and drink and went hungry for you?*'

We owe her. We wouldn't be here without her. Believe me, not a day goes by without me thanking her for something, and yet her way of loving tangles me up. Can scarcely breathe at times when she goes on about the evil in the world, and how the only way to survive is to earn what we need, then hunker down in wild places. Could be right, but not all townies and country folk are bad. Not all of 'em are black-boots and people-traffickers. And even though I've seen with my own two eyes how Old Ones can prey on Young Ones and feed off 'em, I've witnessed kindness on the road as well.

'Let's bust out of this outfit and try and make it on our own,' says Cat when Mama Rose is in bed.

We're lying on our backs on top of a hill, heads in a circle, looking up at the stars. Redwood's with us, keeping an eye on us.

'We could make it on our own. Betcha we could.' With half a nod, Cat would be off in a shot.

'Don't forget Sante's underage,' Redwood reminds us. 'Could be taken into care if you're unlucky. Fostered out to strangers.'

Redwood urges caution, patience. Tells us when we call Mama Rose a worrisome fearmonger and bully, that honest to goodness, she really wants the best for us. Would give her life to keep us safe. Redwood says all the usual things Old Ones say, but the one that bothers me the most is the threat of what he calls 'care'.

From the stories Redwood tells us, to be cared for by strangers is to be halfway down the road to ruin, 'cause 'care' brings a whole heap of trials and tribulation. Churns you up, grinds you down, and then spits you out on the street to nowhere. Strangers wouldn't let me keep Priss, in any case. Wouldn't let me take her into the wild and hunt with her. Just thinking about life without Priss brings tears to my eyes.

'We won't let anything happen to you,' Cat reassures me.

'Never, ever,' says Cobra, folding his fingers over mine.

The truth is, Cobra and Cat could make it on their own. I'm not tall or big enough yet to pass as their equal. What's more, when people see my face in out of the way places, I attract attention Big Time. While the twins, wheaten in complexion, blend in better.

Redwood reminds us of our weaknesses, mine in particular. We listen to him, nod when he wants us to nod, thank him for his advice. Even so, he won't tell us Mama Rose's secret: what she's got on me that I don't know, or what's in that note. Won't say a word, no matter how much we wheedle and plead. So, when the night air turns chilly and we're tired of pretending to agree with him, we turn in.

The back of Mama Rose's truck is where we bed down. Bunks, pull-out table, built-in kitchen with water – when there's fresh water to be had. Home sweet home, the only nest we know. I'm on the top bunk, close to Priss's perch. Cobra's below me, Cat underneath.

I toss and turn, fighting sleep by recalling everything that's happened: the flute, the African, Grey Eyes' ravenous stare. That look keeps me awake a long time, but in the end, sleep sidles up and gulps me down.

When the dream comes it's not as frightening as usual. I'm on Priss, looking through a storm-tossed sky on a scene of carnage. The iron monster ploughs through the trawler with splutters of gunfire. Waves rise and roll as the sea flings bodies to and fro. In the trawler's belly, the tall man holds me up and puts yellow dust and pretty stones in my sea-chest cradle.

This time, however, as I circle the sky with Priss, I look down with her eagle eyes and see a face I've never seen before. A strong, round face, stubbled hair twisted in locks, eyes dark with terror. Hands fumble through a rucksack. Trawler tips. Man slips and falls but holds fast to a prized possession. Lurches forwards, barges past a gaunt elderly man, then fights his way through screaming passengers till he's standing over me: the baby in the chest. Soon as he speaks and I see what's he's holding, I reckon it's him: 'Take this, my child,' he says. 'Learn to play it to keep my spirit alive.' Then he buries a flute in my cradle. Mamadou. He must be Mamadou.

Beside him is a man who could be his brother. Burly, bald-headed. The man in the dream, who usually gives me his dagger, resembles the man in the audience tonight. It's got to be him, for when the trawler smashes into pieces and its cargo of people flail in the sea, he clutches a mast, and lashes himself to it.

I'm calm, curious, from my eagle's eye view on Priss's back, when the night sky crackles with thunder and lightning. A gale-force wind slaps my face, almost dislodging me. The sky splits and a gigantic wolfhound bounds through the storm and barks at me. Growls and creeps so close I feel his hot breath on my face. Grey Eyes.

The dream's warning me. 'Better the mother I know,' I say to myself, 'than the monster waiting outside.'

I shudder awake and reach for the friend who comforts me when I emerge trembling from my night travels. *Priss, are you there? Priss, do you hear me?*

I'm always here, Sante-girl. I've been with you so long, where would I go now?

I tell Priss my dream and a membrane flips over her eyes as she ruminates.

I keep talking, telling her again what I've told her already: a man called Mamadou gave his flute to me. His brother could be the African I saw tonight, a survivor of the wreck that almost killed me. Don't know why, but Grey Eyes frightens me. May be after me.

Eyelids flick back and eyes spark: *And what are you going to do about it, Sante?*

Bird's been with me so long, she knows when I'm running scared. Bucks me up with feathery swish on the ear. I sit up, climb down from my bed.

Cobra rolls over and murmurs: 'Are you all right, Sante?'

'I'm going walkabout,' I tell him.

He groans, flips over and falls asleep again while I step out with Priss.

From when I first recognised my A from my B, from the time I could talk and asked questions, no one, not even Mama Rose or Redwood, was able to answer. Questions such as: where on this wide earth do I come from? And who else has the same blood in their veins as I do? From when I began to realise that not everyone can chat to an eagle the way I talk to Priss, I understood that the best time of the day, by far, to think, is first thing in the morning. Before the sun's up the earth's still and calm, and daylight creatures are too drowsy to create a ruckus with their lungs. They aren't yelping and twittering or preening in the shade of trees.

That's why, when I step into the velvet quiet, and the dream still seems to be riding me, I don't mind.

Waking and sleeping feel much the same round about now. The dream may be hovering close enough to touch, but I know for a fact, I'll be able to figure things out.

Some folk try to run down their thoughts. I hunt. Priss perches on a strap on my hand and then soars, feathers flaunting gold in a charcoal sky. Glides over a stretch of farmland, over crops of maize, tomatoes, grapes. She quivers, then drifts on a current of cool air. Tells me it's too dark to see much. Sky's going to clear soon though and it's going to be hotter than yesterday. But for the time being, she can't smell a whiff of trouble on the breeze.

She can't sense it up there, 'cause most of it's in me. Trouble. On my mind, in my bones. Thoughts twist and leap, until feelings I don't fully understand free themselves and tumble on to my tongue, to help me name what's bothering me: Mama Rose.

I know she loves me, but it can't be right to rule someone you love through fear.

Thoughts winkle out of me and when they're in the open, I decide. Either I obey Mama Rose and live life her way, or learn what I can from the African. Grey Eyes unsettles me, for sure. Even so, if Mama Rose won't let me meet the two of 'em, I'll make it easy for them to track me down. I'll help them find me. That note is *mine*.

Priss on the wing sees movement. Hovers, then

dives for the kill. I hear a shriek and a second later it's over. She brings back her prey, a small, black hare and I let her eat it: eyes, tongue, muscle and blood. Everything.

7

Soon as I get back, I discover Mama Rose has gone to the city with Redwood on his motorbike. I put Priss on her perch and tune in to Bizzie Lizzie's chatter as she dresses in the truck next door. She can't decide which of her many hats to wear to keep the sun off her face. Porcelain-white skin breaks out in freckles at the slightest sniff of sunshine. Swears she freckles easily 'cause she's closer to the sun than anyone else she knows, except Redwood. That's what she told me once. I listen to Lizzie grumbling and start my morning chores.

I take Taj Mahal down to a stream at the bottom of the camp. Let him drink, then feed him outside his trailer as I get ready for my next move.

Strictly speaking, Taj belongs to Midget Man, but since he can only reach parts of him if he stands on a crate, I often help. Today, when he appears, he brushes Taj's legs and tail while I do the rest of him.

Grooming is Midget Man's time for thinking. He savours the stroke of his hand over Taj's coat, the smooth curve of his hind legs, the tender lift of his feet. Usually whispers to him too, like I do, but Midget Man's not himself this morning. Keeps looking over his shoulder, eyes darting from one end of the camp to the other. Twists his moustache, tugs his goatee. He glances at the twins under an olive tree eating bread with avocado, then at Mimi on a stool singing, combing her hair. Can't settle his eyes on anything, not even the beauty of Taj's face, the faint smudge of a dark star on his forehead. Mind can't settle either. Takes me three brushstrokes of Taj's rump to work out what's on his mind: Mama Rose and Redwood. Midget Man's worried about 'em.

When Mimi clambers into the truck, he whispers: 'They went into town to find those men, Sante. Find out what they know and strike a deal with them. Get 'em off your back.'

Doesn't make sense to me, no sense at all. Why would Redwood and Mama Rose do exactly what she told me not to do? Mama Rose is up to something. Knows more than she's letting on too, if she wants to find out what those men are acquainted with. There has to be money involved, if they're considering making a deal.

I look at Midget Man, imploring him to tell me more. He knows what it's like to have people tower over you, tell you what to do, what's good for you.

'No,' he says. Says no but he's struggling with his conscience. Brain's muddled as a maze, with no obvious exits and entrances, and he's lost in the middle of it. Midget Man rubs the brush of hair on his chin: 'I've told you more than I should already, Sante,' he says. 'I daren't say anything else.'

I touch his shoulder, tell him I understand, then ask if I can take Taj for a ride on the shore.

'A few hours should be fine,' he says, fondling Taj's muzzle. 'But be careful not to let him get too hot. It's going to be a scorcher today.'

I promise and make my move. It takes me a while to persuade Cobra to stay put and stall Mama Rose and Redwood when they get back. He agrees reluctantly, and I set off on Taj with Cat, a rucksack on my back.

The campsite's not far from the ocean, and with Priss leading the way, it doesn't take us long to reach it. Taj trots through a field of sunflowers, across a highway, then we head down a hill dotted with lemon trees, to a wide open stretch of beach. It's still early morning, the air bright with human chatter. There's a rattle of cafés opening, the heave and haul of shutters pulled up. Grunts and groans of waiters as they drag tables outside; laughter of men arranging recliners to rent. Priss flies away without so much as a backwards glance, and soon all I can see of her is a fleck on the horizon.

I jump off Taj. Cat follows. We take reams of Taj's finery out of my rucksack and we dress him up. Silver bells and white ribbons, white tassels on his tail. We primp and prettify him, so that by the time we're done, Taj looks like a fairy-tale stallion fit for a princess. I tie a rope around his neck, give it to Cat, then leap on his back while Cat leads us.

We've never done this sort of thing outside the ring before. Never created a spectacle to draw attention to ourselves; never *deliberately* broken cover. That's what we're doing, me most of all. A black girl on a silver stallion. A girl in white cut-offs and T-shirt doing handstands on a magnificent horse. I steady my hands, bend backwards until my legs slide either side of Taj's neck. Then I'm up again, a big smile on my face, to a faint ripple of applause.

As Cat takes us through our paces at a canter, a crowd gathers and the applause grows louder. I stand on Taj's broad back, and with both hands arched above me, do a toe-touch-sky arabesque. Keep my balance. Hold the pose for as long as I can. Drop on to Taj's back again and then do another handstand.

Passers-by pause to stare. Joggers stop running. Traffic snarls to a crawl. A crowd forms around us: mothers and toddlers, folk on the way to work. Most of 'em, intrigued by my acrobatics, stop and gawk, as others smile at me and walk on. All of 'em, I'm sure, will mention me to their friends and families: the black girl on a white horse. And with a bit of luck they'll prattle so much the African and Grey Eyes will hear. And even if they do cut a deal with Mama Rose and Redwood today, they'll be here to see me tomorrow.

This is what I'm thinking, when I sense a presence in the gathering, and hear a plea for help faint as the whimper of a newborn pup. I see her hair first, a tangle of red maple leaves in fall. I catch a glimpse of that hair and feel her spirit reaching out to me. The redhead in the audience from last night. The girl with the worn-down family. I complete a back-flip, and when I'm astride Taj soaking up applause, I look for her.

She's at the edge of the crowd, staring at me with glazed eyes. Mind's a blank, but in her heart I see a pool of loneliness swollen with anguish. Girl's in trouble, for sure.

The thought zings through me, as Cat touches the right side of her nose: our signal for trouble. I look to my right and see a police car slowing down. It stops and a black-boot in blue gets out. Looks at me. Takes off a crumpled cap. Wipes the sweat off his brow and surveys the crowd.

I wanted attention. Got more than I bargained for.

Cat blinks twice at me: should we stay or leave?

Heart hammering, I touch the middle of my fore-head. We're staying.

The man in blue takes out a walkie-talkie and speaks into it.

My pulse quickens, racing faster than I can think.

The black-boot puts the walkie-talkie away. Just as he's about to go, he pauses. Turns and stares at me. Seems to be looking straight at me, but he could be taking in something behind me, something I can't see. He starts to run. I grab hold of the rope around Taj's neck and turn. In a flash, I see what he's seeing.

'Stop! Stop!' the policeman cries. 'Stop her!'

Taj whinnies and rears. I cling to him, whisper in his ear, and as the crowd surges forwards, I steer him to the sea. His legs stretch in a canter, hooves pummelling sand. I squeeze his flank with my heels and Taj Mahal streaks past the policeman, past a gaggle of screaming children: 'Stop! Stop!' they cry. Taj tears across the beach, galloping over a pile of clothes and sandals on the sand, into the sea.

The redhead has walked naked into the Atlantic. She's up to her eyes in it, and even though she's not swimming, she can't seem to hear everyone shouting at her. Can't seem to hear or see. The top of her head is completely submerged when I leap off Taj and fling myself in. I suck in a lungful of air, dive, and swim in her direction. Thanks to Redwood, I'm slick as a seal underwater. I open my eyes, wince at the sting of salt, and, through a whirl of sand, see the girl filling her lungs with brine.

I lunge at her and a tendril of red hair slithers over my face. Wide-eyed with terror, she's almost gone. But then I see it, a last flicker of life in those eyes that reminds me of Priss's prey this morning.

I haul the redhead up in the air. Her arms flap and she hits me. Splutters, heaves out water, tries to drown herself again, but I flip her on to her back on top of me. She twists away, lashes out and I swallow sea. Either I loosen my grip and let her be, or in two shakes of a lamb's tail, she's going to kill me. I hold on.

She struggles and screams, bashes me, then drags me down so deep, I'm about to get away from under her, when the policeman reaches us, and hauls us both in.

It seems the whole of Cádiz is waiting for us on the shore, even Priss. Bird swoops from her morning ramble and lands beside me.

Just as I'm catching my breath, the redhead screams: 'What do you think you were doing?'

She's talking to us: the policeman and me. He's doubled over, hands on his knees, gulping air. Water trickles from his short black hair. He can't talk as yet, so he stares at her – me and him both – as she says: 'I was swimming, that's all. *Swimming*.'

She spells it out in a voice that would make the

Queen of England proud. The same voice Mama Rose uses when we're in trouble and she's determined to browbeat black-boots into submission. Haughty. Bludgeoning. Knows how to throw a veil over the truth, this girl, 'cause if she was swimming, then I'm a mermaid and Taj Mahal is a unicorn.

She shrugs on her shabby green dress and stumbles getting up. The policeman takes her elbow. She pushes him away. Would like to spit at him, I reckon. 'There's nothing wrong with me,' she says. 'Leave me alone.'

I never imagined I could ever end up on the same side as a black-boot, but we both know the girl's lying. She was trying to kill herself.

Her bottom lip twitches as she takes in all the people staring at her. She casts her eyes down, squeezes them shut, and covers her face with her hair.

She's made a fool of me, I know, yet somehow I can't help rooting for her, can't help hoping that she gets on top of the mess she's in. The policeman must feel the same way too, for he doesn't scold her for wasting police time, doesn't write down her name. Tears a page from his notebook instead. Scribbles his name and phone number and hands it to her. It slips through her fingers. I pick it up and read the name on it: 'Federico Angel de Menendez.'

Federico smiles. I put his note in my pocket while he waves gawping spectators away. Stragglers linger until Cat, on Taj, shoos them off: 'Show's over,' she says. 'Time to go home, folks.'

The girl looks up and eyes the colour of honey lick Cat's greens. I feel it the moment they do: the hunger, the sweet sadness in her. The shiver on Cat's skin as she holds out a hand and lifts her up on to Taj Mahal. Cat likes her, wants to sweeten her mouth with maple syrup. I feel it, and in the heat of that moment, as a spark of desire lights between them, I know for a fact that our lives are about to change forever.

8

I know 'cause it's been like that from the beginning
between Cobra and me. I told him years ago that
I plan to marry him as soon as I'm grown. Was
five years old at the time, and from what I recall, he
looked mighty pleased. My head pillowed by his arm,
he grinned, then said slow as molasses dribbling off
a spoon: 'Sante-girl, maybe one of these days I *will*
marry you.'

Leastways, he didn't say no. And from the way he
behaves, the way he looks out for me and holds my
hand when I'm low, I'm still his best girl: even though
once in a while, he does make eyes at strangers.

I think of Cobra when I see the redhead with
Cat and wish he was with us. He'd figure her out in
no time at all and know what to do now Cat seems
moon-crazy. The girl clings to her, head cradled on
the back of Cat's shoulder. Hanging on for dear life

by the look of it, and Cat seems to like it.

With Priss on my hand, I take hold of Taj's rope, and lead 'em to a seaside café for a bite to eat. Cat and the girl don't talk; just stare at each other. Might take 'em a while to get their tongues moving again, so I order breakfast: bread, butter, eggs and bacon, mint tea the way Mimi makes it. Fresh leaves scrunched up in a pot served piping hot. I calculate how much it's going to cost and set money aside from our earnings this morning.

Cat and the girl munch in silence. No time for small talk, these two. No how-do-you-do and, by the way, what's your name? No, sir! They link fingers under the table like Cobra and I do, and gaze into each other's eyes.

I dunk a hunk of bread into my fried egg, stir it around. Take a bite of yolky crust and look at 'em. Priss is eyeing them too. Wonders who in heaven's name the redhead is, while I'm trying to figure out what she's up to.

Mama Rose is always saying you can tell a lot about a person from the way she eats. The redhead eats daintily, chews before she swallows. May be hungry, but she doesn't rush her food. Doesn't wolf it down like Cat and I usually do. Nails may be a bit grimy right now, but her hands are smooth, manicured, nails painted a delicate pearly pink. From what I'm seeing, I'd say she's more of a buyer of bread than a seller of it.

I watch her. Watch the two of 'em gawping at each other, then I say: 'Girl, what's your name?'

She looks at Cat. Cat nods.

'Scarlett,' she says. 'My name's Scarlett Woodhouse.'

'Scarlett,' Cat repeats. 'Cat.'

'Cat.' The girl smiles and Cat purrs.

Under normal circumstances, I'd leave 'em alone to get acquainted. After all, Cat's my older sister. She knows how to look after herself and usually me. But the state she's in, with all that staring and purring, seems to me I'm the Old One here.

'Where are your folks, Scarlett?' I ask. 'Your family from last night?'

Her mouth twitches. I'm beginning to wonder if she's about to run into the sea again, when Cat strokes her hand and says: 'Take your time, Scarlett.'

Cat holds her hand until the lip-twitching stops, and then pours tea into Scarlett's cup. Scarlett sips it, begins to talk. As she tells her story, tears run down her cheeks, and I see a side of Cat I've never witnessed before: tender tabby Cat with kitten; unusually touchy-feely for someone who laughs when Redwood encourages us to hug trees. Cat murmurs over Scarlett, nuzzles against her, patting and caressing, as the story unfolds.

Turns out the rest of the Woodhouse family left town first thing this morning. Borrowed money to buy tickets home.

'I thought we were all going home,' says Scarlett. 'All of us: Jack, my parents and me. They promised! Promised not to leave me again. But when I woke, they were gone. Miguel told me they left me behind as insurance. I'm to stay with him till they're able pay him back.'

My mouth drops open while Cat continues murmuring. Keeps it up, I reckon, to encourage Scarlett to tell us more. Some things, however, are just too hard to speak about, so I ask: 'And in the meantime what are you supposed to do?'

Scarlett tries to straighten her back, but her shoulders droop as words too difficult to utter stick to her tongue. She blushes and hides her face with a blanket of hair. From the look of it, she'd rather drown than go through with what's expected of her. And yet, from what I'm gleaning, she can't very well ask for help from the police. Her folks would get into trouble then.

'Miguel's got my passport, everything,' Scarlett says. 'Won't give it back to me till I've paid off our debt. Says I belong to him now.'

I see a glint in Cat's eyes that spells trouble for whoever's bailed Scarlett's parents. 'You're not his slave,' Cat says. 'Not if you don't want to be. No one has to do anything they don't want to, not nowadays.'

I agree and that settles it. We're taking Scarlett in.

When I get back to the camp, the Old Ones are packing up to leave. It doesn't make sense. Not when there's money to be made in Cádiz and we're not yet covered in clover. But there they are, sorting themselves out. Bizzie Lizzie attacks a line of carpets with a brush and then spreads them in the trucks while Mimi throws rubbish on a fire.

Traces of dust linger in the air; embers of wood spark. Food cartons crackle and melt as Priss yelps and flies to her perch. I'm wondering how I'm going to persuade Mama Rose to stay longer, so I can speak to that African, when Cobra jumps out of the front seat of her truck.

'She wants to speak to you,' he tells me. 'Says we're leaving 'cause of you.'

'But why?'

Cobra shrugs, and then helps me prepare Taj for his trailer. We remove his finery. Just as we start to coax him inside, Cobra stumbles, falls against the trailer and steadies himself. Touches his arm as if it's suddenly numb and he can no longer feel it. Rubs his arm, shakes it. 'Where's Cat got to?'

'She's gone to town to sort out her new friend,' I tell him.

'Where exactly?'

I give him the address where Cat's gone with Scarlett to pick up her things and retrieve Scarlett's passport, if they can.

Cobra shivers, closes his eyes. Groans, holds his head, as his whole body starts trembling. 'Something's not right,' he says. 'Cat.' He whispers her name and a glimmer of fear lightens his eyes.

That's the way it is with Cobra and Cat. The twins are so close, they're able to talk to each other when they're apart, sense where the other one's at.

'She needs my help.'

I'm tempted to ask him how he can be sure, but the dread in Cobra's eyes brightens. 'Got to find her,' he says, and I nod.

Next moment, Mama Rose in overalls, leans out of the truck: 'Sante? Sante-girl! It's time I told you what you want to know. Told you about those men Redwood and I met this morning.'

Mama Rose jumps down, but I'm half-gone already. Cobra runs and I run after him. He leaps on to the back of Redwood's motorbike and I hop on behind. I shout for Priss, and once she's in the air, we're away.

Cobra leans low and my body follows him. Tilts to the

right and so do I. To the left and I'm with him. Two bodies bound in motion straddling a giant panther as it roars down a track, then swings left on to a curve of highway.

My head on Cobra's back, the wind on our faces, we hurtle downhill in our rush to reach Cat. The sky, a pale simmering blue, crouches over us, licking up whispers of heat from the tarmac. A huge yellow sun burns my shoulders.

We climb a steep slope, career down so fast, it feels as if we're flying past trucks, scooters and cars. Zigzag in and out, around a bend that takes us over a wide, open landscape: the Atlantic on one side and on the other, a trail of flowers beside the motorway.

We race past villas and farms, over flatlands. Should have told Mama Rose and the others where we were heading. Should have given her Scarlett's address in the old part of the city: number five, *calle Horozco*, near San Antonio square.

Priss, flying overhead, darts along the shoreline, above high-rise apartments into the old quarter. 'Find Cat,' I tell her. 'Help her.' Priss flies on, and Cobra and I, keeping an eye on her, track her through narrow cobbled streets. Tall, balconied buildings crowd in on us. Cafés, taverns, a church, San Antonio square. Then we zip down an alley marked *calle Horozco*, to where Priss glides in a shaft of light.

'She's here somewhere. She's close by,' says Cobra.

He parks the motor. I jump off and run with him to a block of buildings and find number five. Priss yelps, then gives a high-pitched screech that rips the lining from my gut. Trouble. Big Time.

'What's your bird saying, Sante?' asks Cobra. 'What's she seeing?'

'On the roof. Women screaming. Help them, Priss!' I signal 'attack' and Priss dives.

Down below, I help Cobra push open a large door made of heavy, old wood. We pass through a courtyard in the centre of the building and then Cobra stops. He closes his eyes. Sniffs. Feels the pulse of the house. Shakes his head in dismay, then scrambles up a narrow staircase. Up, up we go, past luxury apartments. Round and round, up five floors, and the closer we get to sky, the more we hear what Priss has been hearing: screams. Screams so loud, my body quakes as we rush on to the roof terrace.

I've been running through shadows so long, the sunlight dazzles me. I hear a jumble of sounds, then figures begin to form and I'm able to see 'em. A barrel of a man punches Cat. She ducks, lunges at him. Scarlett, a satchel over a shoulder, jumps on him, thumps him again and again. He shakes her off as Cat headbutts him. Scarlett screams, and a sleekly-dressed man, black hair oiled in a quiff, grabs Cat from behind while the big one reaches for her legs.

Wings poised, Priss swoops and tears out tufts of

hair. The big man yells, lets go of Cat. She wriggles free and Cobra, behind me, throws her a knife. She catches it and smiles at Quiff. Quiff simpers. A flick-knife springs into the palm of his hand and they circle each other, two tigers about to let rip. Scarlett scrambles behind Cobra and hides.

The big man is about to jump Cat again when Cobra steps in front of him. The man downs Cobra with his weight, tramples him as Priss dives and rips open the man's face. Talons drip blood.

I yell: 'Stop, Priss! Stop!'

I say the words and Quiff looks at me. A moment – that's all it takes for Cat to pounce and plunge the knife into his shoulder. Quiff yowls and gawps at the blood gushing. Flips open a phone, summons help. Slumps over.

'Take her,' Cat says, shoving Scarlett at Cobra. 'Get her out of here quickly.'

'I want to stay with you,' Scarlett whimpers.

'Go!'

Cobra takes Scarlett's arm and they're away down the stairs.

In five shakes, I begin to wonder if they were able to make it as the thud of feet running upstairs sounds from below. A gang, maybe four of 'em, closing in.

Cat slashes washing lines to slow 'em down. Nods, and we run as far away from the stairwell exit as we can. We run across the roof terrace, bodies pursuing us.

I look behind. One of 'em trips over a tangle of washing, but they're fast. Six-packs heaving heft, they trample through a roof garden. They're agile, these men. What they don't seem to realise is that we circus folk earn our living being fleet-footed and nimble. They may be quick, but we're going to show 'em we're quicker.

9

Mama Rose told me not so long ago that
when I was crawling and couldn't quite
walk, before she fully figured out that I'm
more beast than fowl, Priss tried to teach me to fly.
Lured me on to chairs and tables, and helped me take
off, arms flapping. Got me to climb a tree once and
jump out.

'It's a mercy you're still alive, Sante,' Mama Rose
said, when Cobra showed her the dent on my head.

All those early tumbles and cuts mean that, though
I can't fly as such, I'm pretty spry. Can leap and
dive, twist and turn and, thanks to Priss, I've no fear,
whatsoever, of heights.

So when Cat runs across the roof terrace, I glean what
she's thinking and race in front of her. Priss leads the
way and I jump from one roof to the next. Catch my
breath, run to the next roof and jump again. Fall over

a flowerpot. Somersault, leap, legs paddling empty sky. I lunge forwards just in time to catch hold of a strip of cable, and haul myself up. Cat's ahead of me now.

'Stop!' I shout at her. 'We have to go down to find a way out of here.'

She hesitates, looks back and sees only two men after us now. Ahead of us is a roof-scape of satellite dishes, flat terraces straddled with washing lines, clothes fluttering. And beyond, as far as the eye can see, a glittering coastline.

I dart into a stairwell and Cat follows. We run down. A pimpled teenager carrying boxes of pizza passes us. I return his smile. We pretend to walk. Pizzas disappear upstairs and we sprint fast as foxes through a courtyard garden of bougainvillea and jasmine.

We pause at the front door. Breathe slow, breathe deep, then we peek outside. On the left, cars are parked on the street and two women in black hobble along talking. On the right, a Honda. In his haste to deliver hot food, the pizza delivery boy left his scooter running, keys in the ignition.

Cat cackles and I laugh with her as she jumps on the Honda. I slip on behind her, and with Priss guiding us, we make our way back to the campsite.

I don't think I'll ever fully understand Old Ones. Maybe when I'm old myself I'll appreciate why, when Cat and I get back, they behave as if we've lobbed a hand-grenade on to their laps: a Scarlett-coloured grenade that's likely, at any moment, to blow us to high heaven.

Scarlett and Cobra made it, but there's no sign of jubilation. Down by the stream, Mama Rose and Redwood are hearing Cobra out. Could be we've put our lives on the line, but from everything they've taught us – how best to survive, how to co-operate and work as a team – seems taking care of each other doesn't stretch to taking in strangers.

We're travellers and all the travellers I know tend to be wary of outsiders before we let 'em in. Truth is, only Midget Man and Mimi were *born* travelling. Only they are Romany at heart, gypsy through and through. The others *chose* to carry their homes in trucks and keep on the move. Yet when we return to find Scarlett sitting on the back step of Mama Rose's truck, I can tell just by looking at 'em that Midget Man and Mimi are the only ones minded to take her in.

The two of 'em are chatting to her even though Scarlett won't answer back. She stares into space.

'It's OK, darling,' says Mimi. 'You're safe now.'

Midget Man croons a tune, as if Scarlett were a jittery foal he was trying to get close to. Unless I'm mistaken, give him another minute or two and he'll offer her a lump of sugar.

All of 'em look relieved when we appear. Scarlett runs up to Cat and hugs her while Mama Rose steps up to me.

'Are you OK, Sante?' she asks.

I nod, half-expecting her to make us return the Honda to its rightful owner straightaway. She cups my chin. Inspects my face, arms and legs.

'I'm fine,' I tell her. 'A few scratches and bruises, that's all...'

Mama Rose walks over to Cat. Prises Scarlett off her, fingers the bruising around Cat's right eye. 'Sante-girl,' she says to me. 'Get some arnica from the first aid kit. Cobra, pick some of those marigolds in that field. I'll need the petals to make calendula for your sister.'

Cobra doesn't move. He's watching Cat, taking note of how she is with Scarlett: those tender pauses and silences as Cat's fingers trail through Scarlett's hair. He watches his sister and for the first time truly sees the stranger. Scarlett gazes back at him with the limpid eyes of a colt about to bolt. As surely as day follows night and sunshine chases moonshine, his soul opens up to her and – *bam!* – same thing happens to him as with Cat. I hear it; feel the hiss, the tug at his heart as Scarlett lassoes it with a smile.

Cobra gives her one of his cheeky, insinuating grins,

and then fixes his greens on me. He knows what I do now. This one's for Cat, Cat alone. And if he so much as gets in his sister's way, she's going to scratch out his eyes and give 'em to Priss for an afternoon snack. If Cat doesn't keep him off Scarlett, so help me, I will.

There's nothing like a challenge to whet Cobra's ardour. Straightaway, he flashes a smile at Scarlett, and burns a hole straight through my heart. Hurts so much I feel like saying: 'What's she got that I haven't? Look at her! Hunger's scooped her out from within and there's no fat on her body, no curves whatsoever. In fact, her backside's every bit as scrawny as mine is!'

I can scarcely breathe until Mama Rose says to Cobra: 'Get a move on, I need those petals to tend to your sister.'

The moment Cobra leaves, the Old Ones want to know exactly what's going on. Why we've been fighting, stolen a Honda. They want to know where Scarlett comes from, where her folks are. They want answers to a whole heap of hard-to-answer questions, when even I know in my heart, that to keep Scarlett safe from those thugs, we *have* to take her in. No two ways about it. But like I've said already, where Old Ones are concerned, nothing's easy.

Cat tells 'em what she can. Tells 'em everything that Scarlett's told her. Then Scarlett licks her lips, reddens them with the tip of a coral-pink tongue and speaks. Speaks so low everyone has to lean in to hear her. Speaks low and soft, as if she's broken in pieces and can't stoop any lower. But this time, when she tells us how it is, she uses words she couldn't say before, words such as 'pimp'.

The man with the black quiff, Miguel, is planning to pimp her out. He used to be kind to her, but now her parents have gone, he wants her to earn back the money he gave 'em. From the sound of it, the devil himself couldn't be any worse than Miguel.

Scarlett clings to Cat's fingers as she describes her tribulations. Even so, she gets the shakes waiting to hear if the Old Ones will let her stay.

Redwood's eyes narrow. He tugs on the lobe of his ear and asks: 'Where's your passport, Scarlett?'

Mama Rose nods, Bizzie Lizzie too, while Mimi creeps closer and touches Scarlett. Scarlett flinches. Freezes. Won't let anyone but Cat touch her. Lets Cat speak for her as well:

'Miguel still has her passport. We were trying to bust into his safe when he found us.'

Redwood shakes his head, looks up at the late afternoon sky, then scowls at Cat: 'If you insist on acting crazy,' he says, 'you're going to end up crazier than an old coot, and there'll be no helping you, Cat.'

Cat bristles, is about to answer back, but scrunches her face in fury instead. There's no need for her to say anything when she's like that. No need to throw daggers, when she's already hurling 'em with her eyes.

'Cat isn't nuts,' I say to Redwood. 'In case, you've forgotten, you brought us up to look out for each other.'

'Far as I recall, I didn't have a hand in raising her.' Redwood nods at Scarlett. 'If you want to find your way home, young lady, I suggest you go to the British Consul in Cádiz They'll help you out.'

Mama Rose folds her arms waiting for Scarlett's reply.

The girl's mind is thick with cobwebs. Parts her lips, starts to stutter.

'Scarlett needs us!' I cry. 'Needs somewhere to lay her head tonight, food to eat tomorrow.'

'Nothing's as simple as it seems,' Mama Rose reminds me. 'The police may be looking for her already and if they're working with Miguel and his friends, that makes her a liability to us.'

'A great big albatross around our necks,' Redwood sighs.

'A downright curse,' Lizzie mutters.

I can't believe what I'm hearing! Are these the same people who took me in, and saved Cobra and Cat before me? I make fists of my hands, stand square, and face Mama Rose, saying: 'So you think we should leave her to fend for herself? Let Miguel use her to make money? Will someone please wake me up and tell me that this isn't happening?'

I look from one to the other: Mama Rose to Redwood, Bizzie Lizzie to Midget Man and Mimi.

Not a single one of 'em replies, so I turn again to Mama Rose: 'Aren't you the one who's always warning us that some lowlife would love to get their hands on us? Sell us, make us slaves? You said as much last night. Said so to me. And now you want us to stand by and watch that creature Miguel take Scarlett away?'

'Not while I'm around,' says Cobra, handing a pouch of petals to Mama Rose.

'Me too,' says Cat. She strokes Scarlett's hand and takes in the Old Ones: 'Seems the only way to get heard around here is to keep saying the same thing again and again. We young ones have a stake in this outfit and we want Scarlett to stay.'

'Mimi and I agree.' Midget Man speaks and the tide turns.

'Are you sure, Sante?' says Mama Rose.

Scarlett gazes at me, eyes sweet as honey. Her soul brushes against mine a second time and I nod.

'Very well. She can stay with us tonight,' says Mama Rose. 'We'll decide what to do tomorrow. Come along, Sante. I need to talk to you.'

10

I make Mama Rose wait. She has to wait. I can't tear myself away from what's right in front of me: Cobra making eyes at Scarlett. As soon as Mimi started tending to Cat's bruises, Cobra corralled Scarlett. Fetched her a cup of water, a bite of bread and cheese to eat. Behaves as if she's the only girl in the world and I don't matter any more. From what my heart's telling me, Cobra's enchanted, and even though she doesn't register him yet, 'cause she can't focus on anyone but Cat, he hovers over her like Priss does before she dives at her prey.

I've seen that look on my bird so often, I'd recognise it anywhere. It goes deeper than anything you'll ever read in a book. Deeper than the ocean and the sky above it, and it's telling me that Cobra's crazy for her. I watch 'em together and the hole in my heart grows bigger. Truth is, Cobra's never looked at me like that. The white girl may be pale and thin, but I swear, there's something about her that's set him spinning. What puzzles me is that I'm spinning as well.

Mama Rose calls me a second time, then again. Third time lucky. I follow her voice and find her sitting on a cushion in the back of our truck. Redwood's opposite her. On her right is a mahogany sea-chest. From the resolute expression in her dark eyes, seems Mama Rose has been building up to this moment for a long while, longer than yesterday. Those eyes and her clothes tell me this is serious; life and death serious. Must be, 'cause she's changed out of overalls into her thinking gear: an indigo kimono, a band belted around her waist. And in her hair, a black lacquered chopstick speared through a bun on top of her head. In the same way that my thoughts untangle in the grey dawn of morning, Mama Rose's thinking flows freely when she dresses as a geisha. There's a formality about the attire, a measured elegance, she says, that assists her reasoning. She hasn't powdered her cheeks white this time, though her face is ashen.

'Sante-girl,' she says to me when I climb into the back. 'Come here. Let me touch you again, make sure you're OK.'

I'm no longer a toddler learning to fly with Priss, so I don't normally like her to fuss over me. I may have tumbled over the rooftops of Cádiz, but I've no serious injuries to speak of. All the same, given the ache in my heart, I let her.

She smoothes the curve of my cheek, then sidles up to me and hugs me tight. So tight, the jagged edges of our conversation last night, and my frustration with Cobra, tip into tears. And instead of asking questions about who I am and where I come from, instead of demanding to know why she went to see the African and Grey Eyes without me, I curl up beside her and howl louder than a hyena at full moon. 'I don't think Cobra's going to marry me any more, Mama Rose.'

She pats my head, holds me close, and rocks me in those big fleshy arms of hers. Laughs, then says, 'Why do you think I asked you, in particular, if you wanted Scarlett to stay, Sante-girl?'

With my feelings as mangled as they are, I can't find the words to answer.

'Doing the right thing isn't always easy,' Mama Rose smiles. 'Truth be told, I'm proud of you, Sante. You said what needed to be said back there. Not an easy task when Cobra and Cat are behaving like two polecats in heat. Is that it? Is that what's bothering you?'

I sob. All I can think about is Cobra. Cobra and Scarlett. Should be focused on more urgent matters, but just thinking about them excites me. I lay my head on Mama Rose's lap, and squeeze my eyes tight to shut out the world. Cobra especially.

'Now, now, Sante,' Mama Rose says. 'You've got to learn to exercise patience with Cobra. A girl has to exercise patience with any human of the male persuasion. You set your heart on the boy when you were knee-high to a grasshopper, and from what I know about the two of you, there's no one in the whole wide world but you crazy enough to have him.'

Her words, designed to soothe, don't reassure me. In fact, now I've started, there's no stopping my tears and the fury behind them. I'm too angry to talk, ask questions, make a plan. Seems all I can do is wail like a fool. Howl and hiss in a tantrum that starts Priss yelping as well.

Mama Rose cradles me in her arms. 'I told you,' she says to Redwood. 'The child's not ready yet. She's too young to know. Too young to be making decisions on her own.'

Redwood leans forwards: 'Tell her,' he insists. 'Ready or not, it's time, Rosie. She deserves to know what you've done for her and what those men want. And there's no better time than the present.'

I hate it when Old Ones talk over my head. Hate it so much that to stop my caterwauling and sober up quick, I bite my lip until I taste blood. Even so, takes some time for the sobbing to cease while Mama Rose hugs me tighter, cleaving to me. I reckon she doesn't want me to grow up. Doesn't want me to find my monsters and slay 'em.

I pull away from her and settle on a cushion. Wipe tears from my eyes and take her hand. 'Tell me about the African and his friend, Mama Rose. Tell me what happened to my family. Why did they cast me into the sea? I want to know, 'cause I won't be able to fly free like Priss till I do.'

Mama Rose sighs, a long, shuddering release of breath that signals the end of our old life and the start of something new. Then she tells me.

What she describes fits in with what Priss hinted at long ago and what Mama Rose mentioned in passing. I came from the sea, laden with treasure in a sea-chest. Mama Rose grabs hold of the old mahogany trunk, drags it between us, and pulls out a blue-and-green cloth made of strips of woven silk cotton. Strips sewn together with gold thread into what looks like an intricate puzzle blanket. Purple-and-gold between green-and-blue check; wedges of horizontal colour alongside diagonals.

'You came covered in this,' Mama Rose says. She strokes the blanket and then hands it over.

I raise it to my nose and smell the scent of a man in the soft fabric. Musk and cedarwood, a fragrance with a trace of ancient sweat. An image slowly surfaces in my mind and shimmers. As I strain to hold on to it, it fades. I relax and gradually it fills me, seeping into my pores as sensations lap at my feet.

A tall lion of a man, his hands swaddling me in cloth.

I make out a deep rumble of approval. Murmurs of *Sem! Amie! Yo!*

Perhaps the blanket on my lap belonged to the tall man in my dream.

I hear a faint rustling in the shadows and sense a gathering of ghosts hovering close by. I turn. Heartbeat quickens. Blood tingles. Tears sting my eyes.

'You came laden with treasure, Sante. More treasure than I'd ever seen, then or since: gold dust and diamonds. I even found this dagger hidden beneath your feet.'

A picture flickers in my mind and voices I've heard again and again in my dreams whisper to me. I block my ears with the palms of my hands. I don't want to hear them. Don't want my nightmare to be true, yet the voices murmur, resonating down the years:

'Give her this. My dagger to help her in battle. May the child be a princess, a true warrior, valiant in the face of danger yet merciful to those she defeats.'

'May your spear arm be strong, my daughter,' the tall man adds. *'Your legs swift as a gazelle and your heart the mighty heart of a lioness protecting her cubs.'*

If he's talking to his daughter, he must be my father.

Don't want a father. Don't need one, in any case. Tears trickle down my cheeks.

Mama Rose hands me the silver dagger – a sparkling serrated blade above a jewel-studded hilt. 'Diamonds,' she says, rubbing my fingers over them.

Jewels shift and glimmer through a kaleidoscope of tears. I marvel at the warm glow of baubles, touch the blade.

'I used up all the gold dust you brought with you, Sante,' says Mama Rose. 'Used it on food and medicine. Bought our trucks with it as well. I managed to hold on to the diamonds, though. Kept every single one of those precious stones. Have you still got your tutu, child?'

'Of course!'

For as long as I can remember, Mama Rose has always insisted that I look after the tutu well. Never wash it, but swab it clean with a cloth. And when I grow out of it, she makes me a new one. Unpicks the rhinestones from the old one, adds a few more, and then sews them on to a new tutu.

'Give it to me,' she says.

I climb up to my bunk and fetch my tutu, still crumpled from last night's show.

'There they are. The diamonds you arrived with.'

'Diamonds?'

Mama Rose catches Redwood's eye and grins at me. 'There's no better hiding place,' she says, 'than what the eye can see and dismiss in a blink as vulgar circus glitter. This is what's left of your treasure, Sante. Along with the drum and the bamboo flute.'

Mama Rose folds the diamond-studded tutu, puts it on my lap and bites her lip. Chews on it, while she decides how best to say what else is on her mind: 'From the cargo they bundled into this chest here, your people were rich, Sante,' she says at last. 'People from Africa. They must have wanted to start a new life over here. If times were bad then, they're even worse now. Floods, famine, drought ... every disaster you can think of, there's worse to come.'

I anticipate the words in Mama Rose's mouth before she says 'em. If I've heard it once, I've heard it a thousand times: the story of How Things Came to Be This Bad and Can Only Get Worse. How the poor become poorer as money rises to the top. How everyone with any sense is moving north: on foot, on trains, boats and planes to find Greener Pastures. I know the story by heart and, truth be told, it makes me squirm, even though the way Redwood tells it, he should know. He used to make money; dung hills of money. Worked in Wall Street in the USA till he bailed out. Been moving ever since. That's why we live in wild places, live off the grid, 'cause deep in their hearts the Old Ones believe that the way things are, we're doomed. And when the end times come, only those of us who live off the grid will be left standing.

Cat laughs at 'em behind their backs and I do too. We call 'em Doomsters. According to them, nothing's ever going to get better. Cobra, as you'd expect, doesn't dismiss them completely. Says all families are mostly crazy and ours is no different. Have to learn to take the rough with the smooth.

Used to laugh at 'em until they took us one summer to the Spanish beach where Mama Rose found me. There we saw brown bodies lying dead on the shore, women tanning themselves a stone's throw away. Wiped the smiles clean off our faces that did.

So when Mama Rose says: 'Strangers pitch up on our shores and we herd them into camps. They come in broken boats and we let them drown,' this time her words become entwined with my nightmare of a baby thrown overboard as people thrash in the sea. Indeed, her words dwell in me with a ferocity they never have before. Because I'm there. And this is about me and people like me.

'What we're doing is unforgiveable. It breaks every law the human heart tries to live by. That's why I adopted you and the twins. Illegally, of course, but there's not much you can't do if you set your mind to it. That's how come you kids are with me, Sante. For better, for worse, I did what was right.'

That rustling again. The soft shuffle of footsteps inching closer. I turn and the thickening shadows murmur grunts of approval in that strange language: *Amie! Yo! Amie!*

I don't understand it. Don't want to. But there's something else. Something I can't put my finger on that doesn't chime with what I'm hearing.

I stare at Mama Rose. Unable to meet my gaze, she looks down at her hands and says: 'You finally appreciate what I've been telling you, Sante?'

I can't talk 'cause of the tears flowing out of me. I hang my head, confused at that part of me that feels guilty for being in the wrong place at the wrong time.

Mama Rose places a hand on my knee. Still won't meet my eyes, though. Lashes fluttering, she peers at me and says: 'We'll soon be done, Sante.' She pauses, then removes a sheet of paper from inside the trunk, and gives it to me.

Thin and fragile as the skeleton of a leaf dried by wind, the paper's faded with age. I sniff it warily. Smell the same fragrance of musk with a whiff of cinnamon and mangoes. Rotting mangoes. On the paper is a scrawl of round, homely writing similar to my own:

This is my beloved child, Asantewaa, daughter of Amma Serwah and Kofi Prempeh of the Ashanti people of Ghana. I beg you, look after our child and bring her up as your own. Use her treasure wisely, for the riches of Africa are vested in the person of my little princess.

Signed,
Amma Serwah

Is this writing really that of my mother? Are these words the last she wrote before she was mown down by gunfire? Or did she die in the blaze? Or drown in the sea that saved me? I can scarcely believe that the script in front of me, so like my own, was written by the woman who gave birth to me. I try to retrieve the outline of her face, the smile in eyes unfamiliar to me, but cannot. She's always a blur in my dream, lost in a jumble of anxious faces. Even so, her voice returns. A voice shrill with terror:

'My baby! My baby! Save my baby!'

My stomach clenches.

Don't know what I'm supposed to do, what I'm supposed to think. Can't think, not while my mother's panic overwhelms me. I don't want her inside me, but before I can block her, I realise she's always been there. Only now the weight of her emotions crushes my heart, as feelings churn within me: curiosity, horror and then sadness so deep, I could a cry a river and still have tears to weep.

Before she engulfs me, I decide I don't need any more mothers, not with Priss and Mama Rose in my life. And yet, as I read the letter again to get to grips with it, more questions than answers clamour in my mind and curiosity, a hunch-backed cat, slinks between my legs, waiting to be fed.

Hands shaking, body shivering, I ask: 'Who are the Ashanti people, Mama Rose? And how come the riches of Africa are vested in me?'

I look into her eyes and flinch. There's more to be said; something she's holding back that concerns the two of us, and our future.

'Are Ashantis bad, Mama Rose? People we shouldn't associate with, 'cause they behave outside the bounds of the human heart?'

Redwood takes my hand. 'The woman you're named after, Yaa Asantewaa, was an Ashanti queen, Sante. A warrior woman who led her men against the British a long time ago.'

'A warrior?' I say. 'A woman?'

He can see I want to know more, for he moves closer, long arms straddling his thighs: 'I'll tell you all that I know about Yaa Asantewaa and her people in due course. Right now there's something else you should think about.'

Mama Rose blanches. 'Leave it, Redwood!'

'No chance of that now, Rosie.' Impatience adds an edge of urgency to Redwood's baritone and I begin to quake. 'Sante,' Redwood says, 'those men we met in town this morning are part of the same racket that got your folks killed. According to them, what went into your cradle is their property and they want it back. Everything. And if they don't get what they want by tomorrow, they're coming after us.'

Mama Rose smiles and then says with a sigh: 'It's time to move on again, Sante-girl. We're leaving tonight.'

It takes all the strength in me to defy 'em, but I do. I see the gleam in Priss's eyes, remember the sweep and spread of her wings this morning, and know for a fact that to fly I've got to stop running and face my enemies. I take a deep breath, muster my strength, and say clear as a bell: 'You can leave if you want, but I'm staying.'

Redwood's persuasive, Mama Rose too. But this time, the combined weight of their powerful reasoning barely shifts me. I've dug a hole in the ground and I'm burrowing.

They pile on pressure, the way Old Ones do. 'This isn't just about you,' they say. They ask me to think about them, all of 'em, Scarlett as well.

Then they remind me – as if I need reminding – of the tremendous pain people-smugglers, crooked policemen, lowlifers in general, can inflict on a teenager.

I burrow deeper, so deep, they can't reach me with their talking. Truly, the more they talk, the firmer I hunker down. And the deeper I hunker down, the more ferociously I say: 'Trust me. I'll be OK. Priss will look after me.'

Each time I mention Priss, they almost weep. That's how foolish they think I am!

Perhaps it's those African spirits around me: their sighs and groans, cries and whispers. Could be that letter my mother wrote for me, or the power of that warrior queen beefing me up. Don't know what it is; even if the ground fractures and crusts over me, I have to find out more. And that means talking to the African.

I may be younger than her but sometimes I can be just as stubborn as Cat and every bit as fierce. Now that my mind is set, Mama Rose realises that nothing she says is going to change it. Realises that only Cobra can get to me. Mama Rose and Redwood aren't the brains of our outfit for nothing. They know how to play on our weaknesses for the greater good. They yell for Cobra to plead their case, see if he can sway me.

Cobra comes in, one of his snakes around his neck. Been trying to impress Scarlett with his special talent, no doubt. He strokes the snake as he hears us out. Takes the measure of me, then glances at Priss sitting proud on her perch. Sees the same iron gleam in Priss's eyes as in mine, the same blaze of determination on my face, and knows straightaway that I've dug too deep for him to haul me out. No way am I going to compromise, so Cobra says: 'If we want to leave this town with Sante, we're going to have to wait a day or two.'

'We have to move tonight,' says Redwood.

Mama Rose takes the pin out of her topknot,

shakes her straggly hair loose and says: 'If I know anything about villains, and I've met quite a few in my time, Miguel will try and get Scarlett back. And those men we met in town say they want everything Sante's got. We leave tonight.'

Cobra looks at me and I reckon he's thinking what I'm thinking. We haven't said a word about Cat stabbing Miguel, yet the Old Ones seem to know the sort of scoundrels we're dealing with. If they're scared, perhaps we should be too.

The snake at Cobra's neck wriggles down his arm, then twists around it like a writhing, shining bangle. I scowl at him as he asks Mama Rose: 'Where are we going this time?'

Turns out Midget Man's got friends in Granada, Romany friends who'll let us stay with 'em till our trouble blows over.

Cobra pats the head of his living ornament and smiles as a green tongue darts out. Pats the snake a second time and says: 'I'll stay here with Sante if you want, meet those men in town tomorrow and when we're done, we'll catch up with you. Should be easy to find you, if you lend us your motorbike, Redwood.'

Redwood raises an eyebrow. Coughs, glances at Mama Rose, then they both heave mighty sighs, as if the world's going to end much sooner than we think. They confer with Midget Man and Mimi, Bizzie Lizzie too. Argue. *Um* and *ah* some more, until finally they give in.

I reckon they wouldn't be so worried if they were leaving Cobra and I alone in the wilderness. Most times nature's easier to deal with than city folk. But as things stand, there's not much they can do.

Mama Rose slips off the kimono, pulls on her overalls and from a right-hand pocket, brings out the note that the African and Grey Eyes gave to Redwood to give to me. Hands it over.

The paper's thick and velvety, with an address in sloping black letters scribbled over it. I read it and my heart lurches. I pass the note to Cobra. His cheeks pale, he opens his mouth, appalled. I touch the middle of my forehead to signal that I'm staying no matter what and Cobra groans.

While the Old Ones finish packing, Cobra pressures me to change my mind. But the way I'm feeling today, not even the biggest scumbag in the whole wide world or the devil himself could make me do what I don't want to.

Within the hour everything's packed, including Cat's new Honda. She's loaded it into Midget Man's truck without Mama Rose noticing. Mama Rose is too busy, I suppose, seeing that Cobra and I have everything we need: enough money to keep us going for a few days and a roll of canvas for a tent.

Mama Rose touches my cheek, lifts up my chin and, looks me straight in the eye: 'Take care of yourself, you hear, Sante-girl,' she says. 'You're my youngest, so don't do anything foolish and make me old before my time. Don't let my hair turn grey overnight.'

'We'll be fine,' I tell her.

I blink away tears, and when Redwood hands Cobra the keys to his bike with strict instructions that I'm not – repeat *not* – to drive it, I'm to be Cobra's passenger at all times, I nod.

Midget Man writes down the address of his friends in Granada, tells us the name of a pal in Cádiz, Imma, who'll help us if we need her, scrawls down her number as well, and we're done.

Dusk falls and, as crickets start cranking out their love songs, Cobra and I wave goodbye. The trucks roll on to the highway and we're alone with Priss.

11

'You don't have to stay,' I say to Cobra. 'Priss and I can look after ourselves just fine.' There's no better way to begin, I reckon, than how I intend to proceed. Petulant.

Cobra shrugs.

We're making a tepee, three poles and a roll of canvas to build a nest for the night. Bodies bend and stretch, tug and pull, cooperate instinctively. Yet the way I'm feeling, I'm likely to snap at Cobra's heels at any moment, bite him even.

'Sure as hell don't need you,' I tell him. 'I can find those men and sort 'em out by myself.'

'Sure,' he says, positioning a pole.

'Easy as pie.'

A smile tugs at his mouth, and I decide that if he says 'sure' one more time, I'm going to go walkabout.

Take off with Priss for the night; hunt till I'm too tired to feel angry any more.

Cobra secures the tent's canvas, squats on the ground, and smiles as slowly as a snail chewing a seedling. 'Sure,' he says. 'Easy as pie to go back to the very same building we fled this afternoon. It's so easy, in fact, I might as well leave you to get on with it by yourself, Sante.'

I whistle for Priss. She flies down from a big avocado tree. I pull on my leather glove and she settles on my wrist.

Cobra stares at us. At last, he says: 'We have to make a plan, Sante. Work out how we're going to do this without bumping into Miguel and his friends. We need to talk.'

'Don't want to. Don't want to talk to *you* at any rate. Want to be with Priss.'

'I know.'

And he does. Fact is, if you love someone you've lived with your whole life long, chances are, if he likes you too, he knows you better than the palm of his hand. Cobra knows my highs and lows. So much so that even if I am inclined to snap at him, I allow Priss to fly back into the tree, and squat opposite him. Squat and face another problem. How can I stop wanting someone I can't help but feast my eyes on?

His black hair slicked up in spikes tickles the breeze. Cheekbones glint in the first flush of evening. Dusky skin glows. Above us, the sky's the colour of slate, and the moon's fighting for space with the last remnants of the sun.

Green eyes quiz me. 'Who's put a bee in your bonnet, Sante-girl? What's made you mean as a tick tonight?'

Scarlett. I can't bring myself to say her name, but she's here, sitting between us. I feel like a fool reliving the hurt of how Cobra looked at her, when there're so many other things I want to talk to him about. I want to tell him what was in my cradle. Tell him about the letter from my mother, that my real name's Asantewaa Prempeh. And yet, just thinking about Scarlett thickens my throat with tears. After all the wailing I've done today, it seems unnatural that a girl can cry this much and remain standing. Truth is, I want to weep and howl and rant and rave, not just about Scarlett, but everything.

Cobra's palm grazes my wrist and his fingers garland it. 'Don't worry, Sante. We can do this. We'll be OK.'

He touches me, and my eyes begin to leak. Already lost one family. Can't live if Cobra leaves me as well. Those voices in my dream can heap all the blessings in the world on me but, plain as the dirt on my hands, I don't have the heart of a lioness or legs fast as a gazelle's. I'm not a true warrior, valiant in the face of danger. I'm Sante, friend of Priss, adopted daughter of Mama Rose, a scraggy teenager trying not to cry in front of the boy I've loved for as long as I remember.

Cobra folds the palms of my hands in his and fondles them. He holds 'em gently. Kindness loosens my tongue and I blurt out that name: 'Scarlett. You don't look at me like you look at her, Cobra, 'cause you like her more than you like me.'

Green eyes blink, perplexed: 'Didn't know you were the jealous type, Sante.'

He doesn't say it; he thinks it.

'I'm not jealous!' I cry. 'And don't pretend you don't like her!'

He furrows his brow, squints at me, and he might as well tell me straight out that there's not a single thing in the world worth knowing that I know about; not a single fact I can chew on for sure. Squints at me and sees an idiot. He shakes his head in despair and looks up at the evening star.

'You do, Cobra, you do! I saw you looking at her the way Priss looks at a rabbit she's about to eat.'

He shakes his head again and grins: 'I am not Priss, Sante. I looked. I was friendly. Girl doesn't know if she's coming or going. You can't say just 'cause I look at Scarlett, I want her.'

The hand holding my wrist tightens, till I feel the burn: a sizzle beneath my skin as Cobra's eyes remain fixed on mine.

'Are you sure?'

'Sure as the feathers on your bird, the girl doesn't like snakes. I showed her Scales and Bella and she freaked out. Can't make sense of a girl who can't touch snakes and let 'em glide on her skin.'

So Scarlett failed the snake test. My pout eases into a smile that widens into a grin. If there's one thing I know it's this: to get close to Cobra, you've got to like his snakes. I cradle my hands in his and recite one of Redwood's mantras: 'Rattlers, roaches and rats.' The three 'Rs'. Just about everyone's scared of one of 'em. Can't stand roaches myself, but snakes? 'Cause of Cobra, I've no problem with snakes whatsoever. I laugh, and then Cobra and I talk late into the night. I tell him everything Mama Rose told me. Tell him about that strange language I'm hearing as well, the shuffle of ancient footsteps inching closer. And we make a plan.

Early next morning we ride into town for breakfast at the same seaside café I took Scarlett and Cat. The waiter recognises me, calls me 'the black girl on a stallion'. I introduce him to Cobra, and he lets us sit in the same spot as yesterday – in the sun with a glorious view of the sea. I order scrambled eggs and toast and drink mint tea as Priss flies away on her morning ramble.

Ocean's calm today, black in places, with a dark undertow of ripples. On the surface it glitters bright as diamonds, bright as the ones on the dagger in my rucksack.

I finger the weapon and the flute beside it. Touch the note I picked up on the beach from that policeman yesterday. Paper, smooth bamboo, a dagger with a serrated blade, handle studded with jewels. If the African is who I believe he is, he'll recognise it. Feels strange to admit it, but all that loot in my cradle doesn't mean much to me. I'd be tempted to give the African and Grey Eyes everything they want, if it wasn't for my mother and that line she wrote in her letter: *'Use her treasure wisely, for the riches of Africa are vested in the person of my little princess.'*

I don't fully understand her meaning, but it seems to me she wanted me to have those things. How was she to know I'd end up living off the grid where there's not much I can do with a ceremonial dagger? Diamonds are another matter. A bit of money, at the right time, can make the difference between life and death.

I'm trying to figure out the intention behind my mother's words and what I should do, when Cobra returns with a phone from a shop opposite the café. Without the Old Ones around to enforce their rules, Cobra and I ogle it. We've always wanted a phone. We fondle the screen, take it in turns to hold it to our ears. Sniff its surface until we work out how to use it. Then we feed it with minutes, and make our move.

We ride with Priss down the same road we travelled yesterday, from a wide, open boulevard in the new part of town into the narrow streets of the old city. We take a leisurely pace across San Antonio square to the street that sets my heart pounding. Sweat pricks my armpits. Breathing grows shallow, almost peters out, as I begin to grasp the enormity of what we're doing. The building where Miguel and his thugs live, and kept Scarlett, is home to the African and Grey Eyes. They may not know each other, but what if the African and Grey Eyes are working with them? And what if we bump into Miguel?

Cobra parks Redwood's motor, and after we've checked out the street, we choose a hideaway in the shadow of a gloomy restaurant overlooking *five*, *calle Horozco*. We sit where we can't be seen from the dazzling sunlight outside; yet not so far in the dark that we can't keep an eye on the place.

Priss perches on the roof, and while we wait, Cobra and I share a cola. Sip it slowly. Sit up when a van parks and unloads a cargo of food and drinks. Someone's planning a party at number five tonight. Would take Mama Rose's Family Circus over a month to eat that much food, though from the way the Old Ones behave on occasion, they could down that liquor in no time at all.

The van drives away and moments later, Miguel, a jacket over a shoulder, strides out of the front door with his henchman, that barrel of a man. Three ragged lines of scratches run down the man's face; three long lines of stitches. If he wasn't ugly enough already, he's now marked for life by Priss.

Miguel's jacket doesn't quite hide the bandages underneath, the damage wrought by Cat's knife. With a shoulder like that, he won't be able to mess with anyone for a while.

Barrel Man takes a few paces, looks up at the blue morning sky, and almost jumps out of his pants. Hitches them up, points to where Priss is, grabs a bottle and hurls it. Priss stays exactly where she is. Knows an object can't fly high enough to touch her. Flaunts her wings and as she does so, Barrel Man screams obscenities.

Miguel circles and scans the street. Looks every which way he can, and shouts: 'Are those bloody gypsies still around?'

Cobra and I shrink.

'Damn them! Damn those gypsies!' Miguel kicks a tyre and keeps looking around cursing us, as he ambles into an alleyway with Barrel Man.

I don't speak good Spanish, but like I've said already, I've learned the slang words for money and police in just about every language you care to mention. I recognise the words for gypsy as well. Always helps to know what people are saying when they're insulting you.

We wait patiently. Drink one, then two colas. Halfway through the third, the person we're waiting for emerges: the African in jeans and a gleaming white shirt. He walks fast. Cobra nods and we follow him. He buys a newspaper, and then saunters into a café. Orders brandy, coffee. Sits down, flings open the newspaper and starts reading.

Cobra nods again. I take a deep breath, then with most of my heart in my mouth, step up and tap the African on the shoulder: 'Pardon me for interrupting, but I understand you're looking for me, mister.'

He stares at me with muddy, red eyes. Folds the paper, folds his arms: 'Why don't you sit down?' he says.

I do as he asks and Cobra takes a seat beside me.

12

Before I fell asleep in Cobra's arms last night, I made a list with his help, of all the questions I want answers to. First off, facts about my mother and father: the place they came from, what sort of people they were, and why they were on a boat heading for Europe. There's a barrel-load of questions I want to ask. For instance – how did the African manage to survive when everyone else on the boat, except me, drowned? Last night questions swarmed in my head. Truth is, soon as I sit down opposite him, my mind empties, and I just gape at the bloodshot eyes of a middle-aged man. Round, heavy face, skin as dark as my own, and on the table, the hands of a working man: oil-stained, etched with lines. Hands with large, bulbous fingers, which, even when daintily leafing through a paper in a café in Cádiz, are rough and tough. I know this before he takes hold of my fingers and folds them in his.

'Allah be praised! You survived,' he says. 'Our hope for a better future lives!' His mouth jerks in a nervous smile that doesn't light up his eyes, till he downs his brandy.

I take the dagger out of my rucksack, the flute as well, and push them over to him. 'Are these yours?'

He nods, covers the dagger with the newspaper, hands the flute back to me and says: 'Not here, my child. Not while the eyes of the world are on us. Let's go to my home.'

If there's one thing I've learned on the road, it's that you don't go home with strangers. In any case, going into that building isn't part of the plan I devised with Cobra. I may have dreamed about the African again and again, but dreaming's not the same as knowing someone. 'Mister,' I say to him. 'I want to talk to you in public.'

Makes no difference what I want. He gets up and folds the paper, the dagger inside. 'What we have to say to each other is private,' he tells me. 'I can't talk to you in a place where even the walls have ears. You may bring your friend with you if you want, but I'm going home'

I wasn't born an idiot. Don't want to die one either! But then it's not as if I'm completely on my *own*. The African beckons, and Cobra and I retrace our steps and enter the building we hoped never to set foot in again. We trail him up the narrow staircase, round and round, into an apartment on the fourth floor. He opens the door and – *wham!* – it hits you: a place designed to salute the sea and revel in its beauty

White walls, beige marble floors and on the balcony, terracotta pots filled with bay and orange trees. Yet the apartment is eerily quiet. On the floor are Moroccan-style carpets in teal and beige, turquoise and white. Rattan furniture, the same sort I spied years ago in one of Lizzie's magazines. She keeps 'em hidden to remind her of how her life used to be. I once flicked through 'em with Cat, and wondered aloud how Lizzie and Redwood could give up a life of luxury to run away to join the circus.

Some things in the world, I shall never understand. But this I know for a fact: the African and Grey Eyes, his friend, are rich; stupendously rich. Got to be 'cause of the size of that television pinned on the wall. Never seen a TV my whole life long as big as that one! Wouldn't mind perching in front of it for a week to see what comes out.

On another wall, paintings. Not too many, mind you, just enough to draw the eye to the balcony, and beyond that, a view of turquoise sea.

The African disappears. He returns in five shakes with a tray piled high with food: shrimps, slices of ham, strawberries. Drinks too. Lays the food on the table, invites us to sit down and eat, and then pours himself a large brandy.

Cobra rolls a strip of ham and drops it in his mouth. Chews, watching the African. The African stares back. Looks from Cobra to me and then asks the very question I want to put to him:

'How did you manage to survive, child?'

If I were wiser perhaps an answer would trip off my tongue. As it is, I can't say whether it is sheer luck or those prayers they mumbled over me in the boat that protected me. I shrug, go to the balcony, and call Priss. Bird flies down, and I say to the African: 'My bird Priss helped me. But before she found me, those people in the boat prayed over me, gave me their things.'

'We asked Allah to guide you and he did. You remember?'

'Yes, I remember.'

I can tell from that look in his eyes he doesn't believe me. He sniffs and snorts, unconvinced that the shock of a cataclysmic event can stay lodged in a body for so long. 'I dream about what happened,' I say. 'I dream the same dream again and again. The dream won't let me forget.'

One mention of it and goosebumps freckle my arms. I fold 'em to keep warm as the sumptuous hush in the room deepens and the drag of the past flips me back to a place before memory. They're here with me again. Those ghosts from my sea-chest cradle, who want to be heard, but speak a language I don't understand. 'Unless I'm mistaken, mister, you were there as well.'

The African can feel them too. The spooks.

'I can't forget either,' he says. 'It wasn't supposed to happen like that. I was the ship's engineer. We were supposed to take her in before they sunk her out at sea, but the owner brought the date forwards.'

'But why? Why sink a boat full of people?'

He stares at me with dead, leaden eyes. Shakes his head and whispers so quietly, I have to bring my ear in close to hear him: 'To claim insurance. One day later and we'd have got very little. As we both know, my child, if you're not white, your life is cheap in this world.'

He looks over his shoulder, places his hands over his ears and begins to pant and shiver like a puppy taken from its mother. Shivers and sighs in such a way that I'm convinced he's hearing them too: the gentle scuffle of feet as they begin to circle us, coming ever closer to warm themselves on our breath. Invisible fingers reach to touch, to prod, to linger a while longer in the sun.

'What's your name, mister?'

'Isaka.' Hand trembling, he adds more brandy to his glass. Downs it. Pours another slug.

If he carries on like this, he'll end up worse than Redwood when he's flat out after one of his binges. Bemoans the state of the world, the state we're in.

Moans and groans till Lizzie sings him a lullaby to help him feel better. Redwood's what Mama Rose calls a Binge Drinker. From what I'm seeing in front of me now, Isaka is steady as he goes, an all-day drinking man.

His clothes may be spotless, but a pong of booze oozes from his pores as I slip closer to get a sniff of what's eating him. I dip inside him and sense a deep sadness coiled around his heart. Shiver, 'cause underlying his pain, a trace of menace infests him like fruit flies hovering over figs. Could be those ghosts aren't just haunting him, but riding him to wear him down.

Isaka rolls open the newspaper he's placed on the dining table and picks up the dagger. Turns it around as tears roll down his cheeks. 'This has been in my family for generations. What exquisite workmanship.'

He stands, walks to the balcony to admire his heirloom in sunlight. I follow and watch, enchanted by the flash of diamonds as he twists the dagger.

'I was supposed to sell this to the highest bidder and send the money back home to my family in Mali. It was not meant to be. We gave you our most precious possessions, my child. Do you want to know why?'

From the tone of his voice, I reckon he's going to tell me, whether I want to know or not. 'We did what we had to, my dear, because we believed we were at the end of our journey and we wanted one of us, at least, to survive. We faced eternity and gave you the best of ourselves.' He pauses and his mouth twitches in a bitter smile. 'But I survived. I appreciate your gesture, my child, but I believe there was much more than this in your treasure chest.'

He walks back to the table and sits down. I pad behind him, take Mamadou's flute out of my rucksack, place it on the table. Isaka looks at me with those weary eyes of his, rolls his brother's flute back to me, and says: 'The diamonds and gold. I ... they want it back. All of it.'

It doesn't seem right to take back gifts made on behalf of so many people. His intentions are clear enough, for those unseen entities lingering about us respond. A cloud covers the sun. A sea breeze slams a door shut and Priss hisses. The shadows deepen and converge as, almost imperceptibly at first, the diamond-studded dagger on the table starts to turn. Gently, then picking up pace, it moves faster and faster, until it's a whirl of blinding, translucent light. Cobra stands up; his chair falls to the ground.

'Stop it! Whatever you're doing, stop it!' Isaka shouts.

He leaps from the table the moment I do. The moment the dagger, twizzling in a luminous haze, rises shoulder-high, and then flashes past his ear into the wall behind. It judders, turns and drills deeper, until all that's visible is its dazzling hilt.

Isaka crumples to the floor as though he's been

stabbed, shredded into tiny, irretrievable pieces. 'Can't you hear them?' he cries.

I hear a noise like wind-tossed leaves in autumn, the light patter of invisible feet and with it the stench of rotting mangoes that always fills my dreams. Time stops, and we're trapped in the slow-motion glow of a total eclipse.

Isaka crawls under the table. Legs hunched beneath his chin, he hugs himself tight.

Cobra takes my hand, squeezes my fingers as a question surfaces in his mind: 'Is this what you were talking about last night, Sante?'

Doesn't say it; he thinks it. My attention focused on Isaka, there's no time to reply. I reassure the African before I do anything else. Crouch down to his level. My hand on his hand. My hand on his shoulder.

'Can you hear them? Can you hear them?' Isaka whispers.

'I hear them,' I reply. 'They can't hurt you. Ghosts can't hurt anybody, 'cause they're ghosts. Isn't that so, Cobra?'

'They can't hurt *you*,' Isaka wails, 'because they're after *me*.'

Somehow, though he grovels and resists, Cobra and I help Isaka out from under the table. Cobra sits him on a chair while I pull the dagger out of the wall. Tug and pull, till the spirits relent, and allow me to wrench it out. There's a hole in the plaster. I try to give the dagger back to Isaka, but he shrinks from me, petrified. No way will he touch it. He won't touch me either, won't even look at me.

Cobra, about to flee, wraps the dagger in newspaper and dumps it on the table. Then he picks up my rucksack and takes my hand. I push him away. I haven't come this far, defied Mama Rose and the Old Ones, withheld information from them, to leave without getting the answers I'm after. I *have* to know. I have to find out as much as I can about my first family.

I kneel in front of Isaka, grab hold of his chair and pin him down, so he has to look at me: 'Tell me about my mother and father. What were they like? What were they doing on that boat?'

Isaka shuts his eyes. He covers his ears again and then lashes out. Hits me hard on the chin and I tumble to the floor. Priss swoops into the room. Slaps Isaka's face with a wing, extends her talons to claw his eyes. I scream loud as a banshee: 'No! Priss. No!'

Bird clucks over me as Cobra helps me up. 'Go, Priss.' I tell her. 'Wait outside.'

'We've got to get out of here,' Cobra urges.

'This is my call. My family!'

I defy him a second time and fix my gaze on Isaka. He's shaking like a leaf. His fear's contagious, for Cobra, voice shrill with tension, tells me to hurry it up. I can't move. Can't sever this last link with the family that brought me into the world.

'Please,' I say to Isaka. 'Please tell me what you know about my parents.'

I'm on my knees, begging him for a few words, a few details to help me better understand where I come from, when Cobra puts my rucksack on his back. Tugs at me, tries to heave me on to my feet again, but I won't budge. Not while Isaka's rocking in his chair. Back and forth he goes, places a finger on his lips, starts to stutter.

'Tell me. Tell me,' I insist.

His eyes remain closed. Too scared to look at me, I suppose, in case the moment he opens his eyes, he sees those ghosts loitering, waiting for another chance to pounce on him.

'You look like your mother,' he says, his eyes still shut. 'Amma. Her name was Amma. From Ghana. Your parents came from the Guinea coast, my child, and they brought with them everything they possessed to make a fresh start in Europe. Your father carried a pouch of gold dust and diamonds with him. By profession he was a goldsmith, a jeweller to an Ashanti king. Most of the treasure in your cot was your father's. And they paid for it with their lives.'

Isaka opens his eyes, looks straight ahead, but instead of seeing me, fastens on a scene locked inside him. The scene tumbles into me, and I see what he's seeing, feel the sharp twist of his emotions as he gazes on faces beaded with sweat, eyes bright with terror.

We're in the entrails of the boat. People are stumbling, falling over, clutching each other. Men, women, children. The hull of the trawler crashes open, and torrents of water gush in. I see it and feel Isaka's abject horror at the sudden rush of seawater sluicing underfoot.

Water's rising, rising fast as he pulls a suitcase from a locker above. Gropes inside, finds the dagger and places it in my cradle. Says kind words to me, turns as his brother pitches forwards and slips the bamboo flute beneath my blanket.

'Mamadou, stay with me,' Isaka commands.

Mamadou clings to his brother. Blood with blood, skin against skin. A tangle of sound echoes through the boat: the clash of screams, breaking timber. *Boom!* Again and again. The sea swirls around Isaka's thighs. Within seconds it's lapping at his chest. And each time the trawler is rammed, Mamadou's fingers slip and slide. He teeters, falls, is hurled into the night sky, and then crashes into the sea with a resounding roar.

'My brother. My brother.' Isaka whispers Mamadou's name and a jumble of images and noises crackles though me. Broken bodies tossed by waves and then swallowed by the sea. And the wind! A howling wind that serenades the shrieks of the dying. Little by little it quietens. The sea calms and all that remains is the *pitter-patter* of the restless dead who insist on walking with us.

'Forgive me, Mamadou! Forgive me! Leave me, my brother. Rest in peace. Perfect peace.'

I touch Isaka's knee and his shivering stops. The cloud moves away and as sunlight sears the surrounding gloom, the shadows fade.

Isaka is unsteady on his feet. The muddy sheen of his eyes begins to clear. The droop of his jowls seem to tighten, as from one moment to the next, his countenance changes from that of a middle-aged man to a younger, more hopeful version of himself. He touches the back of the chair, the edge of the table. He's gradually finding his balance, when we hear a key turn in the latch.

Isaka tenses. 'Get out of here! Get out quickly!'

The door opens. Cobra and I run at the same time. I head for the balcony; he races for the door. Trick is to divert whoever's coming in while I slip away. Split up, then meet later. We've done it time and time again but today our strategy feels wrong: 'Cobra! Come with me!' I say.

Too late. Grey Eyes walks in and beside him is Barrel Man.

'I told you those gypsies were still around. That damned bird goes with 'em everywhere.'

Barrel Man lunges at Cobra as I jump over the balcony. Ease myself down, swing my legs and drop on to the balcony below. Priss glides to a neighbouring roof and flaps her wings waiting for a signal. If she has her way, she'll attack Barrel Man again, only this time she'll pluck out his eyes.

I'm two floors down now. Only one more to go before I'm back safe on the ground, when Barrel Man leans over and bellows: 'I'm going to drop him!'

I look up. He's dangling Cobra from the balcony, swinging him back and forth.

'You heard me,' Barrel Man says. 'I'm going to drop him to his death unless you climb back right away.'

We're circus folk. Taking risks every day is what we do best. We know how to run and jump, dive and fall. Know how to do somersaults, stretch up to the sky as if we're about to leap over the moon. We may have circus in us, but we're flesh and blood as well. And though we can cheat it at times, there's nobody in the whole wide world that I know of, can defy the laws of gravity.

I fix my eyes on Cobra's greens. They're telling me to keep on doing what I'm doing. Run, 'cause chances are Barrel Man won't dare drop him to the ground. Not in broad daylight; not today.

'I mean it! Get back up here, girl!' Barrel Man lets go of Cobra's wrist and then laughs as he catches him again.

In that instant, clear as if she's standing beside me, I hear Mama Rose reminding me not to make her old before her time. Can't risk breaking Mama Rose's heart any more than I can bear to lose Cobra. Not in this life or the next. Slowly, carefully, I haul myself up, retracing my journey to the fourth floor. Whatever they want from me has to be a whole heap better than watching Cobra die.

13

Soon as I'm close enough, Barrel Man slams a hand on my shoulder, lifts me over the balcony and says: 'Who do you think you are, girl?' He pulls me by the hair and drags me screaming and kicking out of the apartment, up the stairs, on to the rooftop terrace. I'm in his clutches and he's yelling at me.

'Get off me!' I cry. 'Let me go!'

We holler at each other. He takes me by the scruff of the neck, shakes me till my teeth begin to rattle. Shakes and rattles me so hard, we soon have Priss's undivided attention.

She flies from a neighbouring roof to a balustrade at the edge of the terrace. Hops closer on to the pole of a washing line. Yelps at the sight of me being mauled by a huge bear of a man. She's about to attack, when I realise what Barrel Man is up to.

He slips a hand into his pocket and draws out a gun.

Cocks it, but before he fires I'm on to him. I ram my head into his shoulder. Barrel Man stumbles, shoots into sky. Priss wheels away as I cry: 'Go, Priss. Fly free. Stay away from me!'

Priss banks, gimlet eyes uncertain. 'Go, Priss! Go.'

Barrel Man shoots a second time. Misses. Fires again as Priss soars and flies away. He fires again and again till there's nothing left inside the muzzle but hot air. That's when he points the gun at me and pretends to pull the trigger. 'Pow! Pow!' he mouths and looks me full in the face.

What I see is his rage. Rage big as a whale. Big enough to swallow me, break me and spit me out. Barrel Man's crazy with anger.

'Look what your bird did to me!'

He hates me. Hates Priss even more. So much so, that from the look of it, the only emotion restraining him from pulverising me on the spot is the conviction that one day soon his anger will prevail.

'I'm going to get you, girl,' he tells me. 'I'm going to get you good for what your bird did to me. Then I'll take out your bird as well. Shoot her out of the sky and feed her to dogs.'

There's no arguing with him, so I don't even try. I've seen first-hand what hate can do. Hate feeds on hate. Fires up in the belly, blazes through the throat and makes grown men psycho. It would be easier to teach Taj Mahal to spout poetry than get Barrel Man to like me. If he hates gypsies, he's likely to hate illegals even more. Sees my colour, Cobra's too, and wants to trample us. Man's madder than a ravenous hyena.

'Come here, little girl.' His forefinger beckons.

I take a step back, bump into a flowerpot and he's on to me again, a hand at my throat.

'That's enough, Pepe,' a voice growls. 'That girl belongs to me now and if you so much as harm another hair on her head, you're out on your ear.'

Barrel Man loosens his grip, simpers and says. 'Where do you want me to put her, boss?'

Miguel, Grey Eyes alongside him, Cobra in between, nods at the corner of the terrace where a studio room is isolated from the rest of the building by a wide expanse of roof. 'The *azotea*,' Miguel says, and shoves Cobra, wrists tied behind him, in the same direction.

Grey Eyes unlocks the door. Barrel Man hauls us inside, Miguel close behind, and we're crammed into the room. On the right is a window, in the corner, a looking glass.

Miguel unties Cobra's wrists, pushes him on a bed. Barrel Man plonks me beside Cobra.

'You've got something of mine that I want back,' Miguel tells us. 'Scarlett. I want her back, you hear me? And until she returns, you belong to me.'

'Me?'

'Yes, you,' Miguel replies. 'I'm not going to let you go till Scarlett is back in my care. That's what her parents wanted and, as a man of honour, I intend to comply with their wishes. In the meantime, you'll stay here as my guest and fill in for her.'

'Me?'

He must think I'm seriously dull-witted, daft as a dodo, for Miguel spells it out now, so Cobra and I know exactly what's involved: 'Scarlett belongs to me. Until you return what belongs to me, I'll have to make do with you instead.'

Grey Eyes laughs, amused, no doubt, by the glaze of horror stealing over my face. 'And it's not just Scarlett we want back,' Grey Eyes says. 'I want those diamonds your father gave you as well. Indeed, young lady, I think it's time you called that woman who goes by the name of Mama Rose. Call her. Let her know that if she wants to see you again, she'd better bring me what I asked for yesterday.'

Grey Eyes drops our new phone on my lap. 'Do you understand what I'm saying, young lady?'

He says those words and I see red: red rag to a bull red. May be a scraggy teenager, but I'm nobody's lady. Certainly not his! Before I can stop myself and start thinking rationally, strategically, I bounce off the bed and look him straight in the eye.

The cruel eyes of a famished wolf in winter glare at me. He's tall, a full head and shoulders taller than me. Corpulent, face splattered with freckles. An Old One from the north, greedy for southern sunshine.

'Who're you calling "young lady"?'

He smiles. Can't see beyond my size. I take a deep breath, still my vexation and pinpoint another irritation: 'And how dare you talk about the woman who brought me up like that – *that woman who goes by the name of Mama Rose*! If you want me to talk to her, better respect her!'

Grey Eyes laughs at me. Laughs heartily till his face glows red and moist with sweat.

I'm not laughing. No, sir! Fold my arms. Hold my chin up high. May grumble about her, argue and backchat her, but under no circumstances will I laugh about the woman who rescued me, taught me the sacred laws of the human heart and how to survive in the wild. Most important of all, the woman who trained me to hold tight to what I know is right.

Grey Eyes guffaws: 'You mean you don't know? My dear, that woman you call Mama Rose is an imposter and fraudster of the first order. And so is that man you call Redwood.'

Grey Eyes doesn't provide the evidence for his words with yet more hilarity and sarcasm; he shows us instead. Sends Barrel Man downstairs to fetch his laptop, and when he has it, puts on a pair of wire spectacles and fires up the machine. Opens a box on the screen and finds a grainy image of Mama Rose and another of Redwood. The two of 'em are in the clothes they were wearing yesterday. Must have snapped 'em in secret, 'cause Mama Rose and Redwood hate to have their photo taken. One of the abiding rules of our family circus is: No Flash Photography Allowed. It frightens Taj Mahal, puts Cat off her stride. A sudden flare of light and there could be an accident in the ring.

Eyelashes flutter at the screen as I examine the images with Cobra. We peer at 'em. Mama Rose isn't smiling, nor is Redwood. Both look angry, suspicious, and if we didn't know 'em better, might consider 'em downright shifty, like villains in those mugshots in newspapers.

Grey Eyes drags the images from the left side of his computer to the right and millions of faces surface testing 'em against the photos of Redwood and Mama Rose. Eyes, nose and cheeks. Faces, endless faces. Noses too big in some, foreheads too narrow, too small. Mouths too prim and tight, too wide or thick-lipped, until – *ping!* – there's a match for Mama Rose and, soon after, another for Redwood. Redwood is listed under a completely different name, while Mama Rose's name, at least, is familiar. In both pictures they're a lot younger.

I say Mama Rose's name out loud: 'Rosamund Annabel Williams, daughter of Lord Edmund James

Hathaway-Williams of Brecon. Missing. Wanted for questioning.

'Mama Rose, the daughter of a lord? And Redwood?' Cobra asks me.

'Name's…' I pronounce it as if I'm deciphering a foreign language, one syllable at a time. The name of a stranger: 'Cuthbert Xavier Carter the Third.'

Cobra shakes his head, mutters, 'Whoa … this has to be some kind of sick joke.'

He looks from Miguel to Grey Eyes. Miguel shrugs, Grey Eyes chortles. Barrel Man starts sniggering as well, though he has no idea what he's sniggering at. Miguel stares at him and in a beat the sniggering stops. Only one laughing now is Grey Eyes.

'You see,' he says. 'Your nearest and dearest are not who they claim to be. If they've lied to you about who they are, what else have they lied to you about?'

'Too true,' Miguel adds. 'They could be murderers, terrorists, for all you know. You should be grateful we got to you in time.'

I sniff and jut out my chin as the old certainties of my former life begin to ebb away, along with everything I hold dear. 'They're wanted for questioning, nothing more!'

'That may be so,' says Grey Eyes, 'but wouldn't it have been better if they'd let you in on their secret?'

Cobra catches my eye and I keep quiet.

'Now, my dears,' Grey Eyes says, 'it's time you

called your guardians to let them know where you are. You're here as our guests, mine and Miguel's. You'll attend the gathering we're orchestrating tonight. We'll feed you and look after you and you'll play your part until such a time as your people bring us what we want.'

They tell us we're their guests and then lock us up. Properly. Not with a click-and-spring-easy-to-pick lock, but with a Yale lock, deadlocks at the top and bottom of the door. Barrel Man is on guard outside. He wanders up and down the roof terrace on the look-out for Priss. Scans the horizon, disappears and returns with a hunting rifle. Waves the rifle in the air and when he sees I'm watching him, takes aim. 'Pow! Pow!' he croaks. Ugly toad turns and smiles at me.

If I was alone, I'd cover my face with my hands and bawl. Create havoc by ranting and raving, for plain as night is night and day is bright, we're trapped in this nightmare 'cause of me. I insisted on staying when the Old Ones said no. Found Isaka, but when Cobra said, 'Hurry, let's go,' stood my ground. The situation we're in is one hundred per cent my fault.

I hang my head in shame, but Cobra doesn't pile on a barrow-load of blame to add to the burden I'm carrying already. Doesn't make me more dejected by saying: 'Told you so! Told you we should get out fast.' No. He touches the bruises on my chin and lip: Isaka's punch. The ache around my neck: Barrel Man's throttlehold. Eyes closed, my eyelids quiver as the tips of his fingers search my skin for twinges. Cobra eases my pain and the kindness of his touch brings tears to my eyes.

I cry hard, my heart breaking, and Cobra holds me, his scent of peppermint and cloves enfolding me. I savour his smell and snuffle it up as he rocks me back and forth, like Mama Rose does when I'm in despair. 'We'll be OK, Sante,' he whispers. 'I've got your back, you'll see.'

He tries to comfort me but all I can do is wail: 'What am I to do? I can't take Scarlett's place. Can't see a way out of this. Can't!'

Soon as I say those words, I hear Redwood talking to me:

There's no such thing as can't. Kant is a German philosopher who died in eighteen hundred and four. Of course you can find a way out of this mess, Sante-girl. Think it through, kid, and you'll work it out.'

'Thank you, Redwood. Or would you rather I call you Cuthbert Xavier Carter the Third?

'Do you think they'll pimp you out as well?' I ask Cobra.

We've already called the number in Granada Midget

Man gave us. Left a message on the answerphone that we're in serious trouble and Mama Rose should get in touch with us as soon as possible. Grey Eyes took our phone. Said if anyone called us back, he'd speak to them directly.

Cobra, sitting cross-legged on the bed, rests his hands on my knees: 'They can't make you do anything you don't want to, Sante,' he says. 'They can't, not when you're with me.'

'But I don't know the rules of the game they're playing. Do you, Cobra?'

He smiles, one of his slow, reassuring smiles, and says: 'They do what they want. Whatever makes money for 'em they're on to it. What they don't know and can't understand are the sorts of games *we* play.'

He rubs my knees. Soothes my trembling and says: 'Take what happened to the dagger downstairs. Did you see what I saw? Did the dagger rise and fly into the wall?'

I'm wary of where this is going.

'Do you know how that happened, Sante?'

I shake my head.

'Nor do I,' he says. 'But it worked for you. Somehow you were able to harness that power and use it to get the truth out of Isaka.'

'But I don't like 'em, Cobra. I don't like those spooks around me.'

'It was a bit like that with me and snakes to begin

with,' he says. 'Didn't understand what was going on, but then I learned to use my gift.'

I take Cobra's hand, lay it on my cheek. He closes his eyes and as his breathing deepens, I sense he's doing what he does best: delving into himself to summon snakes. Seen him do it in forests, moorland and plains. Dry lands, wetlands. Cobra sits down, closes his eyes and serpents crawl to him out of nowhere. Happens in the sea and rivers as well. Sea serpents and eels slither to where he is. This time, in a rooftop prison in old Cádiz, as Cobra's scent gradually fills the room, my senses twitch and I listen to the wind.

A breeze swings clothes on a washing line. Line wheezes, a chesty old woman struggling up a hill. There's a tinkle of piano music in the air. Courtly, classical, same passage again and again, as someone practises. Down below a woman gurgles at her baby, calling him precious, delightful, her treasure. Coos at him, then sings him a lullaby as the wind dances over rooftops, past windows and balconies, tickling the leaves of creepers and trees.

Sounds around me disentangled, I discern a hiss of movement, the crackle of paper. From my rucksack, propped on the wall, Bella and Scales, Cobra's oldest, most faithful snakes emerge. A brown snake and a black snake. I had no idea he'd brought them with us. They slide and coil on the floor, up a leg of a bed, over a blanket on to Cobra's lap.

He caresses them: 'Bella and Scales,' he says, 'I'm asking for your help. Find your friends. Bring them here. Listen for the music of the flute and come back in your hundreds to dance with me.'

Cobra opens the window in our room, opens it a crack, and Bella and Scales slip into the noonday sun.

14

By the time Concha arrives at seven o'clock, my nerves are jangling. Concha – the woman who's going to get me ready for Miguel's party. She came earlier this afternoon to size me up. Took my measurements, wondered out loud if she should buy me a padded bra to make me look bigger on top. Made me walk up and down the room to see if I could manage high heels. I said no to both. Cobra laughed at the expression on Concha's face when I told her the only boots I'll be wearing tonight are my biker boots.

'It's easy for you to laugh,' I said. 'They're not going to dress you up and parade you like a puppet in front of strangers.'

'Oh, but they are,' Concha tells us. Wipes the smile off Cobra's face and then takes his measurements as well.

I've been walking up and down the room ever since, thinking and plotting, while Cobra stretches on the bed resting, preparing for what lies ahead. Up and down a hundred times over, thinking about Mama Rose and Redwood. Hard to imagine that those closest to you can pretend to be someone they're not for so long. Say as much to Cobra, who replies:

'Let's hear what they have to say before we make up our minds.'

Cobra isn't one to leap to conclusions. Not that my mind's made up. No, sir! But that first whiff of suspicion puts a new slant on our past. And the more I walk, the more the past begins to look like a different place.

'What Grey Eyes said sort of makes sense,' I tell Cobra. 'All that moving about, all that hiding out in wild places. What if we've been living off the grid not because of what's good for us, but 'cause of them? They're missing, wanted for questioning. They don't want to be found. Don't want *anything* to do with the police.'

Cobra swings his legs around. 'Could be our interests coincide with theirs. Could be living off the grid keeps all of us safe. "Could be" has a million faces, Sante. Let's see what they say next time we talk to 'em.'

'But they've lied to us, Cobra!'

I walk up and down, down and up, round and about

in a circle, as frustrated as Priss would be in a cage. I miss the swoop and swell of her, the strength of her talons on my wrist, the smell of her. Heart pounds and I start to sweat. Shiver and shake like a fox in a trap. I trample the ground, gnawing at my tail until Cobra says:

'Sante, you're not going to get out of here any quicker by making a furrow in the floor.'

He puts a hand on my shoulder, turns me around and holds me.

'We're going to be OK, Sante. Long as we're together we'll be fine.' He pulls me to him and hugs me. Then, suddenly, his mouth is searching for mine, and before I can pull away, every single bit of me is crying – eyes, heart, body, soul. I'm sobbing and all of me is reaching out and clinging to Cobra as he kisses me.

So this is what he tastes like. My body wants to stay in the pit of his warmth. Wants to hold on to him for much longer. His scent of peppermint and cloves sweetening my mouth, I tear myself away to clear my head. Didn't know a kiss could touch the bottom of an ocean as deep as this, drag everything up, and yet feel so good.

Eyes shining, Cobra dangles his fingers in the palm of my hand, lifts it, and kisses it: 'Stay close to me tonight,' he says. 'We can look after each other.'

'Stay together, look after each other.' I repeat his words. I'm about say them again, a spell to bind us and keep us safe, when Barrel Man barges through the studio door.

Sniggers at Cobra, his arms around me, and laughs. 'Better make the most of the time you've got now, lovebirds. Who knows who you'll be with by daybreak!'

Concha, behind him, shushes him and shoos him away. She's already dressed for the party: black lace, bare shoulders, black hair swept under a hat with a veil that floats over her face. Tall and elegant. In her hands, a polythene-swathed dress and suit, which she balances on a hinge of the door.

She turns to me, clapping her hands and says: 'You're beautiful.' Concha steps closer and smells the stench of fear on me that even Cobra's kiss can't hide. 'I've got a little something to help you, my dear.'

She opens a huge bag that's even bigger than Mama Rose's and brings out a flask. Pours me a cup of hot, brown liquid. 'Drink it.'

Don't want to drink it. Could be laced with liquor, or worse: a liquid something that eats away at me so they can do with me as they please. 'No thanks.'

'You'll feel better.'

I grit my teeth but in a flash she pries my lips open, raises my chin, and pours the liquid into me. Empties half the glass down my gullet before I start to gag, and then passes what's left to Cobra. I wipe my mouth and taste a residue of thick sweet chocolate with a zest of orange and a trace of something I can't quite place. Warmth floods through my body. Nerves tingle with relief. Body yawns and sighs, stretches, a skylark flinging back its head about to sing.

Within two shakes, I feel as if I'm warbling, then up in the air gliding, higher and higher, on skylark wings.

Concha pushes me into the bathroom. Turns on the taps and when the bath is almost full sprinkles bergamot and lavender oil in the water. I scrub myself and my mind empties. No more visions of shipwrecks. No more *pitter-patter* of the restless dead or *bam-clash* of Isaka and Barrel Man mauling me.

All too soon, Concha hauls me out again, yet the hot chocolate and scented water are still working on me. I'm humming to myself, moving from one moment to the next as if I'm waltzing weightless in a dream.

Concha slips a black petticoat over my head, sits me on a stool and applies make-up to my face. Steps back to examine her work: 'Don't worry,' she says, a glint of ice sparking her eyes. 'They'll only be looking tonight. Looking, not tasting.'

She piles my hair into a bun. Twists it, pins a posy of red hibiscus flowers at the side. Takes down the dress, pulls away the polythene and shows it to me.

I shake my head.

'Try it on,' Concha urges, unzipping the dress. Then, a glint of steel sharpening her voice, she says,

'It'll be much easier for both of us if you don't make me force you into it.'

I put on the dress. Concha zips me up, turns me around. Red silk pinches so tight, my bum sticks out. I stare at the reflection before me. I twist and turn. My likeness twists and turns as well. My reflection echoes me and yet isn't wholly mine. Arms on hips, I look over my shoulder at the apparition staring back at me. Something doesn't fit. And I don't mean the peel-me-off dress I'm wearing. I dress up every day when I'm working, and at times, playing with Cat, I pretend to be older. This is different, disconcerting, as though I'm looking at a version of myself I'd rather not see; a presence that's revealing itself at the same time as it draws me in.

Then it comes to me: it's the face that's tugging at my heart. A face I vaguely recollect from my dreams. Perfect oval, high cheekbones, almond-shaped eyes, ebony skin with a lustrous sheen. And those lips! They look every bit as luscious as the cherry-black fruit they're coloured in. I twist and turn some more. Smile and those eyes smile back at me, as if to say: 'I knew it! I knew I'd see you again. Come closer. Let me look at you.'

I step closer and a distant memory flexes and stirs. I feel the soft curves of a woman's body, smell the scent of mangoes on her breath, as a voice from my past says: 'Asantewaa, my, how you've grown. My princess! My little princess.'

I look around me, trembling as Concha pulls a pair of killer-heel stilettos out of her bag. Dangles 'em in front of my nose as if I should be excited. As if this is my reward for being pliant, my special treat for letting her paint and shape me.

'No,' I say. I say no a second time, then a third. And each time I say it, emboldened by that memory of a distant past, I say it louder and more determined than the time before. That forgotten muscle stretches and yawns, warming up for what is yet to come. If resolve has a face, I reckon it's mine. Concha puts the heels away, I pull on my biker boots, and I'm done.

15

Cobra and I walk into the party hand in hand, Concha and Barrel Man either side of us. Cobra in white tuxedo, bow tie and black jeans, as if we were going to a school prom. Concha pushes us in. Straightens my back, by standing straight as a rake herself. Lifts her chin and all eyes turn to look at her, then at Cobra and me.

We're used to folk staring at us. Step into the ring and heads swivel. This feels different, the room especially. What looked light and airy in daytime is cramped, crowded with indistinct shapes and a combination of smells: wisps of cigar smoke and the salt tang of the sea underlined by a heady crush of sandalwood. Room's dim, candles flicker in silver candelabra and chandeliers. Faces, distorted by wavering shadows, loom and leer, while the eyes of strangers weigh us up, like lumps of meat they're planning to eat.

My heart skitters. Cobra's fingers tighten around mine but I can't stop trembling. In my mind's eye I complete the rituals I go through every time I perform. Kiss Priss, touch her feathers for luck, rub sawdust on my hands, and I'm on. Shoulders back, big confident smile. I sense a change in Cobra as his chest expands and his greens light up. He catches my eye, smiles and flashes open his tuxedo. Tucked in the inside pocket is Mamadou's flute.

I pull Cobra closer and kiss him on the mouth. All it takes is a single kiss, a quick nip of his lips and my trembling eases and the party fades away. I make-believe it's just me and Cobra telling the whole wide world, and anyone else who cares to know, that we're more than friends, and better than kissing friends, we're together.

'Enough of that,' says Barrel Man and pulls us apart.

He hauls Cobra to the far end of the room while Concha, hand on my elbow, guides me to an alcove by the balcony. Barrel Man hurries back and stations himself in front of where I tried to escape a few hours earlier. Ugly toad has no idea what we've got planned for tonight, no idea at all. None of 'em do.

Midget Man and Mimi are always telling me that the best way to take the measure of a dangerous situation is to listen to it. Listen to the wind and you'll sniff any trouble coming your way. Sniff it out, and you're better prepared to deal with it; better prepared to fix your gaze on it and slay it.

I close my eyes and the room presses in on me and reveals itself in a tinkling of glasses and clink of ice. Slugs of liquor swill down gullets. Tongues slither and slurp, scooping out oysters. Liquor. Seafood. Insidious chatter. Beneath the insistent buzzing of old men and women are the nervous tweets and twitter of young ones. The wind never lies. Even before I open my eyes to try to understand what's going on, I sense that I'm eavesdropping on predators and those they prey on.

My eyes open and what was dim becomes clearer as a blur of colours riot around me: sombre, evening pigments in purple, burgundy and blue. Sudden flashes of jewellery: pearls, diamonds, rubies. Pendulous earrings on sagging earlobes, lumpy necklaces around scrawny necks, and on thin, limp wrists, ornate bracelets of a bygone era. Gaunt-faced women, hair topped with tiaras, open their arms. Fusty-looking men lick their lips. And all of 'em, every single one of the old folk at the party, swarm like bees over young ones. At the heart of the proceedings, a ringmaster orchestrating the event with the help of Miguel, is Grey Eyes.

A glass of whisky in one hand, a cigar in the other, he moves in the shadows from one group to the next. Flicks ash on the floor and I notice that the little finger sticking out from his glass is much smaller than the other. I study him closely as he makes connections, introductions. An elderly man kisses the hand of a flaxen-haired teenager. Her eyes flinch, even as her lips open in a smile. She offers the old man a drink, sits down beside him. Strokes his legs, paddles her paws in his.

Gnarled fingers tremble over taut flesh, over shoulders and arms. Fingers quiver over pale cheeks, snuffle against the neck of the girl to savour the sweet scent of youth and capture it.

Scarlett. She could be Scarlett. She could be me. My stomach heaves and churns.

'Is this your first time? Don't turn around...'

A voice behind me, little more than a whisper.

I nod.

'Name's Ayesha,' the voice says.

'Sante. Sante Williams.'

A birdlike creature sidles up beside me. Oil-black hair swept up, brown eyes glittering tears. Tears of anger, I believe, for her body beside mine quivers with rage as she mutters through gritted teeth: 'I could ... I could...'

Before she can finish what she's about to say, Concha hisses: 'Ayesha, you're here to work, not talk. Find someone. Entertain them.'

Ayesha sighs and darts into the crowd.

Feeling as though I'm about to retch, my mind fixes on Cobra. Where is he? Can't see him in this light. I inch forwards but Concha holds me tight. I search the room, looking for the shape of him, a gesture, a movement that tells me, this is Cobra. I cringe, for everywhere I turn, I see the same thing again and again. Grey Eyes introducing Old Ones to those of us in uniform. A polite kiss of introduction, followed by a discreet pinch on the arm and stroking of skin as someone murmurs: 'Very nice. Good bones. *Marvellous.*'

I can't do this. Got to find Cobra, get away from here. But Concha has other ideas. She holds me, makes me watch.

The swarm of movement shifts, a gap opens, and I catch sight of him at last. Only person I know who throws his head back in laughter like that is Cobra. Caught like a fly between two of 'em.

'This one's mine,' a wizened vulture of a woman cries.

A man, skin wrinkled slack like a lizard, grabs Cobra's wrist and replies: 'No, he's mine.'

Grey Eyes intervenes. Hands Cobra over to the vulture. She hops around him, squawking with glee, while Cobra, half an eye on me, winks. Least I think he winks. Could be blinking back tears for all I know. He must be winking, for he sits the woman down on a chair and starts plying her with strawberries.

'Straighten your back and smile!' says Concha, running a finger down my spine. I stand tall but can't for the life of me bring a smile to my lips. Not while my innards are leaping and twisting.

'Smile! Smile for the Captain, he'll be with us soon.'

'The Captain?'

Concha's violet eyes glimmer. 'I got you ready especially for him.'

'Who're you talking about, Concha?'

'He'll like you. You're his type.'

'Who?'

'No need to worry about that. All you have to do is smile!'

My senses twitch at the acrid scent of trouble. Goosebumps prickle my arms. I gulp for breath. Someone's staring at me.

Concha wouldn't dare ask me to smile if she felt the intensity of those eyes crawling over me, trying to lick the brown off my skin. Don't like it one little bit. He's watching and waiting, a man of deadly intent, pinched in spirit. I feel it in my gut. Trouble on the wind and it's heading my way.

'Smile! Or I'll slap you,' Concha hisses.

I glare at her. She flares up and raises her hand as Grey Eyes saunters towards us. Beside him is a tall, thin man with the face of a walking cadaver. Man's old, stained yellow by evil. A devil with a dead man's eyes and a shark's smile. He walks with an ebony cane topped by a lion's head.

'Young lady,' says Grey Eyes. 'You look wonderful tonight.'

Ice-flecked eyes look into mine. I feel the cold cut

of diamonds on a moonless night and taste the slow burn of success smouldering within him. Grey Eyes is in his element: a maker and shaker of events, a breaker of hearts. Can't wait to get his hands on my treasure to add to the money he's making here tonight.

'What a pleasure to see you like this,' he says. 'Out of your filthy jeans and T-shirt at last.'

He's got me where he wants me all right, and he likes it. Smiles, then frowns at the sight of my boots and I smile right back at him. Doesn't like that. No, sir! Not one little bit.

Grey Eyes hands his drink to Concha. Puts a hand on my shoulder and twirls me around. 'Concha, darling, you would have excelled tonight, if only you'd persuaded our guest to put on footwear befitting the occasion. You've failed me, Concha. I expected more of you.'

Concha, her attention on the man standing beside Grey Eyes, ignores his comment. She pinches my bum, puts her arm around my waist to show me off. Nods at the tall man with death on his face. He squeezes the muscles on my forearm.

I fix a smile on my face as he stares deep into me with eyes that could freeze a corpse. My heart leaps, smile congeals, feelings recoil at what I sense inside him. Pus. Pure pus. I look around again for Cobra.

He's still sitting with the old woman, still feeding the vulture berries. Cobra nods at me, and his greens tell me to hold on, keep calm. We'll make our move soon.

The tall man weighs my hand by holding up my wrist. Lifts my chin, stoops over me. Grimaces, exposes a row of sunken teeth and indicates I should do the same.

I show him my teeth. 'Exquisite,' he says in a voice cold as the grave. 'Where did you find this specimen, Wolf? What's your name, young lady? Are you for sale?'

A blaze of anger engulfs my throat and burns the inside of my mouth. I bite my tongue to hold the anger in place. Gulp down that red rag of rage. Could snap at the man's fingers, bite down on 'em, bust my head on his chin. Could shatter his teeth, kick his shins, trip him over but I won't. Not today. Don't dare disrupt Cobra's plan by getting myself evicted. Can't, under any circumstances, let Cobra down! I smile instead. For our plan to work, I've got to be here for Cobra.

'Wolf, you haven't answered my question, what's your price for this beautiful young thing?'

'Mister, I'm not for sale,' I say. 'Never was, never have been, never will be.'

'Everyone has a price, young lady.'

'What's yours?' I reply.

He chortles: 'I like your spirit. It helps to have something to work on. Be a good little girl now, tell me your name.'

I put on my circus smile but as the smile spreads and warms my soul, that feeling of dread returns, and I realise that to survive this ordeal, I need help. Big Time. Help to steady myself and hold my nerve.

'I'm waiting...' He looks at me, the power of his intent oozing like poison from a boil. He wants to annihilate me.

In the pause between his question and my reply, I gather my wits. If I didn't know who he was before, I'm now convinced he's the man Concha calls the Captain. Before I tell him my name, I call on the power of whatever it was that made the dagger fly. I call on those spirits who helped me earlier. Call 'em by saying the name I was born with, as well as the name I've acquired, in the hope that those who saved me from drowning will hear my heart hammering for help. I hold my head up, push my chin out, and even though from the tip of my topknot to the end of my toes, inside and out, I'm quaking, I say with as much authority and pride as I can muster:

'Name's Asantewaa Prempeh, daughter of Kofi Prempeh and Amma Serwah of Ghana-land. I'm Asantewaa, also known as Sante, daughter of Mama Rose Williams of Brecon, head of a family circus, which includes Cobra and Cat, Midget Man and Mimi, Redwood and Bizzie Lizzie. We're family.'

The three of 'em, Concha, Grey Eyes and the Captain, laugh so hard you'd think I was funnier than

Redwood and Midget Man on a good day, Mimi and Bizzie Lizzie too. You'd think, if you didn't know any better, that I was scream-out-loud, tumbling, farting-clown funny. They laugh, 'cause they don't know that Asantewaa's the name of a warrior queen, a ferocious leader of men. Don't know, don't care. Truth be told, I don't know much more about her either. But their laughter hurts me, and whatever hurts me, I'm discovering, rouses the wrath of the spirits that came out of my sea-chest cradle.

The three of 'em cackle so much, they start to cry. Concha dabs the corner of her eye with a lace handkerchief. The Captain snorts. Then, out of nowhere, Isaka appears, puts an arm around me and says to Grey Eyes: 'I thought we'd agreed. The girl is our guest. She and her friend have no place here.'

'That may be so,' Grey Eyes replies, 'but they shouldn't have taken Scarlett, should they?'

Isaka shakes his head. 'We agreed,' he says and with his arm still around me, looks me full in the face. His eyes are clear now, like the eyes of a newborn baby intent on nebulous, flickering shapes; phantoms he alone can see. His arm slips, then Isaka gathers me in again: 'What have you done to her? Concha, did you do this?'

'And why not?' Concha replies. She shrugs and pouts, then drifts into the crowd of revellers, black lace exposing slashes of pale skin.

'Do you realise that you're the image of your mother, child?' Isaka says to me. 'If I didn't know otherwise, I'd have sworn she was with us tonight.'

Grey Eyes chuckles: 'Isaka's been seeing a lot of ghosts recently. You've brought the past to life again, young lady.'

I bite my tongue and act coy as the Captain scowls at Isaka. Taps his stick on the floor. Twists the lion's head in his paw. Clear as the day is bright, he wants Isaka out of the way so he can make his play, but the African sticks to me like a limpet. Stares at me, amazed at the transformation Concha's wrought on my face.

'Unbelievable. You're exactly like your mother.'

Isaka says variations of the same thing over and over again. If he tells me once, he tells me a hundred times. I look like my mother. He calls her name and the more he does so, the more impatient Grey Eyes and the Captain become. They whisper to each other as unbeknown to them shadows start to gather around us. Shadows thicken, footsteps quicken, and little by little I begin to realise what Isaka is doing. He may have been part of this racket, but he's on my side now, and is showing me the way. Talk about them and they make their presence felt. Call them and they appear: spirits of the restless dead and my mother, Amma. Amma Serwah.

I whisper her name and a breeze rustles the leaves of shrubs and creepers on the balcony: purple bougain-villea, sweet-smelling jasmine. Summer fragrance wafts over the gathering and first one candle, then a second is snuffed out. A third candle splutters and then, as if heaving a collective sigh of relief, every single candle in the room, flutters and dies.

In the commotion, Cobra shouts my name. Whistles and I slip through a fug of cigarette smoke and bodies towards him. Whistles and I come, alert in the darkness, to his call. My fingers fumble over faces. Touch the old crone's nose, hear her vulture screech and I tumble over Cobra.

'Lights! Turn on the lights! Will someone *please* turn on the lights?'

We squat in a corner. Cobra gives me Mamadou's flute and as I start to play, I sense Mamadou's hand reaching to me from a chasm between life and death, which is less than a hair's breadth away. I let him in and a joyous song of long life and good health ripples through me. Mamadou plays and my fingers dance as Cobra, beside me, closes his eyes. He breathes deeply and very soon they come. Up the street, crawling along creepers, gutters, rooftops, over walls, over every hurdle: stones, crates, and bottles that separate them from Cobra. And when they arrive, they slither under the door, over the balcony, through windows. Wave after wave of 'em. A heaving, swirling mass of snakes lighting up the room in a writhing moondance. Cobra calls 'em and they come. And then the screaming starts.

Shrieks to make the blood curdle and freeze. Bone-shaking, nerve-rattling screeches. Again and again. Cries of: 'What's going on? Lights! Lights!'

The lights come on and the screams grow louder as bodies tangled with snakes, squirm on the floor. They came to dance for us and they do. They jump and jive, twist and turn, leap and sway to the sound of my flute. Swarm over Cobra, kiss him with forked tongues. They shower him with affection, and then as quickly as they came, they disappear. Even so, all the shrieking and hollering goes on for a long time. So long that I know for a fact Grey Eyes won't be holding a party like this again any time soon. Not here, at any rate.

16

Mama Rose is forever saying that of all the creatures on God's earth, snakes have the worst press. I once asked Redwood why this was so. 'Listen, kid,' he said, 'I'm not a theologian, but the way I see it, it all comes down to what the Bible says about Adam and Eve. How that serpent lured Eve to take a bite of forbidden fruit. Some folks believe that tasting that darned apple has led to endless trials and tribulations for the human race. Reckon that's why, since kingdom come, no one's had a good word to say for snakes.'

Right now in Grey Eyes' salon, I'd be lying if I said I was sorry for creating havoc. Far from it! I'm grinning from ear to ear at the mayhem. Spilled food, smashed plates and glasses. Bottles and tables upturned. Chairs trampled as those vultures and lizards scuttle and fly out of the room.

Cobra and I beam. Don't know about him, but I'd do it all over again to see the rage on Grey Eyes' face. Beetroot-red, eyes blazing ice. And the Captain? Horrified. Slumped in a heap, ebony stick on the floor.

Grey Eyes cries: 'Get them out of here. Quickly. Miguel, Pepe, move the merchandise!'

Miguel marshals terrified young ones and herds them from the room, while Barrel Man bundles Cobra and me upstairs. He opens the studio door, locks us inside. But not before I see how truly frightened he is. His skin is bleached so pale, Priss's talon marks on his cheeks look ghostly under the light of the moon.

As soon as we hear him stumble downstairs, Cobra puts a finger to his lips and we listen to Grey Eyes barking out orders below: 'Tidy up! Move, man! Move! Yes! Mop the floor. Of course you should sweep everything away first. What happened? How the hell should I know?'

We hear a flurry of activity beneath us: tables righted, chairs put back in place, the ferocious suck of a vacuum gobbling debris, the *swish-slop* of a mop. Then the sound of footsteps climbing up to the roof. Two, maybe three, men walk across the terrace towards the studio door. Footfall too light for Barrel Man's trudge. Grey Eyes and Miguel, perhaps. But the third man?

'Isaka?' I whisper to Cobra.

He shakes his head.

Sure enough, the footsteps are too slow for Isaka.

I hear the *tap-tap* of a cane. The Captain.

What if he's coming to take me away? I'd rather die than feel the breath of death on my face again. I'm shaking so much Cobra grabs hold of my hand.

'It's OK, Sante,' he says. 'It's OK.'

He holds me still as one after the other the locks on the door are released. A key turns in the latch and the door swings open. They walk in, Grey Eyes and Miguel. Behind them, even more ghastly than when he glowered at me in candlelight, is the Captain.

'What did you think you were doing?' cries Grey Eyes. 'You've ruined everything! Everything.'

Miguel circles us. From the look of it he thinks we're beasts fresh out of the jungle. Wild, unnatural. 'Let's get rid of them, Wolf,' he says. 'They're more trouble than they're worth.'

'What? And let them keep Scarlett? Are you losing your nerve, my boy?' The Captain thumps his cane on the tiled floor and purses his lips in displeasure. 'That redhead will earn us a fortune. And once I've broken this one in, she will as well.' He nods at me.

Merchandise. That's all we are to him. I'm minded to knock him down, then dive between Grey Eyes' legs and out of the room on to the terrace. Jump from roof to roof and fly as free as my bird. I would if I could, but Cobra's holding my hand and with every fibre of my being, I know that he's urging me to stay calm and be still. Cobra squeezes my fingers. I clasp his tightly as the three of 'em glare at us.

'I've met snake-charmers before,' says the Captain, caressing the golden head of his cane. 'Once, on my travels in the South Seas, I met a delightful young woman who shared your gift. She could charm snakes out of trees and make them do her bidding. Wrapped me round her little finger, and I admit, I loved her dearly until she betrayed me. Do you know what happened to her then, dear boy? Do you know what her neighbours did to her?'

He taps his cane on the floor. Three taps and we're ready to hear more.

'Of course you don't. How can a stripling such as you have any inkling of the dark heart of the human soul? They burned her alive. Set fire to her hut and fields. Trussed her up and set her alight. They claimed she was a sorceress, a witch. How they came to that conclusion, I'd rather not say…'

He presses a finger to his mouth. His lips twitch on the verge of laughter, then relax into a smile as he inhales: 'Ah, the fragrance of burned flesh before sunset. Exquisite! If I were you, dear boy, I'd be very careful indeed how you use your gift here. We Spanish are religious people. So remember, if you dare cross us again, if you jeopardise our little enterprise in any way whatsoever … *gobble, gobble, gobble!* Trussed turkey in Cádiz.'

Cobra tenses but holds his tongue. Keeps it tied, while his greens hold the Captain's gaze before the old man turns to me.

'As for you, I believe you forgot this.'

He retrieves my bamboo flute from his pocket. Waves it in front of me, and as I reach for it, throws his cane to the ground and lifts the flute higher. Then he takes it in both hands and snaps it in two. 'You will never spoil one of my parties again. Never, you hear me?' He chucks pieces of bamboo on the floor.

I tumble to the ground, hugging the broken flute to my chest. I blub like a baby, fingering the jagged shards.

My first heirloom, the first gift from my treasure-chest cradle. They can keep the ceremonial dagger if they want. But this? I hug the pieces tighter. Before I knew that my full name was Asantewaa, before I knew who my parents were and learned that they'd named me after a ferocious Ashanti queen, I kept the only link to my past close to me, and played my flute like a friend.

'Mamadou,' I whisper. 'Mamadou.'

A hazy silhouette grazes the edge of my vision and flits away.

I stand tall. Wasn't named after a queen for nothing. 'Mister,' I say to the man with the mark of death on his face. 'You've made the worst mistake of your life. I may be a plaything to you, a toy to be tossed around.

I may not amount to much in your eyes, but this flute was given to me by a master musician from Mali, Mamadou.'

The Captain snorts. Grey Eyes too. Miguel backs away.

'Mamadou?' he says. 'Isaka's brother?'

I nod.

Miguel drags the fingers of his left hand through his thick black quiff as uncertainty flickers on his face. 'He was on that boat with Isaka? The boat that you ... Papa?'

The Captain jabs his cane into Miguel's shoulder. Miguel winces, his shoulder still painful from the fight with Cat.

'Yes, he was on that boat,' I say.

I'm about to spill a whole heap of beans and tell 'em what I think of their bullying ways, their horrible party, when I notice Cobra rubbing the right side of his nose.

'Enough,' he signals.

And yet I feel it bristling in the air; a secret thickening, growing fat. A secret stifled by defiant glances from the Captain to Grey Eyes; that jab to silence Miguel, his look of consternation. I brace myself to do what I didn't dare to earlier. Take a breath and delve into the cesspool that's the Captain. Feel the pride in him; pride burnished with contempt. Rootle deeper, graze the wiliness of his power and see him for what he is:

a seething, breathing glob of evil. Listen in, and it hits me. *Wham!* And I'm quivering, 'cause I glimpse what he doesn't want me to see: a jigsaw of fire and stars as an iron monster tramples a trawler. It's then that I know, as surely as the moon waxes and wanes in the night sky, that somehow or other the Captain is linked to the death of my parents.

'Yes, Mamadou was on that boat,' I tell 'em. 'And when I play this flute, his music lives and so does he. You can try to hurt me as much as you want, mister. Fact is, no good comes to those who hurt me. And that's a promise.'

The Captain dismisses my threat by turning his back on me. Turns his back and the urge to punish him for breaking Mamadou's gift and everything else brings bile to my mouth. Priss. If I had my way, I'd get Priss to pluck out his eyes and gobble them up. Rage boils inside me as I watch him reach for the door. Then, all of a sudden, he pauses. Faces me again, listening. He hears it. We all do.

From a distance at first and then closer, a flute is playing. Pictures form in my mind as a song vibrant with colour – red, turquoise, purple – conjures new horizons. I see the flowing robes of men leading camels over a vast expanse of desert. A human caravan. Low notes tremble, high notes flutter and as the music soars, reverberating through our prison, the Captain looks at me and shudders.

'Stop it,' he cries. 'Whatever you're doing, whatever trick you're playing, stop it this instant.'

It's hard for a man who's used to obedience to appreciate that not everything is under his control. Says jump, people jump. Not this time. There's a whole world in here that can't be seen, that has rules of its own and is pursuing its own agenda. And it's whirling around us painting pictures with music.

'Stop it!' the Captain thunders.

I show him the broken flute. 'It's not me,' I tell him. 'I'm not doing anything.'

'Me neither,' says Cobra.

'Then who?' The question slips out of Grey Eyes' mouth before he can stop himself.

He's rattled. They all are.

'*You* did this,' I say, jabbing a piece of bamboo at the Captain.

He shakes his head, stamps his feet. 'Stop it!' he says. Flings his cane to the ground and covers his ears to block the tempest of sound raging around us. The more he protests, the louder the music roars. The naked light bulb above us swings, and in a corner of the room the cheval mirror creaks. I glance at it and catch a glimpse of what I think at first is my reflection. It shimmers, then darts away, as the face I saw earlier today tugs once again at my chest. My reflection moves, yet I'm standing still, fingers linked to Cobra. The bulb dims, then glows.

Slowly, relentlessly, Mamadou's music invades every nook and cranny of our jail. And with it comes a breathing, heaving sensation of tiny fluttering wings that mass and teem, until the prison cell throbs with a tornado of invisible insects about to lift off the roof. Then it stops, and the silence that ensues is every bit as unnerving as what came before.

We hold our breath. Every single one of us clutches on to what we hold most dear. Cobra slides a hand around my waist. I gather his fingers in mine.

Huddled like sailors on a storm-tossed sea, Grey Eyes and Miguel crouch beside the Captain. Miguel helps him up.

'Father,' he says, 'Let's go.' He hands the Captain his cane.

The old man stiffens. 'I'll deal with you tomorrow,' he says to me. Then he mumbles, mostly to himself than to anyone else: 'I saved Isaka. We saved him. You'd think that was enough. No, this is the gratitude I get. Give these people half a loaf and they want it all. What was I supposed to do? We couldn't pull every single one of those damned illegals out of the sea. We couldn't take any more. Give me your hand, Miguel.'

Tenderly, Miguel offers his hand. The Captain clutches it. Back bent, eyes tiny pinpricks of fear, he mutters: 'They've come to get me, my son. The angry spirits of the drowned.'

Miguel leads the Captain away as Grey Eyes bolts the studio door.

Now I'm convinced. The Captain was there. He was there when the trawler my parents were travelling in was mown down by bullets and destroyed. My parents were left to drown in the sea that saved me.

17

That night, before I fall asleep in Cobra's arms, I know I'm going to dream that dream and it's going to reveal my mother this time. I know, just as surely as Cobra knows that Cat's on her way to us, and she's bringing Scarlett with her.

'What about the others?' I ask him.

His fingers garlanding my wrist, he lifts my hand in the air: a dark brown arm beside a wheat-coloured one. I twirl my thumb, rotate my wrist, and keep quiet as Cobra communes with Cat. From the way they're able to talk to each other when they're apart, I reckon they must have been holding hands in the womb, those two.

'The others are coming too,' Cobra says. 'But Cat and Scarlett are on their own.'

'Why?' I sit up.

Cobra pulls me down again, and turns me, so I'm

facing him. His greens lick my face; his fingers stroke my thigh, and that rush of emotion that surfaced when he first kissed me flashes through me again. I smoulder and crackle as he says: 'It's not as if I'm on a phone to her, Sante. Can't ask her questions or hear her voice. I *feel* her. Feel she's eager to reach us. Anxious.'

As anxious as my mother is, I suppose. Her presence has been lingering about us all day, interceding on our behalf and protecting me. I push her out of my mind, concentrate on Cat. 'If she's with Scarlett, where are the Old Ones?'

'My guess is that they're planning on getting help from the police.'

'They can't! Mama Rose and Redwood are missing, wanted for questioning. They're outlaws! They can't break their cover now.'

'This is an emergency,' Cobra reminds me. 'Trouble doesn't come much bigger than this.'

We're in trouble all right.

I smooth down the spikes of Cobra's black hair, kiss the lids of his greens to reassure myself he's real. Stroke him, trace the sinews of his arms and thank my lucky stars that I'm not living this nightmare on my own.

After Grey Eyes bolted the door and left us alone, Cobra placed a saucer of water in a corner. Teased Bella and Scales out of the inside pocket of his tuxedo and let them drink until, satisfied, the snakes slipped into my rucksack to sleep.

'They're worn out,' Cobra said.

'Me too.'

Don't know why, but that simple admission sparked an avalanche of laughter and we reeled with a step-away-from-cliff's-edge hysteria. We laughed recalling the faces of those lizards and vultures in the snake-infested room. Finally, Cobra paused and broached the subject I was trying to forget: the ceremonial dagger, its levitation and whirling, the tumultuous roar of Mamadou's music tonight.

'What do you think's going on, Sante? What are your spooks after?'

I sit on our narrow bed, hands hugging my ribs to ease the pain of our outburst: 'I can't say, Cobra. The only thing in the whole wide world I'm sure of right now is you. I'm glad you're with me, beside me. I'm glad you're my friend and more.'

'For sure.'

The back of his hand grazed my cheek and then brushed the lobe of my ear as my eyes embraced his. 'I appreciate it must be hard to make sense of what's going on,' he said. 'But after everything that's happened today, you must have an inkling of what they want, Sante.'

His fingers squeezed mine, urging me to talk.

I didn't know how to put words to the feelings and thoughts jumbled up inside me. I still don't. Don't know how to separate what's happening within me from the turbulence around me. Priss. Priss would help. I felt the urge to go walkabout with her to tease out my confusion. Just thinking of Priss brought tears to my eyes.

I gulped 'em down: 'Priss has got my tongue, Cobra, and what's in my mouth is tied. I can't seem to find the words to place on it to make sense of anything. This is too deep for me, too complicated.'

'Try, Sante. Try your best,' he replied, quoting Redwood.

All he had to do was quote him and in a blink of an eye, I could hear Redwood talking to me as if he was standing beside me: *'Whatever you do, kid, always do your best, always give your best.'*

I closed my eyes, heaved a sigh, and did what Redwood advises we do in a Tight Situation Without an Easy Way Out. When a predicament confuses me; when I'm spitting with rage and can't see what's in front of me, Redwood tells me to calm down, breathe slowly, and then say whatever comes into my head. 'Cause more often than not, the body has answers the mind can't fathom.

'Trust your instincts, kid,' I heard him saying. *'You may not realise it yet, but deep inside, you know the answer to every problem life will fling at you. The trick is to let it out.'*

I stilled my mind, then uttered the first thought that came: 'Everything connects to my dream and the boat I was in. The dream tells me, and Isaka confirms that the boat, a boat full of migrants and refugees, was rammed. All of 'em drowned except for Isaka and me. I was put in a chest...'

I got up and started to walk around the room.

Up and down, round and about. Touched the walls, the door frame. Trailed my fingers along the dents and curves of our studio cell by doing the closest thing to hunting down my thoughts I could think of – pacing. Truth is, without Priss – her certainty, the spark of her fierce eyes – I felt hopeless, empty. A total waste of space. I gathered my wits, pushed the thought of Priss aside, and as my body relaxed and I exhaled, with my very next breath my tongue untied, and it came to me:

'The sea-chest. As soon as Mama Rose opened that chest and gave me the rest of the gifts those people entrusted me with, everything changed.'

I remembered that hunch-backed cat of curiosity and felt it slinking between my legs again, almost tripping me up.

Cobra's greens pleaded with me to dig deeper. It might as well have been Redwood standing in his shoes, Redwood who turned around. But it wasn't Redwood. It was Cobra, his face brightening as he said: 'And?'

'Everything's changed 'cause I want to know more. I want to find out exactly what happened. I have to know, 'cause I feel 'em around me.

'Like me and Cat?'

'I guess. Can't talk to them as such, but I know they're there. I hear 'em, Cobra. See 'em flitting around at the back of my eye. In that mirror, the uneven corners of this room. Hiding behind dark edges. I think they want me to help them. Don't know how exactly...'

My nose twitched. I eased the itch to hide my uncertainty. 'Sounds weird I know, but...'

'Go on...'

'I think they want justice, a day of reckoning.'

Cobra took off his tux. Hung it up. Then, with his knack of putting into words what I can't quite grasp but is clamped deep inside and terrifies me, he said: 'Are you sure they're not out for revenge, Sante-girl? Are you sure they're not using you?'

'I don't think so.'

'Then what?'

'Remember that time Mama Rose took us to the beach where she found me?'

'Won't forget that in a hurry. A trip to the seaside and what do we see?'

'Dead bodies. Remember those women sunbathing next to 'em? Remember?'

Cobra winced in an effort to erase the image from his mind and sat down on the bed.

I settled beside him. 'I reckon those spooks want the same sort of things we do, Cobra. They want their lives to matter. They saved me, I think, so that at least one person in the whole wide world would remember 'em. And I do. The dreams make sure of that.'

The scene on the beach seared within us, Cobra's fingers trembled. He leaned over, picked up fragments of flute from the end of the bed, and slotted 'em together. 'I can mend this if you want, Sante,' he said. 'Make it good as new for you and Mamadou.'

'He doesn't need a flute to play with now. Doesn't need it as much as I do.'

Cobra put the bamboo pieces in my rucksack, then reassured me that if the Old Ones involve the police in our trouble all will be well.

'But what if the police are already involved?' What if…'

The endless possibilities and permutations of a connection between the Captain, Miguel, Grey Eyes and the local police propel me off the bed.

They're all connected. Must be. I recall those faces leering at us in candlelight and I cringe, then shiver in fury: 'Betcha the police are in on it. Betcha they get a cut of whatever the Captain and his crew make.'

Cobra sighs and beckons me back. As he rubs my nose with his, I gather him in my arms and bring out the full radiance of his smile with a promise: 'We're going to get out of this mess,' I assure him. 'Somehow or other I'm going to dream our way out of here tonight.'

He laughs, holds me tight. 'You're my girl, Sante,'

he whispers. 'For ever and always, my very best girl.'

I don't say a word. All I can to do is smile, 'cause I'm half-asleep already.

18

When the dream comes I'm less than a speck on Priss's back. My face pressed into her neck, my hands stretched over her wings, we're carried by trade winds across the Straits of Gibraltar to Africa. Priss soars and glides, swept by currents over mountain ranges, then purple valleys seeded with date palms, grapes and guava.

We cross a long, winding river and I cling on, telling Priss how much I've missed her, how she'd better come and rescue me soon, 'cause I'm losing my mind without her. I talk to my bird, and as I do so, her pulse beats in time with mine, and we merge. Her gold-brown feathers swaddle my skin, her beak seals my mouth, and before I have time to blink and take stock, I'm seeing the world as Priss does.

Below us, as far as the eye can see, rolling hills of shifting sand.

Above, a mottled morning sky with a hint of rain to come.

We fly south across a vast expanse of desert. Dry riverbeds etched in the landscape peter into trails strewn with empty water bottles made of plastic and hide. Beside them, the remains of travellers picked clean by vultures: a skull, a leg bone, a decomposed arm, its right hand stretched in a final prayer to the sun. A convoy of lorries and cars pass by. A caravan of camels led by a man swathed in black. He stops, gazes at the golden bird darting through a cloud, then continues on the trail.

I am Priss and Priss is me and we're flying free!

We press on, undaunted by the desert terrain. Then, out of nowhere, a sheet of lightning illuminates the sky. A clap of thunder sounds, and below us a whirlwind sucks in a huge mound of sand and spits it out. The wind dances and spins round and round, churns hidden pebbles, stones and long-forgotten bones. Stirs 'em up and flings 'em at us.

A feeling of dread creeps into my being. Priss climbs higher, but the wind chases us, a dark, roiling curtain of sand. Her feathers bristle, she picks up speed, and terror paralyses me as the stench of death freezes my blood. It's them. I know it's them pursuing me.

In the swirl I detect the evil eye of the storm. I see it, and straightaway two faces emerge sculpted by wind and dust. Grey Eyes. And beside him, the Captain, cast in rubble and sand.

I'm dreaming, I tell myself. *Only dreaming.*

Wake up, Sante! Wake up! I try to open my eyes, but the dream has me firmly in its paws. My grip on Priss tightens, but my enemies are so close that evil fills my nostrils. Head tingles as they laugh at me. And yet the more they cackle, the more I taste the truth of what I saw in the Captain last night: malicious contempt. If he can't use me, he'd rather see me dead at the bottom of the sea.

A blink of an eye feels like an hour in dreamtime. Contorted images merge. The trick is to tease 'em out, decipher 'em, catch 'em. I remember my gift, squeeze my eyes tight, and Priss plummets, then surges forwards below the debris and dust of the sand storm. Closes her eyes and I can't see a thing. Heartbeat slows and gradually, as the storm subsides, the icy chill of death leaves my blood.

We journey over savannah: grassland and stubble, hobbled acacia trees. Baobabs, giant scarecrows, dangle bulbous fruit on their arms.

We veer west and parched savannah turns into tropical forest: silk cotton trees, mahogany, ebony, teak. And in-between forest spaces, adobe thatched villages give way to zinc-roofed towns and sprawling cities with buildings that scrape the afternoon sky.

Priss glides down and settles in a home in a forest glade. In the middle of a courtyard, surrounded by rooms with white-washed walls, is a fruiting mango tree. The fruit is unusually large, spectacularly golden in hue. I see them and a spasm of fear stabs me from head to toe. I shouldn't be here. There are sacred spaces in the wilderness, places bathed in the dreams of the dead, which should be left untouched. This is one of them.

I should turn and run as fast as a gazelle chased by a cheetah. I would if I could, but under the tree is my mother, Amma Serwah, a mango in one hand, while in her other arm, she holds a baby. I step closer. Blink twice. Blink again.

It's strange to see myself as I was: bare-chested in a nappy, my neck beaded with sweat. Feels weird. Weirder still when my mother lifts me up, burps me and hands the baby to me.

Can't say that I've ever held an infant as small as this before.

The baby cleaves to me and her flesh becomes my flesh, and I see my mother as she does: large eyes smiling down at me, fingers tickling ribs, while the sun shines through the leaves of the magnificent tree. Leaves glimmer bright, a halo of dappled light around my mother's head. And dangling from a branch, a golden mango shivers, ready to drop.

I reach and try to touch it. Wriggle my fingers and toes. Gurgle in greedy contentment. I should be happy, and yet the moment I smile, my eyes start to leak tears, and my chest heaves with a jangle of emotions that erupt in sobs.

Priss. I want Priss. Her fragrance, the familiar shelter of her wings. I need her right now because every little bit of me, inside and out, is hurting and breaking into pieces.

My mother lifts me up, and in a flutter of an eyelash, I'm fourteen again. She wipes the tears off my face. Flicks a feather from my neck, rubs my shoulder, teases a finger through a lock of my hair. And all the while, as she caresses and folds me gently in her arms, the look of love on her face takes my breath away. And my tears flow, a never-ending river into a sea of sorrow.

My mother holds me, gazing at me with brown eyes as dark as my own. She holds me until, of all the questions I'd like to put to her, one I never thought to ask slips off my tongue: 'How could you throw me into the sea? How could you leave me?'

Without hesitation she replies straight from the heart in a language that needs no translation. 'I didn't leave you. Your father had to tear you from my arms to save you. We travelled because of you, my child, to find a better future. We paid for our passage in full. Paid in dollars. Thousands of dollars. But when that iron ship ploughed into our boat and shattered our dreams, your father and those around us answered my call to save you.'

'My father. Where is he?'

My mother looks up at the mango tree, gazes anxiously at the ripe mango above her, the sap seeping from its stem.

Wants to pluck it, I reckon. Eat it before it falls splat on the ground.

Tears her eyes away, then nods in the direction of a white-washed room. Nods and a door swings open. In the cool cloistered shadows, a man sits at a workbench smelting a strip of gold. He registers my presence and beams at me with a smile that reminds me of Cobra: a sunshine smile that encircles my heart and lights me up from the inside out.

The tall man in my dreams.

A lion of a man in a tawny robe. Broad-chested, skin the dark brown of a polished conker. Straight nose, generous mouth, blue-black eyes in a face lined by laughter.

Smiles at me, then glances at the same ripe mango my mother did.

Hurriedly, he picks up a pair of pincers, lifts the gold. Taps it into shape with a dainty hammer and rushes out. Slips a bangle on my wrist and as I admire it, he says: 'My gift will protect you, Asantewaa. It will help you walk with your feet firmly on the ground in step with our ancestors. You should go now, my daughter. Be lucky. Walk good!'

'But I've only just arrived.'

'So it seems. And yet before that mango drops, you must be gone from here.'

This is indeed a sacred place for the dead. Even so, I don't quite believe him when, to underline the danger I'm in, my father adds: 'A delay could cost you your life, Asantewaa. Be on your way.'

Can't be right to leave when I want to linger and get to know 'em better. Taste the food they like to eat, learn to speak their language. There's a bundle of things I want to find out about them as well. I want to hear stories about the queen I was named after. Hear tales of belonging, tales about my grandparents, tales only they can tell me. And after they've told me everything they know, when it's my turn to fill the silence between us, I'll tell 'em about Mama Rose and her Family Circus. Tell 'em about dancing on Taj Mahal. That back in real time, they call me Sante, and Priss is my friend. Might mention Cobra, given half a chance. Most important of all, I'll let 'em know about the scam that got them killed. There's so much that I want to say, and yet when I open my mouth all I can do is whimper: 'Don't you want me to stay?'

'Of course we do, but this is not your place, Asantewaa,' says my father. 'The moment that mango drops, you'll be trapped here with us.'

Seems he's speaking for the both of 'em. His face is resolute; my mother's is tormented.

Then I hear it. That rustling again. The soft shuffle of footsteps inching closer. Shadows flit and flutter around the tree, murmuring approval.

Amie! Yo! Amie!

My voice trembles: 'Can't I do *anything* for you? Help you somehow?'

Even before he replies, the set of my father's jaw is answer enough. My heart lurches, skips a beat as it dawns on me that I shall never call this man 'Pa', never rest my head on his shoulder and snuffle up the fragrance of cedarwood on his clothes. I'm a trespasser here. But having lived without them for so long, the sight of my parents mesmerises me.

Feet freeze, fingers stiffen.

Mind slows to a trickle, wits scatter, and for the life of me, I can't find the strength to leave 'em.

I'm spellbound. Must be, 'cause I find myself forgetting how the evil eye of that storm pursued me and almost did for me. Instead I'm thinking: *Of course I can get back! Never been trapped in a dream yet. Might as well pluck that mango now; get this foolishness over and done with!*

My father, catching my drift, shakes his head. And as my mother reaches out to me, he slips a hand around her waist and pulls her close.

'This is not your place, Asantewaa,' he repeats.

'This is a place for unquiet spirits of the drowned; a place of shifting sands for restless souls trying to find a way home. Leave us, before it's too late. Wake up! Wake up quickly.'

Amie! Yo! Amie!

I hear them, sense them circling me as the putrid touch of death by drowning splashes my skin. I feel them and taste their wrath. But truth be told, I'd endure anything, the kiss of death itself, just to be with my parents a moment longer.

'This is our home,' I insist. 'This is where I was born.'

'This is a dream, my child. A precious interlude to thank you, encourage you. Take heart, all will be well. Walk good!'

My father's grip around my mother tightens as her eyes devour my face, taking note of every feature, the twist and turn of every lock on my head. She savours me and then trembles when a breeze shakes the branch and the mango sways. The leaves of the tree hiss.

Amie! Yo! Amie!

'Are you going to leave me again?'

'Asantewaa,' my mother replies: 'If you joined us in our watery grave, they will have won.'

'Who are *they*? Tell me! Tell me what to do to help you!'

Her brown eyes twinkle, brimful with love. Her shoulders slump, as my father stands firm: 'You already know who they are, Asantewaa. And you know in your heart that every day you're alive, you're helping us.'

'I'll do whatever you say. I'll do it straightaway.'

A nerve twitches at the side of my father's mouth. 'Go, Asantewaa! No more questions. Time has run its course and you know what to do. The answer to every challenge lies within you already.'

Could be Redwood speaking. Old Ones! Give 'em a chance and they spout riddles at you. Yet there's truth in what he's saying.

The breeze gathers and whistles through the leaves of the tree. The tree shakes. The ground tilts and I stagger. Eyes swivel. Mango drops.

My father leaps and catches it before it touches the ground.

Leaps as he cries: 'Wake up, Asantewaa! Wake up!'

I hear insects first: screeching cicadas followed by the piercing shriek of monkeys and cormorants and an insistent beating of wings. A slow drum roll of sound, as shadows surround my father and shout with one voice:

Amie! Yo! Amie!

I call Priss, try to wake up.

Sunlight dazzles my eyes. I stumble. Hit my head on the ground.

My mother folds my hand in hers and for a second that seems to stretch for eternity, I'm a baby gurgling on her lap again and she's polishing off that mango.

Sucks it dry. Throws it on the ground. Grins at me, jiggles me on her lap and with arms flailing I start to laugh. And with the scent of mango on her breath, she kisses me. She kisses me again and again and each time she kisses me, I know I shall never let her go.

19

'Wake up, Sante! Wake up!'

Cobra's voice.

I grapple, manage to grab hold of it, cling on with all my might as it hauls me out of dreamtime.

Cobra; my lifeline.

I say his name, but the only sound that comes out of my mouth is the grating of chattering teeth.

'Sante? Are you OK?'

I take a gulp of air and snatches of memory stick to me like grit.

The tree. The bump on my head. The light within me snuffing out as a gossamer thread of life snapped. The curious sensation of drowning, before others lap at my feet. My mother and father and then the rest of 'em. The unquiet spirits of the drowned: passengers and crew of the bulky trawler we travelled in, an elderly man, Mamadou with his flute. They gather around me dripping puddles of saltwater. Hovering, murmuring.

'The ancestors answered our prayers,' the old man whispers. 'They can't deny us now. The girl must live.'

'Will she be all right?' someone asks. 'Will she wake up before it's too late?'

Deftly, quickly, my mother rubs my hand. The old man pats my back as my father places a chip of kola on my tongue and urges me to chew.

A sour taste floods my mouth and a burst of energy galvanises me. I try to sit up to shake the fuzziness out of my head, but the shadows won't let me. They hold me down. Whisper hocus-pocus in my ear as my mother says: 'Husband, our daughter is every bit as obstinate as you are.'

'And whose eyes encouraged her to stay? Mine or yours, dear wife?'

My mother thumps my chest, rubs it hard.

I drift in and out of consciousness, and as I slip and slide between this world and the next, I think: *So this is what it's like to die*. The thought lights a flame within me and straightaway I remember my promise not to make Mama Rose old before her time or turn her hair grey overnight.

I try to sit up again. This time it's my mother who holds me down.

'Close your eyes, Asantewaa,' she says, and her

breath changes. The scent of mangoes disappears, replaced by the bitter salt tang of seawater.

Water's deep, so deep the smell of it tells me it's pitch-dark; cold as the grave.

'Close your eyes,' she says. The shadows croon with her. Mamadou taps his flute with a shell to keep time as my mother sings me a lullaby that makes me yearn to stay in her arms for ever:

'Go back to sleep, little babe,

You and me and the devil makes three.'

I shut my eyes and she sings some more:

'Don't you weep, pretty babe,

Come lay your bones on the alabaster stones
And be my everlasting baby.'

My mother continues massaging my chest, teasing tension out of my muscles. Long, deep breaths set my heart pumping again, while the world around me slows to a crawl.

'Go to sleep now, Asantewaa,' my mother says. 'Close your eyes.'

My eyes flicker open. Can't close 'em yet. Not until I see her face again. As the tide of my dream retreats, my mother shrinks from me and takes on another form.

The whites of her eyes sparkle brighter than diamonds.

Coils of seaweed loop through her hair.

She gasps, and what was once her mouth erupts, teeming with tiny, writhing fish.

She touches me and I cringe, for her hands are as cold as marble, fingertips wrinkled from brine. And her robe, encrusted with mother-of-pearl, shimmies with the bloom of jellyfish. What should be a smile blisters into a mask of pain as she returns to her watery grave.

I scream, lay my head down, and wake to Cobra shouting my name.

I hear him, feel him shaking me.

Eyelids flutter open. I want to obliterate the last image of my mother's face while I attempt to retrieve the best of her – eyes as dark as my own, rib-tickling under the tree, the scent of mango on her breath.

'Sante?'

My vision clears and I see Cobra.

I collapse in his arms and hug him with all my might at the thought of how close I came to never seeing my circus family again. Never caressing Priss's feathers, going walkabout with her. Never walking hand in hand with Cobra, paddling fingers with his, or sampling the different flavours of his mouth. My heart aches and I tell myself that as surely as the night sky glitters with stars and I burn at Cobra's touch, I'm going to see this through. Going to claim justice for my parents and those who drowned with them. And as for those lowlifes who would have me dead, they are *not* going to win.

'Were you dreaming again, Sante?'

He wipes the sweat off my face, plucks a tail feather out of my hair, and when I start twizzling the golden bangle on my wrist, his greens light on me. Looks at me strangely and says: 'You've been travelling at night again. What happened this time?'

Words won't come. I roll my tongue in my mouth. Flex it, tap it against my teeth, but when I try to talk, I stutter and start crying instead.

'Slow down,' Cobra says, rubbing my arms.

He wraps his tuxedo jacket around me and takes me in his arms, the way Mama Rose does when I'm spooked. Says the same things as Mama Rose as well: 'Easy, Sante. Relax. Everything's going to be fine.'

He rocks me in his arms and when my tears have dried and my chattering's over, I tell him.

'I travelled with Priss last night. Travelled to Ghana-land and met my parents. My father gave me this.' I turn the bangle around. Twist it and smile as it shines.

Cobra knows me better than the lines on the palm of his hand. Knows that though at times I may skirt around it, may even try and avoid it if I can, I always end up telling him the truth.

Cobra's cheekbones glint. Fear sparks on his face. He's even more alarmed than I am.

He drops my hand, stands up. Starts pacing the floor like I did yesterday. I guess it's his turn to feel jittery.

'What's going on, Sante?' he says. 'Why's your pa come back now to claim you?'

I roll his tuxedo into a pillow. Lay my head down and yawn: 'He gave me this gift to keep me safe, is all.'

Seems the bangle means a whole heap more to Cobra than to me: 'Don't know why any better than you do. I wanted to tell 'em about you, but there wasn't time.'

'Had time enough to make you that thing you're worrying on your wrist...'

Cobra circles the room like a trapped puma. As he turns, I sense what may be bothering him. The tall man in my dreams. 'My pa's dead,' I whisper. He's stone-cold dead in a watery grave, Cobra.'

He walks three paces, turns, and stops bang in the middle of the room. Stops and it overwhelms him. Fever. High fever. 'Cat,' he says. 'Cat's here.'

We scramble on to the bed, look out of the window.

It's early morning, the sky a pearly grey with ripples of herringbone-pink splashed across the heavens. Another hot day. Slumped on a chair, asleep in a corner of the roof terrace, is Barrel Man, rifle at his side. Head nodding, mouth drooling spit. Dreaming, I guess, for suddenly he jumps, opens his eyes.

We duck. When we look out again, Barrel Man's dozed off.

Then I see a flash of golden feathers, a stretch of wing and Priss lands at the edge of the terrace. Behind her is Cat. Didn't hear her jump on the roof, but I saw her leap, catch hold of a line of cable and haul herself up. Quiet as a cat she is, stealthy. Slung over her shoulder is a blowpipe, a pouch at her waist with darts. Sometimes uses 'em when we go hunting with Priss in out of the way places. Poisoned darts kill fast. Could be she's only drugged 'em today – dipped 'em in one of Midget Man's potions. Could be she aims to maim and not kill. Never quite know with Cat.

She climbs on to the roof terrace, crouches behind a potted palm tree and looks around. Sees us watching her.

Cobra points at Barrel Man, puts a finger to his lips.

I signal to Priss. Tell her to hold back, keep still.

Priss throws back her neck and, with a gimlet eye fastened on Barrel Man, opens and closes the razor-sharp tips of her talons.

Cat inches closer, is about to take aim when Barrel Man opens his eyes with a start. His rifle drops to the ground and he jumps. Sniffs trouble. Stoops to pick up the weapon and spies Cat. Sees her, then feels a stab of pain in his neck. His eyes dim. Right hand flops to his side. Rifle clatters to the ground again as his left hand gropes his neck. He pulls out the dart. And as he stares at it dazed, Barrel Man sways, and crumples to the floor.

In a twinkling, Cat pounces on him and rummages through his trouser pocket. Pulls out a rosary, a phone, a strand of string.

'Where's the key to your place?' she mouths.

Cobra slaps his chest and thighs and mimes: 'Look in his other pockets.'

Cat rolls Barrel Man over, pats her hand down his thigh. Pulls out a battered pack of cigarettes. No key.

Fumbles through his jacket. Finds a flask of whisky. A wooden crucifix. Still no keys.

Cat gestures: 'What should I do?'

'Keep on looking,' I hiss. 'But whatever you do, hurry up, before Barrel Man stirs.'

Cat shoves the whisky, phone and cigarettes in her pouch. She picks up the rosary and crucifix, about to stash them away as well, when Barrel Man's forefinger quivers. Suddenly, his hand jerks and he lunges for Cat's ankle.

She spins, stamping on his hand. Before he has time to howl, she stabs another dart in his neck. The big man's out for the count. It's then she sees it. Puddled in a roll of muscle around his neck, a thick gold chain. On the chain are three keys. Cat yanks them from Barrel Man's neck, tosses the chain in her pouch and runs to the door.

She releases the deadlocks. Drops a key. Tries another and – hey presto! – the door opens at her second attempt. And there she is, a fat-cat grin on her face, the key jangling on her finger: 'Come on. Let's get out of here.'

I take my rucksack, put my biker boots inside. Cobra slips on his tuxedo and we're off with Cat and Priss over the rooftops.

Priss leads and we follow. We hurl ourselves from one roof to the next. Leap over flowerpots, clamber up potted palms and garden trellises. Reach the top, stretch and jump. Crawl up guttering and as we vault over an iron guardrail, Cobra's tux catches. He tears himself free and we run. Run fast as leopards down a spiral staircase to a courtyard and, in two shakes, we're outside again.

Scarlett, goggles over her eyes, a black beret hiding her hair, is waiting for Cat on the pizza-delivery scooter.

Cobra looks left and right. Left again, and spies Redwood's bike where we parked it. He fiddles with the electrics, hotwires the motor, and we're off.

20

We don't slow down till we're several kilometres out of town, a stone's throw from our former camping ground. We pause, get our bearings, then press on to the only place we know where we'll be sheltered, out of sight. The closer we get to our hideout, the harder Cobra pushes Redwood's bike. He overtakes Scarlett, waves, and she follows with Cat, while Priss circles overhead. We turn left up the dirt track, and after bouncing through a lemon grove, Cobra brings the bike to a halt in a cloud of dust.

It doesn't seem possible that less than two days ago our trucks were parked here. Taj Mahal's trailer was over there. I watered him in the stream. In a blink of an eye, I'd adorn him with bells and white ribbons, slip on my turquoise tutu, and step into a world of wonder. Fact is, life with the Old Ones suddenly seems a million years away, when all that remains of Mama Rose's Family Circus are dried tyre ruts, clumps of horse manure, and scattered ashes from Mimi's last bonfire. Would turn the clock back if I could, set about things a different way. But what's done is done, and it's time to take stock.

I pull on my leather glove and Priss comes to me. I squeal with delight at the mighty heft of her, the flash of her fiery eyes, the hard shine of her beak. I coo and gurgle until Scarlett parks the scooter and Cat hops off.

'Found her hiding on a roof close to yours,' Cat says. 'Minute she saw me she flew over. Must have been keeping an eye on you, Sante. Waiting for you.'

I nod, inhaling the heady fragrance of my feathered friend. Suck her in, snap my tongue, cluck, and Priss responds. She flexes her wings and swoops into the avocado tree.

In an ideal world I'd go walkabout. Step out of time for a few days and figure out what to do next. Work out what the bangle on my wrist means. Mull over what the spooks really want from me and how Isaka, Grey Eyes, Miguel and the Captain fit in. I'd be off with Priss if I followed my heart. But my heart's pulling me in two directions at the same time. The part of me that's leaning towards what my head tells me is right prevails. I'm part of a crew now, and whatever's happening isn't just about me. I may be a catalyst, but Scarlett's involved as well, and because of me, so are Cobra and Cat.

'We came as soon as we could,' says Cat. 'Left the Old Ones behind and set off.'

She kisses the tip of her forefinger and places it on Cobra's lips. He pulls her into his arms and hugs her. 'Are you OK, Cobra? And you, Sante?' Cat brushes away a tear.

Never seen her moved to tears by hugging Cobra before.

'Come here, little sister,' she says, and wraps her arms around me.

The Cat I know isn't what I'd call the hugging type. Likes to hiss and snarl, bite and scrap. Cat is softer somehow. And flitting over her face is the same sunshine smile as her brother's.

Must be Scarlett's doing. Loving Scarlett's made her insides melt and tenderised her soul. Seems Cobra's got Scarlett on his mind as well. He's staring at her, trying to figure out what the girl's got inside that's transformed his twin. Him and me both are asking similar questions:

What lies behind the honey-lick of those wild eyes, the unruly beauty of that hair?

Cat links fingers with Scarlett, and the four of us squat on our heels and talk.

First off, we catch up; fill in the gaps. I tell Cat and Scarlett what I didn't get a chance to tell 'em before. I tell 'em about the treasure in my sea-chest cradle and the ghosts of the restless dead.

Cat frowns. 'Are you sure this is for real, Sante? Or are spiders spinning cobwebs in your head again?'

'What I'm saying is as real as the dirt on my hands.'

I show 'em the grime on my palms, and when Cat's satisfied that I'm not joshing her, I tell 'em about the ceremonial dagger, the mysterious music from Mamadou's flute. How those thugs broke it and the music played on.

Cat scrunches her face again. Her brow furrows, and as her mind swings into gear, her greens sizzle with excitement. 'I remember now,' she says. 'That strange music you played when we did our first gig in the cathedral square. The music riled Cobra's snakes, weirded them out. Spooked 'em. Spooked everyone.'

I nod. 'All I have to do is talk about 'em, Cat. Say their names and the spirits make their presence felt. Call 'em and they appear. Hurt me and they'll frighten you.'

'Can you call 'em right now?' Cat looks over her shoulder. Grins at me.

'I could, but I shan't, 'cause this isn't a silly make-believe game I'm playing. It's about life and death. For real.'

Scarlett tugs at a strand of hair and wraps it around a finger. She's crouched so close between Cat and me that I feel her breath on my face when she asks: 'Any idea why the spirits are doing this, Sante?'

It's the first time she's called me by name, and

I notice freckles on her nose, like a sprinkling of cinnamon on white, buttered toast.

I choose my words carefully; think before I speak. I've asked myself the same question again and again and yet I'm still searching for a convincing answer. 'The way I see it,' I say at last. 'The way I feel when they're around, I think those ghosts are looking out for me, pushing me in a direction I can't quite make out. Not yet, at any rate. But when I think about it, I'm pretty sure they want a day of reckoning. Want their lives to matter.'

I turn to Cobra for confirmation. He nods. Scarlett does too, and I go on: 'They helped Cobra and I wreck Miguel's party last night. Blew the candles out, gave Cobra a chance to summon snakes. You should have seen those Old Ones running for their lives!'

Cobra chuckles, then smiles a dazzling snake-oil smile that reveals the whites of his teeth. Smiles and I beam at him, feel that crackle in my heart, and a sizzle hot enough to spark a fire in a bundle of twigs. I grin.

Scarlett blushes. Twists a curl behind her ear, lowers her head: 'You were at one of their parties?' she asks. 'Did you see the others? Did you talk to them?'

'We saw 'em. Spoke to a girl called Ayesha.'

'Didn't get a chance to speak to anyone else, though,' Cobra adds. 'They hustled us out of there as soon as the lights came on.'

Scarlett's eyes gleam toffee-black. 'I never got to speak to them either, but from what I picked up from Miguel, they come from all over Europe. Some come from Africa, as far away as Thailand. Miguel says they'll do just about anything to get a foothold here. Anything.' Her voice fades to a whisper: 'Did you meet the Captain?'

I don't reply straightaway. My mouth opens and I gaze at her, wondering how it is that someone who claimed to have spent a single night in Miguel's care, knows as much as she does. Cobra catches my drift. Holds his tongue, gives Scarlett a chance to talk.

She flushes and Cat covers her fingers with a hand. Scarlett grips it so tightly Cat's knuckles turn white. Both of 'em swallow. Cat nods and then Scarlett says: 'To begin with Miguel was my friend. I thought he really liked me because he made me feel special.'

Cobra and I lean in, eager to hear more as Scarlett's voice trails away. I try to delve inside her, but whatever trail she was on has disappeared. Tears trickle down her face.

We wait. The silence between us deepens and the weight of Scarlett's distress coils around my chest, almost crushing the breath out of me. The girl's hurting, aching all over. Then it hits me! *Boom!* Of course! She was in Miguel's clutches before we were, so she's felt it too: the shame of it, the humiliation.

I catch a glimpse of what's running through Scarlett's

mind and begin to recognise the shape and size of 'em: vultures playing with rubies, bald-headed lizards chins sagging, heads jerking up and down. She's been there. Saw what we did.

'Dying's too good for 'em,' I say to Scarlett. 'Those Old Ones at Miguel's party could die a thousand times over and then some, and it still wouldn't be punishment enough. They made me feel that I was as ugly as a mole rat.'

Scarlett stifles a sob. 'They did that to you too?'

I nod. 'Ugly as mole rat and worth less than a speck of dust.'

'That's what they do best,' Scarlett replies. 'Pull you apart, trash everything you hold dear, so they can use you. You too?'

'They broke my flute,' I remind her. 'But before that...' I look at Cobra. He takes my hand, presses it, and I say: 'Before that, they said Mama Rose and Redwood aren't who they claim to be. Said they're outlaws, wanted by the police for questioning.'

Cat's jaw drops: 'You're kidding us, right?'

'Can't say for sure, one way or the other until we talk to 'em,' says Cobra. 'Were they OK when you left them?'

'Soon as they got your message they lost it completely, but that's Doomsters for you.' A glint of anger, like a knife slashing air, flashes in Cat's greens. 'Something goes wrong and the sun's never going to shine again. Going to be hurricanes and storms from now till Doom's Day. Went mental. All of 'em.'

She brings Cobra and me up to speed, and pictures flow into my mind. I'm in Granada with the Old Ones: watching 'em, eavesdropping on what they said.

Mimi howls: 'My darlings! What's going to become of them now?'

Bizzie Lizzie, not to be outdone, stamps her foot and hollers loud as a jabbering crow: 'I knew it! I knew no good would come out of this. We should have stopped her. But then I've never known a child as obstinate as Sante Williams. Girl's going to be the death of me, I swear!'

I hear the two of 'em ranting and raving while Mama Rose stands, rigid as a statue, a webbed hand clutching a chair. The only part of her moving, a finger on her left hand, quivers.

'Mama Rose couldn't talk,' Cat says. 'Couldn't walk or talk for a full hour. Needed all the whispering Midget Man and Redwood could conjure between 'em to make her sit down.'

'And Midget Man?'

'Took it in his stride,' Cat tells me. 'Said he had faith in the two of you. When he couldn't take Mimi and Bizzie Lizzie's hollering a moment longer, he sneaked off on Taj Mahal and picked up your scent on the wind. Said the signs he sniffed out, combined with the omens he saw in the sky, told him that in the end, we're all going to be fine. Right as rain. He came back in time to help me prepare my darts. Set off with Scarlett before sunrise. When we left, the Old Ones were huddled together talking, trying to figure out what to do for the best.'

Cobra takes in Cat's words and asks: 'So by the time you left, they hadn't gone to the police?'

'Not as far as I know.'

If I needed further proof that ours is not a typical family of everyday folk, this was it. The Old Ones are definitely hiding something. A taste of sour milk seeps into my mouth as the possibility that living off the grid is a cover for something more sinister and troubling tightens its grip on me. But why all the lying? Why? Thanks to Grey Eyes and Miguel, I'm like a fly caught in a web of suspicion that's tearing me away from those I love most in the world.

And suspicion, I'm discovering, breeds uncertainty. I'm trying hard to stay focused, when Cat lets slip that while he was helping her prepare her darts, Midget Man extracted a promise from her.

'Made me swear that as soon as we returned to Cádiz, before we tried to get you two out from under Miguel, we'd look up that old friend of his, Imma, a dancer. Said she'd help us find somewhere safe to stay.'

Then I remember: 'Midget Man gave us her name as well. Gave us her number.'

'Just as well we called on her,' says Cat. 'She warned us that Miguel and his gang want Scarlett back and they're looking for her. Told us to get out of town pronto. Then she gave us the name of a place we could stay once we sprang you. Her brother's place. Two hours north of here. Drew us a map. Said we'd be safe there.'

Cat takes the map out of her pouch. Shows it to us, and while Cobra and I look at it, shakes out a cigarette from Barrel Man's crumpled pack. Lights it. Passes it to Scarlett, who sucks it greedily.

The Cat I knew wouldn't light a cigarette for anybody. She didn't smoke. Said cigarettes were bad for us. Used to drink, though.

Right on cue, Cat pulls out Barrel Man's flask. 'Whisky,' she says. Takes a slug from it, and then hands it to Scarlett. Scarlett swallows, pulls a face, and offers the flask to me.

I say, 'No.' Cobra does too.

Next moment he scrunches up Imma's map, tosses it on the ground, and says: 'Two hours away is two hours too close to those lowlifes for my liking. We should clear out of here completely. Head for Granada, meet up with the Old Ones, and leave the country.'

Scarlett inhales again. Blue doughnut-shaped rings glide out of her mouth, then she says in a haze of smoke: 'It wouldn't be right to leave the others. I owe them. They explained what was expected of me...'

Her voice dips, once again, to a whisper. And once again I can't help wondering if what she's saying is the whole truth and nothing but the truth. And if it is, why she reveals it in dribs and drabs, contradicting what she said a moment before.

Scarlett closes her eyes. When she opens them again, her pupils are dilated and resemble those of a startled fawn. Suddenly, she throws back her hair and her face changes yet again, as wariness gives way to determination. 'We've got to get them out of there,' she says. 'Get them to safety somehow.'

The girl's too twitchy to trust, and chances are that under pressure she could end up the wrong side of crazy. I know this, and yet what she's just said chimes with my sentiments exactly.

Cat and I nod while Cobra shakes his head: 'Have you lost your minds? Are you seriously considering tangling with people-smugglers and sex-traffickers? Those folks we met back there are the worst people in the world. Think again, Sante.'

And to Cat, he says: 'I don't know what that girl's done to you, sis. You've given your heart to her, maybe, but there's no need to lose your marbles as well.'

Cat sharpens her claws. Don't see it, but I hear it in her voice. 'That girl's got a name, Cobra. Say it.'

There's no chance in this world or the next of that happening any time soon. No chance of Cobra taking orders from his twin. Can tell from the set of his mouth that he has no intention of allowing Scarlett's name to pass his lips. In fact, he refuses to say it three times, so I end up saying it for him: 'Scarlett. Her name's Scarlett.'

'Of all the hare-brained ideas I've heard, this one beats 'em all!' Cobra gets up, brushes down his black jeans then kicks the balled-up map high in the air.

Priss hisses at him from inside the avocado tree. I answer her cry with a soothing whistle. She flies down, picks up the map and drops it in my lap.

'Listen,' Cobra says, circling us. 'If the Old Ones won't do it, let's do it for them. Go to the police. Ask for help. Show 'em where the others are. Identify those crooks and get them banged up.'

Cat pulls one of her I-can't-believe-what-I'm-hearing faces and sniggers.

Scarlett chuckles.

It's not always wise to laugh at Cobra. Can make him mad, mean as spit. Can't help but smile at him, though. After years of mistrust, years of hiding out in wild places, of giving the authorities, black-boots especially, a wide berth, he wants us to ask 'em for *help*? Might as well celebrate Christmas with the devil.

And when Scarlett says: 'I don't suppose you know – why should you? – but Miguel's best friend is head of the police in Cádiz,' she hits the nail on the head.

'There you go,' says Cat.

But that doesn't stop Cobra, who's every bit as pig-headed as his sister. Doesn't listen to her. No, sir! Says variations of the same thing again and again. Calls us 'numbskulls', 'clueless'. Protests. Tries to talk what he calls 'sense' into us, which only makes matters worse. The more he rails at us and questions our sanity, the deeper we dig ourselves in, while Scarlett sits back, a hint of a smile on her lips.

At last, I put my hand on Cobra's leg, and make him squat with us again. 'You've had your say,' I tell him. 'Let's vote on what to do next. Those in favour of helping the others…'

I put up my hand. Cat and Scarlett link fingers and wave their arms in the air.

Cobra stands up, wipes the dust off his palms. Might as well be washing 'em from what I can tell, 'cause plain as the sun in the sky, he wants no part of the blame for what happens next. 'Outnumbered and outmanoeuvred by fools! So be it. On one condition – the minute your eggs start to unscramble, the three of you are going to say loud and clear, under my direction: '*Cobra told us not to do this, but did we listen? Hell no!*'

We girls whoop with laughter, and in-between back-slapping and hand-clapping, we make up our minds. We're going to go to Imma's brother's farmhouse, regroup, make a plan to help the others. We're going to set 'em free and scupper the Captain's racket.

For Scarlett and I, getting even with the Captain and his friends is as personal as it gets. For the sake of my parents, and those who drowned with them, it's time to take care of unfinished business. And even if we're not able to make everything right, we'll do all we can to make 'em a whole heap better.

21

It turns out that Carlos Garcia, Imma's brother, used to work in the entertainment business like we do. Made a bundle playing flamenco guitar while Imma danced to his tunes. Gave it up to run the family farm full-time. A tall, thin man, brown curly hair flopped over an eye, I take to Carlos as soon as I shake his hand. Firm and dry.

'I was expecting you,' he says.

The dog at Carlos's side licks my fingers. Dog's a red setter called Tortilla. Nuzzles me as his master says: 'Imma called early this morning and told me all about you guys. I gather you know an old friend of ours, Elvis Gomesh.'

'Elvis who?'

Carlos smiles: 'Elvis Gomesh – known to you, most probably, as Midget Man.'

Mama Rose and Redwood, now Midget Man?

'Never knew Midget Man was called Elvis. Did you, Cobra?'

Cobra shakes his head. Cat shrugs, takes Scarlett's hand, and Carlos ushers us into his home.

We all take to him – that is – Cobra, Cat and I do. Scarlett's nervous, wary, even though before we set foot in the house, we sniffed it out. Checked the exits and entrances in case we need to get away in a hurry. Most important before we called out Carlos's name and knocked on the farmhouse door, we took the measure of the place to get a sense of who lived inside the rambling old house.

I closed my eyes and breathed deep to gauge the scent of the building and hear the echo of past lives that once lived in it. The perfume of wood-smoke laced with a whiff of wild rosemary wafted out of warm ancient brick, built and extended by generations of farmers. A farmhouse baked in the swell and glow of a rolling landscape of hills. Someone's home, as well as a dwelling place for animals: for behind the reassuring smells and sounds of the house – the footfall of someone walking down stairs, the bark and snuffle of a dog – was the snort of animals roaming in fields, the whinny of stabled horses.

'Feels good,' Cobra said.

Cat nodded, and despite a sliver of anxiety on Scarlett's face, I knocked on the door and Carlos let us in.

First off, he feeds us. Makes cups of milky coffee, then fries bacon and eggs. Cuts us huge slabs of bread, spreads butter on it, and takes the food outside. We sit at a long mosaic table under a chandelier fitted on a canopy of grapevines and figs. Down below is a swimming pool and, beyond the wooden gates of a bottom lawn, flowering meadow and grassland gradually rise into hills that become rocky, mountainous peaks.

I could go walkabout with Priss for days up there. Clamber up those hills, climb those magnificent peaks. I devour the view and, hungry for a spell of solitude with my bird, I forget to eat. Gawp instead. Tortilla jumps up, steals a slice of my bacon.

'Down, dog,' Carlos shouts. 'Good boy.'

Dog slinks away and as I eat what's left on my plate, Carlos jokes that we're yet another band of Imma's runaways. Reckon she must have helped others before us. In any case Carlos tries to tease us, and when we don't laugh with him, asks the question, which of all the questions in the world, we'd rather not answer. 'What are you running away from?'

A knife clatters on the flagstones. Scarlett bends to retrieve it. Cobra looks at me. Cat does too. Next thing I know, Carlos's eyes are drilling into me and he's talking as if I'm the leader of our gang, the one with an answer for everything.

'If you're going to stay here,' he says, 'I need to

know something about you. Why you've come to me for shelter.'

From under the table, Tortilla's cool nose prods my knee. I stroke the soft, red shine between his ears, and as he snuggles closer, licking my fingers, Priss swoops and nestles on the bower.

Carlos looks at my bird, then looks at me waiting for my reply.

An explanation pushes at the back of my throat. I try to talk. I *um* and *ah*, mutter a few words, stumble, then stop.

A frown crosses Carlos's face; another question sparks in his eyes. The more time he spends in our company, the more puzzled he appears.

I mumble, attempt to tell him our story but it weighs heavy on my tongue and defeats me. I may have taken to Carlos, may like his dog as well, but after everything we've been through, I'm not foolish enough to think I can *trust* him yet.

He flips back his hair, pours himself more coffee and says: 'I let you in because of Imma. If you want to stay here, the least I expect from you is a degree of openness in exchange for my hospitality. Now, if you can't be straight with me, you'll have to find shelter elsewhere.'

Takes a sip of coffee, savours the taste and lowers the white china cup.

I stroke the bangle on my wrist and words tumble

out of me: 'We were kidnapped by a German man in Cádiz and his friend, Miguel.'

Just saying the name ignites a convulsion of hatred in Scarlett. 'Miguel Zaragosa,' she cries. 'He … he…' Scarlett shudders. Then, eyes bright with accusation, she stares at Carlos: 'Miguel and his father, José-Mariá Zaragosa, hurt girls like me. They meddle with us. Peddle us.'

'It's OK, Scarlett. It's OK,' Cat says.

She tends to her, holds her close while Cobra takes Scarlett by the hand and lays his fingers over hers. Cups her fingers, warms them with his breath as hushed tears fall.

Carlos presses the palms of his hands together and murmurs: 'José-Mariá Zaragosa. Imma's runaways mentioned his name. They called him the Captain. I understand your predicament now.'

Carlos shows us to a spare room – a large covered space above a garage where, once upon a time, a previous owner bred doves and pigeons. What Mama Rose would call a Glory Hole – a dumping place for things no longer used but no one can be bothered to get rid of – Carlos calls a pigeonnier, a dovecote.

Piled in clusters at the far end is discarded furniture: garden chairs, a broken beechwood table, on top of which is an ancient vase of dried purple flowers.

'You'll have to tidy this up,' Carlos says. 'I'll bring you some bedding. That's the broom cupboard. Sweep the floor, make mattresses out of the blankets, and you should be OK.' Carlos looks at his watch. 'I'll give you an hour to sort yourselves, then I could use your help mucking out the stables. In the meantime, I'll call our mutual friends in Granada, let them know you're here.'

It doesn't take us long to tidy. Open the windows. Mop the floor. Clean and dust till the place is spruced and buffed. We consider mucking out with Carlos, but decide instead to concentrate on what's fired us up. We sit on our mattresses. Scarlett removes Barrel Man's phone from Cat's pouch, rummages through it and shows what's inside it to Cat.

'Barrel Man has a family!' Cat gasps.

Scarlett, more attuned to gizmos than the rest of us, flicks through the photographs on the phone while Cobra and I lean in to look.

There he is: Barrel Man, round as a tub, arm in arm with Miguel, at a bar. Then again with a thin woman, most probably his wife. On their laps are two girls. Butterball-plump, they look more like their pa than the woman at his side. Wife's as plain as an old tin pail, yet her timid eyes appear kind.

'Do you think he bullies her?' I ask, recalling how Barrel Man relished dangling Cobra by the arm and almost throttled me on the roof terrace.

'Wouldn't be surprised,' says Scarlett in techno-savvy, screen-rat mode.

Screen rats don't talk much. Don't know how to, I reckon. Another reason the Old Ones consider it wise to hole up in wild places. Claim ordinary folk can't communicate any more, 'cause talking's been bred out of 'em with the overuse of technology. And when the end comes with unceasing floods, hurricanes, wild fires and pestilence, everyday folk – those whose brains have become wired to gadgets and gizmos – won't be able to say boo to a goose. They'll say boo to their screens instead. That's what the Old Ones say. Don't usually agree with them, but of one thing I'm certain: whatever's in those machines is mighty powerful, 'cause it's drawing me in too.

I look over Scarlett's shoulder while Cobra searches my rucksack. Brings out Bella and Scales, drapes 'em around his neck before he takes out what's left of Mamadou's flute: two pieces of broken bamboo. Inspects 'em, cleans 'em by blowing off the dust, then sits down, cross-legged, and begins mending my heirloom with glue from an old tube he found somewhere.

Scarlett is still sifting through Barrel Man's phone, and at the same time Cat, forefinger flitting across a screen, hunts through Scarlett's. Grins. Starts rocking back and forth in silent laugher, lets out a whoop of delight, and shoves Scarlett's phone at me.

On the screen's a snapshot of Scarlett in school uniform: navy blazer, blue checked dress, a straw boater jammed on her head. Same eyes, same red hair but back then she was living another life altogether. 'Scarlett! Is that you?'

Lips twist in what passes for a smile. 'Used to be,' she tells me.

Like so much about her it doesn't make sense. The girl in the photograph's rich with the imperious elegance of a dancer; a dancer who's never had to brush or polish her shoes herself, that's for sure. And another thing: poor kids don't go to school dressed like that. Can't afford to. So how come a girl as pampered as the one in the photograph ended up trying to drown herself on a beach in Spain? And how did parents who could once afford an expensive school for their daughter wind up begging on the streets of Cádiz?

Questions hang in the air as Scarlett continues scrolling through Barrel Man's phone. His whole life is stashed in there: phone numbers of everyone who matters; numbers for the Captain, Isaka and Concha. Scarlett writes them down.

There are photos of Barrel Man lounging on a yacht with Miguel and Grey Eyes. Barrel Man, an arm around Concha. Concha, complexion parchment white, in the black-and-pink costume of a matador; Concha, followed by endless images of boys and girls of all ages and races in a variety of skimpy costumes and seductive poses. Their faces, every one of 'em, expressionless.

I may not be used to playing with 'em yet, but any creature with a brain the size of a flea can see it's downright dangerous to store your whole life in a gadget. Especially when it can easily fall into the wrong hands. Always thought Barrel Man was a toad. Didn't realise just how much of a fool he is as well.

Tap, tap, tap. Press, scroll. Scarlett's finger trawls, creating a rhythm punctuated by occasional pauses and grunts of disgust.

'This is dynamite,' she says. 'This could blow the lot of them clear out of the water, high into the sky. This could land 'em in prison for years if we get these pictures to the right people...'

She can't stop looking as reams and reams of images surface from the inner workings of Barrel Man's phone. Despite her revulsion, I begin to sense that she's digging deeper and deeper, grappling with the task at hand like a hungry pup at the teat, for a reason. 'Is there one of you in there?'

Scarlett looks at me. Not a sideways half-glance 'cause she's more intent on what's on the screen, but a full-on stare that raises the hairs on the back of my neck.

Cinnamon freckles shimmer and glow, eyes glitter hard as diamonds. She curls her mouth in a scowl and then suddenly bites down. A drop of blood swells on her lip. Lip trembles, and I stare, bewitched, dazed by what I'm seeing. Even so, I'm aware of a sharp intake of breath and a blur of movement as Cat hands Scarlett's phone to Cobra. He gazes perplexed at the screen before he gives it to me. I don't look at it, 'cause I can't take my eyes off the blood on Scarlett's lip. It balloons, is about to spill over when, her eyes still fixed on me, she scoops it up with the tip of her tongue.

'I told you... I told you...' she says in answer to my question.

She doesn't have to tell me. Scarlett, I realise, has to look at *everything* in case deep in the bowels of Barrel Man's contraption are images of herself with the same haunted desolation on her face; which means, if I'm right, that she was at Miguel's for much longer than the single night she claimed to begin with.

Unsure what to say, how best to explain herself, Scarlett rearranges her legs. Crosses 'em. Uncrosses 'em. Looks at Cat. Summons her by patting the empty seat beside her.

Cat sits down again. But this time, instead of lounging over Scarlett as she usually does, she raises her knees to her chin and hugs them. 'What really happened to you and your folks, Scarlett?'

A growl of thunder rumbles above the pigeonnier

as wind whirls through a grove of olives and fig trees. Leaves rustle. Ancient bark creaks. The air inside and out heaves, saturated with the cloying sensation of imminent rain and niggling unanswered questions.

I browse through the pictures. No wonder Cat wants to know more. No wonder the tips of her fingers are white with the strain of not touching; the pain of holding everything in, when she's tight as a tick about to burst. Can't be easy loving someone with webs of suspicion wrapped around 'em; especially when that someone's the girl whose life I'm shuffling through.

Scarlett with her parents and her brother during easier, happier times. Could be any group of rich folk, any one of the families I've looked at and envied for as long as I can remember. Families I've wanted to snuggle up to and infiltrate: a *proper, normal* family with a ma and pa and two children – a flame-haired teenager beside a boy. Could be any family, if it wasn't for the fact that standing behind 'em, an arm around each of Scarlett's parents, is a face I recognise: Miguel, a smile on his lying, cupid lips.

I slide a finger over the screen, the way Cat's been doing, and more images pop up: all of 'em of Scarlett and Miguel now. Scarlett in a sun hat on a beach. Tousle-haired Scarlett sleepy-eyed in bed. And in each of the photographs, she's entwined with

Miguel, hugging him as if they're not only the best of friends but much more. Miguel on a bar stool, a hand over Scarlett's, while Scarlett in a green bikini, eyes hidden by a visor, sips a drink the same colour as her swimsuit. Crème de Menthe – Bizzie Lizzie's favourite. And there she is again draped over a sofa, a well of secret knowledge brimming in her eyes.

Blasts of wind scour the farmhouse, whipping up dust. Windows rattle in the pigeonnier. Thunder sounds and a moment later, lightning zips across the sky, illuminating our faces.

'I asked you a question.' A chink of ice in Cat's voice does the trick. Scarlett sits up. Cobra does too, alert to a shift that tells those of us who know her that Cat's claws are out.

I hand the phone back to Scarlett. She looks at it and her cheeks flush. 'I heard you,' she says to Cat. 'It's just…'

She drops the phone, reaches out, then recoils as Cat hisses:

'Don't touch me. Don't you dare touch me again till you tell me the truth about you, your folks and Miguel.'

Scarlett tries to speak, but when words won't come, emotions flit over her face like a spray of cards in a hasty five-card trick. Tight-lipped fury. Uncertainty. Spasms of fear and love, which slip into a look guaranteed to give her the Cat she's after: a Cat's who's pliant and tender and is completely on her side. Mouth half-open, Scarlett cautiously meets Cat's gaze, then beats a hasty retreat. I would too if I were her, 'cause from the ferocity in Cat's greens, she has no intention, whatsoever, of taking any prisoners today.

'Please, Cat,' Scarlett whispers. 'Please.'

Cat shakes her head. 'Ain't going to work this time, Scarlett. Asked you a simple question and I'm waiting for your answer.'

'You want to know what happened to me and my family and Miguel? You really want to know? Are you sure, Cat? *Really*?' Scarlett shivers. Goosebump-blotches appear on her arms and she hugs herself to keep the storm raging outside as far away as possible. 'You don't want know, Cat. If you care for me at all, you don't want to know. *Please*.'

'Oh, but I do, Scarlett. I do.'

'No, you don't!' she says and begins rocking back and forth, to and fro, again and again, as if in order to reveal crucial facts about her life, she has to enter a trance – a safe place in no-man's land where she can talk without fear of hurting.

Back and forth she goes, faster and faster, until almost panting, she asks, one more time: 'Are you sure, Cat? Are you really sure?'

'Tell me the truth for once! All of it in one go! And this time make sure that every little bit of what you say is one hundred per cent, hand-on-heart truth, the whole truth and nothing but the truth, so help me God.'

Reckon the truth may be a moveable feast, as far as Scarlett's concerned, and belief in God not an option she takes very seriously, for she spits out: 'So help me God! Thank you, God, for my mother and father. Thank you! Thank you for parents who think of themselves before they consider my brother and me. Parents who feed their addictions before they even begin to think of feeding us. Use us, more like it, me especially.

'Did you know drugs eat you up, Cat? They do. Drugs devour you. Gambling too. Put the two together, worlds collide and bad things happen. Unspeakable things. I'm not talking a bit of dirt on your hands or mud on your shoes. I'm talking up to your neck in it, swimming in filth. Can't wash yourself clean after that, 'cause the stink never goes away. Attracts bluebottles and flies. Maggots hatch. Then along comes the biggest maggot of them all, Uncle Miguel. Takes a long hard look at me, and gives the *adults* in my family even more money, more drugs. Says come to Spain, why don't you? Make a fresh start. And… And…'

Tears streaming down her face, Scarlett freezes, then begins to tremble, a petrified deer blinded by headlights.

'I'm listening…'

'Stop it, Cat!' I cry. 'Can't you see what you're doing to her?'

A strand of red hair falls like a lick of night over Scarlett's face. Shadows play across her freckles and in front of our very eyes, from one moment to the next, the redhead changes yet again.

'You're listening, are you, Cat? Well, listen good. You're always telling me that everyone has a special talent, aren't you?'

Cat nods. 'Yes, that's what Mama Rose says. Everyone has a special gift.'

'Everyone, including me?'

Cat nods again: 'Everyone, Scarlett.'

Scarlett trails her tongue over her lips. Makes 'em shine bright as rubies, then smiles a sly, secret smile that makes my skin crawl. Cobra's too, I reckon, for I sense him flinch beside me.

Scarlett shakes out her hair, circles her face with a finger: 'My special gift, Cat, is my face, my eyes. What you see here.'

She lays her hand on Cat's. Leans closer, so close that tendrils of red hair tickle Cat's cheek. 'When you've seen what I've seen,' she says, 'you learn to use everything you've got to survive.'

'Everything?' says Cat.

'Wouldn't be alive, if I didn't,' Scarlett replies.

The scars in her run deep, far deeper than any of us imagined. Even Cat. A tear wells in her eye. Cat places Scarlett's hand on her cheek: 'Did you love him very much?'

'I thought he would make everything better,' she says.

'Did you love him?' Cat persists.

Scarlett nods. 'I loved him enough to think that, maybe, if I loved him more, I could do what he wanted me to do. But I couldn't, Cat. I can't.'

Scarlett starts rocking again. Even so, Cat can't help but ask, a plaintive meow in her voice: 'Do you…? Did you…? Do you love me at all?'

'Can't you see, Cat? She's too far gone, she can't hear you now!'

Cat points a finger at me: 'You stay out of this! You too, Cobra.'

Cobra shakes his head and as he does so, waves Mamadou's mended flute in the air. Curled around it, tongues flicking in and out, are Bella and Scales. Diverted for an instant by the strange sight of a flickering, writhing flute, Cat peers. A second is all the time it takes to dart behind her, crouch beside Scarlett, and draw her into my arms.

What else am I supposed to do? Saved her from drowning, didn't I? Welcomed her into our circus family, so, whether I like her or not, whether she's scary, good, bad or in-between, a downright liar or a vixen, wily as a thief, she's partly my responsibility.

I stroke Scarlett as I would a chick with a broken wing. Stroke her, as Cobra says: 'You're pushing your girl too hard, Cat. You're going to lose her, if you go on like this.'

'Hush now,' I say, voice soft and low, like when I'm soothing Taj Mahal by whispering in his ear. 'It's going to be fine, Scarlett. You wait and see.'

I do my best to steady her, reassure her. Cradle and rock her until Cat, relenting, joins me. And together we keep Scarlett warm as the storm rages outside.

22

The moment Scarlett falls asleep, her head nestled on Cat's lap, the storm hits its stride. Thunder creaks across the dusky sky, lightning streaks it, brightening the brickwork of the house. Rain lashes at the windows and when the sky lights up again, stark silhouettes of trees glimmer in the downpour. The storm clamours, and a curious sensation creeps into the pigeonnier, rising from the floorboards like sudden gusts of air.

I listen to the changes taking place: Scarlett's shallow breathing slows, Cat's suspicion eases, while Cobra paces the length of the room with Bella and Scales around his neck. There's an angry turbulence in the air. I smell it, absorb the weight of anxiety smouldering within it, and sense – distinct as an itch that refuses to go away – familiar phantoms increasing, pressing in on us.

Silent as a snake, Cobra turns, face grim. 'Time we worked out what to do next,' he says. 'Time we decided if we're going to take her with us or leave her here with Carlos.' He nods at Scarlett.

Cat covers her with a blanket. 'She needs to rest. We all do. As Mama Rose is always saying, once we've had a good night's sleep, everything will fall into place. We'll know what to do, how to do it, and whether Scarlett will be a help or a hindrance.'

'A hindrance most likely.' Cobra caresses the heads of the reptiles adorning him. 'The girl's slipping and sliding, sinking deeper into crazy. She's trouble all right and will weigh us down like a ton of bricks.'

'May be so,' I reply, 'but let's sleep on it, like Cat says, and see how Scarlett is tomorrow.'

That's what I say, but what I really mean is: I wish Mama Rose and Mimi were here to talk to, Redwood and Midget Man as well. 'Cause the way I'm feeling, I need 'em more than ever before. I'm missing the Old Ones – their voices, their quirks, their cracked, doom-mongering ways. Unless I'm mistaken, Cat is too.

A girl with the mighty heart of a lioness shouldn't be thinking this, I know, but cross my heart and hope to die, I'd give away everything I have – all my heirlooms, even Mamadou's flute – if the Old Ones would only knock on the door and help us clear up the mess we're in. In fact, I wouldn't mind one little bit if at the end of it all, Mama Rose sits me down and says:

'Told you so! Told you you were too young to cope on your own. And I was right, wasn't I?'

Could be she's going to make me eat huge helpings of humble pie for the rest of my life. Could be, if I was able to turn the clock back, I wouldn't do what I've done, but this I know for a fact: leaving Scarlett with Carlos would be a mistake. 'We can't just dump her on him, Cobra. It's not fair. Poor man's done enough for us as it is, and we're going to need all the help we can get to call out the Captain and destroy him.'

Cobra shrugs and says: 'All the more reason not to take Scarlett with us. Girl's a liability, plain and simple.'

Even Cat, who's stroking Scarlett's hair as she tosses and turns in her sleep, nods in agreement. I usually go along with the two of 'em but this time I hesitate as an idea whispers in my ear. Can hardly hear it till it hollers at me in such a way that I can't imagine why I didn't think of it before. Every once in a while the very worst of liabilities creates infinite possibilities.

'Wait a minute.' I rootle about in my rucksack and as I do so, I see him as clearly as if he were standing in front of me: the black-booted policeman on the beach. Bent over, catching his breath, dripping salt water on to sand. The black-boot who helped me drag Scarlett on to dry land. I retrieve the note he gave her, the note she dropped that I picked up and stashed away. It's creased and soiled, but I can still read the name on it: *Federico Angel de Menendez*.

I say his name out loud. 'He told Scarlett to contact him if she needed help. More or less said the same thing to me too.'

I hand the paper to Cat. She looks at it and sniffs. Sniffs it a second time, as if her senses are so acute she's able to get a measure of the man from his scrawl and the paper he uses. Pick up his scent and glean whether he's trustworthy or not.

'Scarlett says…' Cat glances at her and corrects herself. 'She said all the black-boots in Cádiz work for the Captain. They know everything about his racket and keep quiet about it 'cause he pays 'em off.'

'That may be so,' I say. 'But you never know. They can't all be crooked. Can't all be getting a cut of the Captain's game, can they?'

Cobra stops pacing and faces me: 'We should ask Carlos for advice. Bet you he knows who can be trusted and who to steer clear of.'

A curved beak taps at the windowpane and at that very moment the golden bangle on my wrist begins to burn and throb. I shake my hand as a scorching sensation sears my bones. I twist it, try to take it off, but then again Priss's insistence grows, and I'm torn between the bangle and my bird, pain and relief.

Tap, tap, tap. Double tap. Priss's beak raps a sharp tattoo from the ledge outside. Taps urgently, begging for help the only way she can. Taps and yelps like a fledging about to be swept away by the storm.

I clamber on to the windowsill. Tug and pull at the latch, even as the golden gift on my wrist sizzles and my insides flame.

Cobra stretches to help me, touches my hand, recoils: 'You're burning up, Sante. What's going on?'

He looks outside and senses that something's there. Priss's rap becomes a *thwack* and her impatience tips into frenzy.

'Quick, Cobra! Help me!'

For the first time ever, he avoids grazing my skin as we prise the window open.

Priss hops inside. Flies from one end of the pigeonnier to the other. I follow the swoop and spread of her wings, inhale the dank odour of her feathers in the hope that if I can only concentrate hard enough, the fire raging within me will abate. And that what Cobra grasped but I saw outside will disappear, scattered by the storm.

I focus on Priss, though with each breath I take I know that they're out there waiting for me, and that something fundamental has changed. Instead of waiting for me to call 'em, they're out in the stable yard summoning me with all their might; dragging me into their orbit. And with every whisper of magic they possess, they're reeling me in as surely as a fisherman draws in his catch.

I try, once again, to take the bangle off my wrist. It tightens, pulses with heat, and I shriek. Priss shudders. So do I.

Cobra hovers. The love-shine in him claims me as his eyes tell me to stay close to him. But we both know he can't keep me from 'em. 'Cause if he tries to restrain me, he'll burn up too.

Antennae twitching, Cat gets up from beside Scarlett. 'Cobra, Sante? What's the matter?'

Scarlett stirs. Turns over. Is about to settle again when she sits up, pupils dilated midnight-black. Silky with sleep, moving as if half in a dream, she trails fingers through her hair. Smiles, then stares past me through the window into the darkness beyond. The window creaks battered by wind and rain.

'Tell me what's going on,' says Cat.

Scarlett sighs and in a heartbeat replies: 'They're here aren't they, Sante? They've come for you.'

I nod, gather my wits before they fry up completely. Cobra and Cat circle to corral me: 'You've got to let me go. Can't take this much longer…'

'Fetch water, Cat,' Cobra says. 'Douse her with water.'

I run for the door. Cobra blocks my path. All I have to do is touch him and the intensity of the fire raging inside me, the *thump-thump-thump* of my bangle will clear my way. I hesitate, wishing I could turn back time and touch Cobra like I used to, feel the snap and crackle of the spark between us, instead of the throbbing of my father's gift.

'Are you leaving me, Sante?' Cobra asks.

'Never!' I cry. 'Not in a thousand years. You've got to let me go, Cobra. Those spooks can't hurt me any more than they're hurting me already. And they don't mean to, I'm sure of that.'

He remains where he is.

Unable to contain the red-hot heat forcing me outside, I moan: 'Cobra, if you won't let me go, you might as well take one of Cat's daggers and be done with me now!'

At last, Cobra moves, and I step into the stable yard.

23

Slowly, deliberately, I walk to the throng of ghosts. Walk; don't run. Too scared to run. Walk as fat drops of rain splash my face and drench my clothes, soothing the fever on my skin. I stick out my tongue and the rain cools it, healing the blistering pain in my mouth.

The closer I get to 'em, the calmer I feel. Could be Midget Man's whispering in my ear, 'cause what I'm hearing is: *'This moment is* meant, *Sante. From time immemorial it was ordained.'* Whether it's Midget Man or my deepest self talking, I know that before I was even thought of and conceived in my mother's womb, before my parents got on that boat and surrendered me to the sea, something somewhere decided that this place, of all the places in the world was where I'm supposed to be right now.

The flames in my belly dwindle. The sizzling on my

wrist fades. The golden bangle returns to its former state and I'm in front of 'em: a gloaming, restless mass of spirits marooned on a circle of dry land.

Rain leaps and dances about us and, in a twinkling, a whirlpool of light swallows me. Light flickers, a frenzy of fireflies. Voices murmur, and as the ghosts warm themselves on my breath, I detect the vague outline of faces: the nub of a nose, the curve of what might have once been a mouth. Shapes shift, merging one moment, then a heartbeat later, prompted perhaps by an invisible thread of memory, contours reassemble into what passes for a face. My mother's. My father? A hint of mango with an undertow of cedarwood tugs at my nose. I hear a trace of my mother's lullaby and even though I can't see them, I realise they're within and about me.

My eyes gradually adjust and I glimpse Mamadou in their midst, beside him the elderly man. Soon as I recognise him, Mamadou sighs with relief, lifts his finger, reaches to me and brushes my forehead with a touch that shakes me to the core.

As plain as day follows night and daylight is brighter by far than moonlight, my mind clears and a sequence of pictures, vivid as a waking dream, forms. It's all there. Every little bit. One scene after the other: everything we have to do in the next forty-eight hours to call out the Captain and set the others free. And at the heart of the plot, the key that will unlock the bolts that secure the Captain's door, is Isaka.

Headlights dazzle the stable yard.

Brakes squeal. A truck horn blasts and the cargo of lost souls scatters.

Another honk, and suddenly there they are in all their noise and glory: Mama Rose and the remnants of our family circus.

'Good grief, Sante, what are you doing out in the rain? Quickly. This way.'

Mama Rose hustles me through the stable yard to the house. Carlos, Tortilla barking beside him, lets us in. After rustling up a towel, Bizzie Lizzie wraps her arms around me. 'Almost gave us a heart attack seeing you out there. Almost ran you right over.'

She strips off my clothes, dabs my face dry. When she's satisfied that I'm no longer wet, Lizzie drags me to the sitting room where Mama Rose is building a fire.

Of all the lessons Redwood has taught me, the one that can most make a difference between survival and lingering death, is how to keep warm in the cold. May sound crazy, but running barefoot in the snow warms the soles of the feet a treat. Showed us how to rub sticks to spark a flame. Can take for ever. So when you're shivering, icy cold, the easiest way to warm up is to build a fire with kindling, matches, fire-lighters if you have 'em, though a leaf of newspaper will do just as well.

Teeth chattering, heart pounding at the enormous risk in the task still ahead of me, I watch Mama Rose go through the motions. Bundles kindling in a stone hearth, lights it, then blows until it catches and roars. Watch her as Lizzie, all arms and legs, cherry-pink hair bobbing above her head, plonks me down. Goes back to the truck to fetch dry clothes. Tut-tuts and fusses, while in the kitchen the rest of our crew and Carlos heat up a casserole.

Mama Rose piles on logs. Flames lick 'em and as sparks shimmy up the chimney, Cobra and Cat and Scarlett slip in. 'My babies,' Mama Rose crows. 'Thank heavens you're safe! Come and give your old mama a hug.'

Cobra obeys while Cat, greens hard as emeralds, waits her turn. When Mama Rose embraces her, Cat stiffens. Might as well hiss and spit like the creature she's named after. A single gesture at the right time can say more than a thousand words. Mama Rose takes in Cat's brazen stare and fondles her cheek nonetheless. Hugs Scarlett and then scarpers with Lizzie to the kitchen.

'Are you all right, Sante?' Cobra asks.

I nod, squeeze my eyes to say I'll fill him in later. He may not know it yet, but we have a plan to discuss and act on. Cobra slides his hand beneath mine and by mutual consent we don't speak. None of us Young Ones do. Hold our tongues in place to eavesdrop on the Old Ones in the kitchen.

Carlos's baritone plays tag with Midget Man's tenor; dances between Tortilla's yelps and barks as snatches of conversation drift down the corridor.

'Well, I never,' says Lizzie.

'I knew it! I knew something like this would happen.' Mimi.

Redwood rumbles in reply, then Mama Rose hushes and silences 'em all. A heartbeat later, Carlos is talking again.

From the dribs and drabs I piece together, Carlos is filling 'em in on our story. I smile at Scarlett. She lays her head on Cat's shoulder. Cat folds her into her arms as Cobra's hand, held in mine, tightens around my wrist. He warms my fingers but, as I start to play with the golden bangle on my other wrist, he frowns.

We listen in. And without discussing anything further, we glean from the banter of our eyes – those glances and winks we use to communicate in the ring – what we're going to do next: wait for the Old Ones to come to us and then ask 'em a whole heap of questions, such as: 'Who are you, Redwood? What's your real name? And what's yours, Mama Rose? And while we're on the subject, Midget Man, why did you stop calling yourself Elvis? And you, Mimi! Is Mimi your proper name? Is Bizzie Lizzie yours?'

I've a million questions piled on my tongue and when the time comes, true as the whites of my eyes, I shall be the one asking 'em. I know, 'cause since I was knee-high to a grasshopper, Cobra and Cat have smuggled questions they daren't ask into my mouth.

The Old Ones stop talking. We hear the clatter of plates stacked on a tray, the heave-haul of kitchenware, whisper of voices conspiring and then, all at once, in they troop, noisy as nestlings about to be fed: Mama Rose at the helm with a platter of food, Redwood bringing up the rear, a bottle of wine in each hand.

The moment I see them, I get a whiff of how they intend to play the cards they've been dealt: as if nothing whatsoever has changed and everything's as it was before I opened my sea-chest cradle. Before Grey Eyes and Isaka stumbled on me, and led us to Miguel and those others. If they're going to pretend everything's the same, I swear to every god there is that for as long as I draw breath, I'll never get my head around Old Ones!

'Welcome home, my lovelies,' says Midget Man, handing out plates Mama Rose serves food on. Chicken and chorizo casserole with potatoes and salad.

Cobra, Cat and Scarlett tuck in. My meal on my lap, I look from one to the other, Mama Rose to Redwood, Midget Man to Mimi. Take in Lizzie's pink halo of hair. Savour the nooks and crannies of faces I've loved all my life; faces I was once more accustomed to than the dark sheen of my skin: Midget Man's snub nose,

Redwood's loping grin and Mama Rose. Can't help but stare in wonder at the curious glow of her dark, pebbled eyes.

'Is everything all right, Sante-girl?' she asks.

Forks dangle mid-air as everyone stops eating and gazes at me.

'What is it, sweetie-pie?' Lizzie asks.

Mimi sighs. 'Must be the shock of everything she's gone through, poor darling. A life of adventure takes its toll eventually, and I'm sure you've had more than your fair share of scrapes, Sante.'

My jaw drops. Scrapes? Adventure? Where to start? What to say? Rage rises and before I have time to blink, I cry sharp as a cockerel at first light of day: 'In case you've forgotten, Cobra and I were *kidnapped*. Kidnapped, meaning held in captivity for a ransom for a whole day and a night. And what did you lot do? Did you come and save us? Did you ask the police to look for us? You did nothing. *Nothing!* Now tell me, who are the adults here?'

I glare at 'em. Glare so hard, forks cease to dangle and are placed carefully on plates. Midget Man rubs his goatee while Redwood, tugging at the lobe of his ear, murmurs: 'That's young 'uns for you. Insists on taking off on her own and now she's back with us safe and sound, seems she wanted us to send in the cavalry all along.'

'Life doesn't work like that, sweetie,' says Lizzie.

Mama Rose puts her plate on the hearth, opens her arms, beckons me closer. I shake my head as words tumble out of me. The very same words Mama Rose uses at the first hint of a lie: 'It's time for truth-telling, folks! Who are you, Mama Rose? What's your real name? And you, Redwood? Or should I call you Cuthbert Xavier Carter the Third?'

Amid splutters and gasps, a ghastly calm descends. The Old Ones stare at each other: wives glance at husbands, Carlos at Midget Man and then all eyes swivel and drill into Mama Rose. And somehow, all of it – all the staring and blinking – is to do with a long-buried secret. I grit my teeth and like a dog scrabbling for a bone, refuse to let go: 'I asked you questions. Least you can do is reply.'

Redwood takes a sip of wine and says: 'Where did you hear that name, kid?'

'From the same person who told us that your real name, Mama Rose, is Rosamund Annabel Williams, and you're the daughter of Lord Edmund James Hathaway-Williams of Brecon. Same person who told us the two of you are "Missing. Wanted for questioning."'

'What's his name?' Redwood again.

'I call him Grey Eyes, but his name's Wolf. Don't know his surname yet, but he works with the man who took Scarlett – Miguel – and Miguel's pa, the Captain.'

Redwood takes another sip of wine. Peers at me and

my confidence ebbs, defiance trickles away. Carlos steps in.

'The Captain is not a man to cross,' he says. 'He's dangerous, highly influential, a *gaditano* called José-Mariá Zaragosa.'

Firelight flickers and fades on her face as fear ripples through Scarlett. Can't have her howling the house down, so the moment she parts her lips, I jump in quick: 'Miguel and his pa meddle with Young Ones. Peddle 'em like they tried to with Scarlett. Like they tried with Cobra and me.'

A horrified hush rushes through the Old Ones, crushing any trace of movement, leaving 'em frozen in time.

Silence clamours. I hold my breath waiting for an explosion of: 'I told you so! I told you, Sante! But did you listen?'

I count one. Two. Three. Soon as I hit four out it comes, even worse than I expected, 'cause what I hear is a frightened squeak crawling out of Mama Rose's mouth: 'Did anyone...?'

I shake my head.

'And you, Cobra?'

Cobra shrugs. 'Nothing I couldn't handle. Others aren't so lucky.'

Cobra digs out Barrel Man's phone from his jeans and the images we flipped through earlier scuttle like crabs from the screen into the room.

Takes less than a minute for the Old Ones to grasp what we're showing 'em. Gawp and shudder, shaking their heads. Carlos grabs the phone and stamps the crabs dead by switching it off. Cat takes it from him and pockets it.

More glances as all eyes including mine lock on Mama Rose. She fidgets, heaves a huge sigh and it's then I feel it again: that worm of anxiety from the night Mama Rose took Isaka's note and shoved it in her bra. Thicker, bigger, heavier than ever before, it crawls from the depths of the earth and wriggles into the open.

Mama Rose senses it as well, for she says: 'Sante, Cobra, Cat – might as well include you in our circle tonight, Scarlett, since you're here – it's time I told you something I should have mentioned long ago.'

24

Turns out truth-telling takes time. Time enough for the Old Ones to pile more food on their plates, empty two bottles of wine, and then drag up a case of booze from Carlos's cellar and start swilling it down. Eat and drink like it's Christmas tomorrow to erase the scuttle stain of crabs and what we told 'em. Redwood throws another log on the fire, we cosy up, and when all eyes are on her once again, we give Mama Rose the floor.

'A long time ago when I was much younger than you are today, I upended everything my parents stood for. Didn't feel right to live in a great, big house in the country when outside our gates my pals were poor as church mice.'

Pictures of Mama Rose as she once was leapfrog over the ones in Barrel Man's phone and jostle for attention. An age-old house appears in my mind and

I catch sight of Mama Rose as a baby. Chubby cheeks, white bonnet. Mama Rose at seven, skipping, playing hopscotch.

'I gave away the family silver: all our cutlery and candlesticks. Didn't go down well with my parents and so they packed me off to boarding school. The very best, of course, where they tried to instil in me rules rich folk live by; rules that say that things are the way they are 'cause that's how they should be. The rich man in his castle, the poor man at his gate.'

The Old Ones chuckle, Redwood loudest of all.

'Last time I counted,' Mama Rose says, 'I reckon that by the age of sixteen, I'd been expelled from at least ten schools. But I was clever. Went to university and it was there that everything fell into place and I discovered exactly who and what I am...'

More pictures crystallise and I recognise Mama Rose, a young woman strutting in a pair of high-heeled shoes. Red, like the slash of lipstick on her mouth today.

She notices me staring at her, mouth half-open, the food on my plate untouched. 'Eat up, Sante-girl,' she chides. 'Eat your food while it's hot.'

Truth is, I'm more interested in what she's saying. And nibbling at my curiosity are yet more questions about the woman who raised me. Questions I never thought to ask until now. Where was she born? Who else apart from Cobra, Cat and me has she loved deeply, sincerely? I want to know more and more. For instance, what in heaven's name is holding the Old Ones back from discussing the contents of Barrel Man's phone? Must have rattled 'em. Rattled 'em good.

I take a bite of cold chicken, make a stab at the salad, and more images leap into vision in anticipation of what Mama Rose is about to say. I'm catching the drift of her all right; she's coming through loud and clear.

Mama Rose, a clenched fist in the air, marches with a raised placard in her hand. Marches singing, then shouting and fighting. Did a whole heap of fighting by the look of it. Fought and felled people with her fists!

'I suppose you could call me an anarchist,' she says. 'Hate governments of all sorts, rules, fetters of any kind. Threw stones, lit fires. Got into trouble. Trouble enough for all of us here at one time or another to be labelled terrorists. In two shakes of a lamb's tail, blackboots were over us like 'roaches in a sack of sugar. Said we'd leaked secrets. State secrets. That's how Mama Rose's Family Circus was born. We changed our names, acquired new skills, and went underground.'

'Did you, Mama Rose? Did you leak secrets?'

She smiles at me. 'It was a very long time ago, Sante. The world's changed since then. Walls that divided us are down, and although new ones seem to be going up all the time, the police have bigger fish to fry these days. Even so, we prefer to lie low.'

Cobra, his plate empty, sits up. 'What's an anarchist?' he asks.

'A dude who doesn't need black-boots on his tail to behave,' Redwood replies. 'We believe in freedom, son. Absolute freedom to do what we want to, when we want to do it.'

'And not a moment before,' Lizzie chimes in.

Mimi nods, Carlos and Midget Man too.

'We refuse to answer to anyone but ourselves,' says Redwood. 'Want to live with the wind in our hair, the sun on our faces.'

My cheeks pucker in a grin, 'cause true as the blue in the sky, next time Redwood wants to teach me something new, next time he reminds me to do my chores, I'll say: 'I refuse to answer to anyone but myself. I want to fly free like my bird Priss.'

I can almost taste how sweet it would be to always do as I please, when a splash of mango juice wets the tip of my tongue. I sit up and sense Scarlett, half-hidden by Cat, urging me to ask a question that concerns us all. Scarlett thinks it and straightaway the question hops out of my mouth: 'Freedom to meddle with Young Ones whenever and wherever you want? Freedom to sell us and pimp us out? Really?'

All eyes turn to Mama Rose again and I can't help but wonder at the connection between Scarlett and me. Felt it this afternoon when she realised my spooks were in the yard without even looking. I think of Scarlett, then tumbling hotfoot behind her, dwell on the weirdness of my family. Being Doomsters was bad enough, but this? My family of misfits an anarchist terrorist cell? Even as I listen to Mama Rose, my mind's in a spin as I try to understand what's within and around me.

'Freedom to molest and traffic Young Ones isn't the sort of freedom I'm talking about, Sante.'

'So why didn't you come and fetch us?' Cobra replies. 'Why didn't you call in the cavalry like anyone else would have done?'

Mama Rose plays for time. Chews the inside of her cheek and I consider a possibility. Whatever crimes they committed, it'll take days of pestering to get this lot to talk. Yet if they know how to operate outside the law, perhaps they can help us bring down the Captain and Grey Eyes. All the more reason to listen closely to what Mama Rose says next.

'We didn't go to the police on principle, Cobra. Black-boots are agents of the state, thieves and liars. After what they put us through all those years ago, I shall never ask them for help again. Never!'

'Never?' Cat sucks her teeth in disgust. Eyeballs the closest creature to a mother we have, and cries: 'You've been lying to us for years and you *dare* call other people liars? You've all *lied* to us!' Pent-up rage flushes her face. 'Every second of every day when you dragged us from one godforsaken hellhole to another, from some witch's bum of a place to a damp, smelly creek in the back of beyond, you were lying. Said you were looking out for us, keeping us safe, when in fact all that traipsing around was always about you!'

Mama Rose flinches.

'Seemed to me the older you got,' she replies, 'the more I felt it was never the right time to tell you.'

Mimi stifles a sob. 'The long and short of it is we didn't want to let go of any of you.' Rubs tears from her eyes and turning to Cat, she says: 'We did everything we could to help you thrive, and more. We made mistakes, for sure, but, Cat, darling, where's your gratitude?'

Might as well ask a snake to say please before it strikes. Tell a lion to smile before it roars. There's no stopping Cat now: 'Oh, you're good,' she says. 'Very good. You twist and turn the truth and yet you want *me* to be grateful when *you're* the ones who said that lying's a kind of betrayal. The worst, the most deadly kind.'

Tears start to spill down Mama Rose's face. 'The three of you were so young, you could easily have let our secret slip. We didn't have a choice!'

Now it's Cobra's turn to talk. I watch him warm his tongue as he weighs up his words. Wants 'em to come out just right: 'When we were in Cádiz locked up on the roof, I said – "Sante, we should hear what you Old Ones have to say about this name-changing business before we make up our minds."' Redwood nods. We all do. 'So what do you expect us to think when you've told us again and again that no matter how desperate our world may seem, we *always* have a choice. And the choices we make are what makes a difference.' Cobra pauses, lets his words hover, then slowly sink in. 'Could be our interests coincided with yours. Could be living off the grid kept all of us safe. Fact is, we trusted you to do right by us, but it seems from the start, you did what you've taught us to despise – you lied.'

Anger still ripe in her, Cat jumps up. 'I'm going to leave this outfit! I'm out of here.'

Tries to take Scarlett with her, but Scarlett pulls her back down. Scarlett glances at me. A single glance and I hear her appeal to haul us back on track. Somehow or other, despite their hatred of black-boots, we need the Old Ones on side to achieve our goal.

I fix my gaze on Cobra. Even with the little he knows, he's way ahead of me, already searching for a chink in the Old Ones' armour; already probing 'em to find their weakest link. 'Carlos,' he says at last. 'We need your help to find out if a policeman called Federico Angel de Menendez is clean.'

'And how can we get those pictures on Barrel Man's phone,' I chip in, 'to someone, anyone, who can help us scupper the Captain's racket?'

The Old Ones stare at each other again. Heads cocked, eyes plead as a mixture of emotions splurge into the open: hesitation, panic, deep alarm. There's no need for words, for what I'm hearing as clearly as if each and every one of 'em is voicing their deepest fear out loud is: *This is dangerous. This could scuttle our plans to toe the line.*

Feelings pull and shove in different directions and even though no one moves an inch, I sense a tussle in each of 'em, a tug of war between 'em as a group. On one side are Midget Man, Mimi and Carlos. On the other, urging extreme caution, tight-lipped and strait-laced, are Redwood, Mama Rose and Lizzie.

I'm watching 'em closely, when a jab of pain pricks my heart, and I sense Lizzie's determination harden. She folds her arms as a cloak of sadness settles around her: 'You promised, Redwood! You promised!'

'I know, Lizzie. I know,' Redwood's face confirms.

Silent exchanges spark and smoulder like dying embers in the grate. Feet shuffle, eyes blink. Passions skitter, twist and turn, until Redwood pulls the lobe of his left ear – a sign, which I know from experience, means his insides are melting. He's relenting. Tugs his ear a second time and faint whispers of doubt surface alongside an urge to rebel and right ancient wrongs. His resolve shifts and a transformation occurs. All eyes needle Mama Rose and once again she nods.

'Come this way,' Carlos says. 'Let's do it.'

And we begin.

Take a computer, any computer. Once upon a time, according to Midget Man, Redwood was a dab hand at 'em.

'Used to be a hacker,' Midget Man tells me. 'Broke into computers and stole their secrets. FBI, KGB, there wasn't a contraption in the whole wide world Redwood couldn't worm his way into.'

We're gathered in Carlos's study, a place with books everywhere. Books on thick wooden shelves, on an old mahogany desk, books piled high on a tiled floor.

Carlos sits down at a computer. Revs it up and Redwood lurches forwards. 'Let me do it,' he says. 'I'll make it impossible for them to trace those images back to you. Then I'll dig into Menendez's police file while you make calls to check if he's clean.'

Opposite me, Bizzie Lizzie's topknot quivers. Eyes and nostrils flare. Haven't spent years as a member of Mama Rose's circus without learning how to spot the first sign of trouble. As soon as Lizzie's nose twitches, out it comes.

'Redwood,' Lizzie says, hauling herself up to her full, dizzying height. 'Redwood, you promised. Promised on your father's grave that you would never again touch one of those things. We gave up everything, Redwood: our apartment in Central Park, our furniture, our art. We even gave up family and friends and still I stuck with you. And in exchange you promised. Put your hand on the stone Bible of your father's grave and swore…'

Eyes on fire, Redwood cries: 'God dammit, Lizzie! Yes! I did all of the above and we both of us know I was as drunk as a jackass at the time. What's more, I'm an atheist, Lizzie! An atheist!'

I've never heard any of this before, but then, the way we've been living off the grid, I've never once seen Redwood in front of a computer. Hands poised over the keyboard, beads of sweat glimmer on his brow, while an inner light illuminates his weary clown face. And there's something else I can't quite place, a love-shine in his eyes that slips, from one moment to the next, into a fiendish, ravenous glow.

'Be careful, Redwood. Be very careful indeed,' says Lizzie. ''Cause if you push me to the brink, it'll either be me or that *thing*.'

I stare at that thing and feel the same magnetic power that drew me closer to the screen of Barrel Man's phone.

Redwood's fingers settle on the keyboard, rapture fills his face. Plumps out his cheeks till even his lips turn up in a smile: 'I made you a promise, Lizzie,' he says. 'Can't deny it, 'cause I did. Truth is, would you rather hooch and moonshine kill me? Or I help our young 'uns with this *thing*?'

'You ain't got a chance in a million of helping anyone!' Lizzie snarls. 'You're out of practice, Redwood. Wasn't it you said that these contraptions change quicker than the blink of an eye?'

'It's like riding a bicycle, my dear. Once you know how, it never goes away. And maybe I'm not as out of practice as you think.'

To my horror, Lizzie shrieks and does a Cat. By which I mean she tugs at her hair. Pulls out a clump of pink, gazes at it bemused, and then yells in despair. Behaves badly Big Time. Doesn't stop Redwood, though, doesn't take that mad gleam out of his eyes. No, sir! Spurs him on 'cause he roars, lets out a whoop of delight, and he's off.

Quick as a flash, he sucks out the photos and numbers from Barrel Man's phone and sends them to an old girlfriend of Carlos's. Maria works for a tittle-tattle tabloid in Seville, a newspaper in which nothing's too scurrilous to print. Indeed, the bigger the scandal, the better.

Carlos calls Maria, explains what she'll soon find in her mailbox. Who the photographs belong to. Rustles up the name of a friend of Maria's – Henrique – who Maria claims can give Carlos the lowdown of who's who in the police force in Cádiz. Who stinks, who's clean, who's on the Captain's payroll and who wouldn't touch him with a bargepole.

Carlos talks to Henrique while Redwood, the

fanatical glow still on his face, finds out more about Federico Angel de Menendez.

'See that shine in Redwood's eyes?' Scarlett whispers in my ear. 'That's what my father's looks like when he's on a high-stakes roll. Could bite him in the bum and he wouldn't know.'

I reconsider my family yet again. Do Old Ones everywhere try to shield their Young Ones from what they fear most in the world? Are they always driven by dread in case what overwhelmed them may undo us as well? No computers, no phones, 'cause in his heart of hearts, Redwood's a dedicated screen rat?

Cobra squeezes my hand as Redwood enters the home page of the police force of Cádiz. Rummages around until he has to enter a password to retrieve individual police files. Tries variations of a theme and soon all of us – except Lizzie – are leaning in, willing him on. Rolls the dice again. A third time. Fourth time lucky, I suppose, 'cause – hey presto! – he's in.

'Your friend Menendez received a commendation for bravery last year,' Redwood tells us. 'Looks like the real thing. Does he check out with Henrique, Carlos?'

Carlos nods.

'Now,' Redwood says, looking me straight in the eye, 'Wolf-man, Grey Eyes, whatever you call him. Would you recognise him if you saw him again, kid?'

Mama Rose hovering behind me, pulls me away. 'No, Redwood,' she says. 'You've done enough!'

'Man kidnaps our young 'uns, tries to traffic 'em, traffics other folks' kids and you want me to let him be? I shall be careful, Rosie, won't leave any trace of where I am. Do you trust me, Carlos?'

Carlos gives his consent.

Pictures and words bounce on to the screen. Redwood lunges at the keyboard again as his body, hunched over the contraption relaxes with concentration. *Stab, stab, lunge!*

'Gotcha!' Redwood presses a key and an emblem of a globe framed by olive leaves, a sword behind, scales of justice below, appears.

'INTERPOL.' Cobra reads the word out loud and before I can blink, Redwood's performing the same trick Grey Eyes showed us a day before. Photographs flood the screen.

'Describe him to me,' Redwood says.

Before I draw breath, Cobra rattles off a description of Grey Eyes: 'White, German male. Around five foot eight. Heavy set.'

'He's got grey eyes,' I add. 'And his name's Wolf.'

Reams of photographs appear.

'Any other distinguishing features?'

I close my eyes and Grey Eyes's jowly face surfaces. Distinguishing features, I say to myself, inspecting the flushed, open pores of his sweaty profile. Distinguishing features. 'Yes, on the right side of his chin are tiny pockmarks. But there's something else,

Redwood. The tip of the little finger of his left hand is a nail short of a full finger. Sliced off most probably.'

Redwood taps in the information, and suddenly there he is. Grey Eyes a bit younger, less jowly, perhaps, but much the same. 'He's on their radar already. Wolfgang Richter. Trades in people and children. Served jail time in Hamburg and then disappeared. What's the address where he stashed you kids?'

Cobra tells Redwood, who carefully copies Grey Eyes's photo from the screen, types in his address in Cádiz, and then sends it to Maria in Seville.

Redwood turns the computer off and snaps it shut. 'There you are. In a day or so those scumbags of yours will be dealt with in the court of public opinion. And if you're lucky, Menendez and his black-boots will be on to them as well. Are you satisfied now?'

I smile in gratitude at Redwood.

'Thank you,' says Scarlett.

Cat grunts, then says: 'You did what you had to, Redwood. Doesn't mean I'm going to stay. Can only speak for myself, but I'm keeping my options wide open. All of 'em.'

'All of 'em?' Mama Rose replies. 'In that case, there's a chance you won't go away and turn my hair grey before my time. What would I do without you, child?' Mama Rose fingers the curve of Cat's cheek, and in that brief moment of tenderness, Cat closes her eyes. Opens them with a sigh, and Mama Rose bustles us out of the study.

'Time you young ones got some rest,' she says. Then, as an afterthought, she adds: 'Redwood and Lizzie, I want a word with both of you.'

We leave 'em to it.

Later that evening in the pigeonnier, Scarlett recovers the scrap of paper on which she wrote the numbers from Barrel Man's phone and gives it to me with her phone. The screen lights up as I begin tapping in Isaka's number. Cobra's hand slams on my shoulder. Spins me around and says: 'We've done enough, Sante. It's over! The end!'

I shake my head, shrug him off, and mutter: 'Not!'

Cobra tries to grab the phone. I chuck it to Scarlett, who throws it to Cat. Cat laughs while Scarlett, a kiss-me-lick-me smile on her lips, watches as Cobra says, very slowly – as if I'm on the crazy side of stupid – what Redwood said earlier: 'With that friend of Carlos's on their case, those young ones are going to be safe, Sante. There's no need for us to meddle any further.'

'No need for you, perhaps,' I reply. 'But us girls are of the same mind on this. We're leaving early tomorrow morning before the Old Ones can stop us.'

Did I taste a splash of mango on my tongue before I spoke? Don't think so.

Cobra greens glitter. 'You're not telling the Old Ones you're going?'

Cat twizzles her nose, lifts an eyebrow in disdain, and chuckles: 'Tell 'em? Can't speak for you, but we're not morons, Cobra!'

'You're worse than morons!' he says. 'The three of you have lost what little brain you were born with!'

Cat lobs the phone into my hand and, before Cobra can stop me, I tap in Isaka's number. Phone purrs in my ear and to my surprise, Isaka replies as though he was expecting my call.

Tells us where to meet him.

Tells us how best to prepare for the Captain tomorrow. Turns out, tomorrow's his birthday. With a bit of luck, a fair wind behind us, and Isaka's help, we're going to deliver a present that he'll never forget. And neither, it seems, will Cobra. Looking every bit as venomous as the serpent he was named after, he turns away from me and makes up our bed.

25

About an hour after midnight, when I'm deep in sleep, the dream comes to me with a ferocity that gnaws into my bones. This time, instead of the cargo of lost souls, Scarlett looms large in the entrails of the boat.

She's trapped, floundering. We all are, everyone, including me. No longer a baby swaddled in a sea chest, a miracle at the heart of the dream, I'm Sante Williams, circus performer, fourteen years old. Old enough to know that a dream's just a dream, even though this one's got me so tightly clamped in its jaws, I can't move. Hands and feet heavy as mud, all I'm able to do is stand and stare as Scarlett's freckles glimmer, then fade. She looks straight through me, disbelief on her face, as she says in my voice: 'Where am I? What am I doing here?'

I've been on this boat many times before. But for a

moment I can't make out if I'm seeing the wreckage through Scarlett's eyes or my own, while all around us the Young Ones at Grey Eyes' party stumble as the boat is rammed a second time.

Voices ricochet as timbers splinter. Boat creaks, then the curve of the hull cracks open. Torrents of water gush in and Scarlett, her face glazed with terror, screams. Water rises and Scarlett's distress at the sudden rush of sea sluicing underfoot overwhelms me, releasing the paralysis in my limbs.

An overhead rafter falters, then falls. On it, a coil of rope unfurls and slithers.

I inch forwards and as the sea swills about us, lapping at my thighs, I stretch out, fling one end of the rope to Scarlett, and then pull her towards me.

'Scarlett, stay with me,' I cry, uttering words that sound vaguely familiar but I sense aren't my own. 'Stay with me!'

Words spoken by someone else a lifetime ago; not my words, then whose? Time folds in on itself, echoing the past; and as it does, I haul Scarlett into my arms.

I've endured fragments of this dream over and over again. Woken frightened and confused. Felt the dream seize me; shake me about, and yet this time it feels hobbled, twisted somehow. So different, I freeze as a growing sense of unease chills my blood. Fear slices through me as I realise that someone else behaved as I'm doing, and did exactly what I've just done. Someone before me, and it didn't work, 'cause right at the end of it all a life was severed, a human heart broken.

Memories pulse within me, and as the dream speaks, I remember. What I'm summoning are scenes that Isaka and Mamadou lived through. Scenes I gleaned from Isaka in Cádiz. Which means, if I'm right, within seconds the water around us will rise to my chest. And each time the trawler is rammed, Scarlett's fingers will slip and slide, before one of us is hurled into the sea.

'Hold on, Scarlett,' I whisper and a jumble of noise crackles as I recall what happens next: the wind will howl and broken bodies tossed by waves will be swallowed into the deep.

Boom! The hull is hit again. Sea surges about my chest, my neck.

'Move your legs, Scarlett. Keep afloat.'

Teeth chattering, she clings to my waist. Then, eyes fixed in horror, her feet start to paddle. Both of us slip-sliding away.

Far off in a distant land, feathers brush over my face, and Priss hisses in my ear.

Someone shakes me, tries to wake me. But the dream has me in its teeth and refuses to let go.

Scarlett or me? Who will it be?

'Wake up, Sante. Wake up!'

Cobra's persistence prises the dream open and I surface into real time, gulping for air. Eyelids lift and there he is; breath warm against my breath, cheek close to mine. 'You were dreaming again,' he says.

Half-asleep, I pull away, muttering Scarlett's name. Cobra tries to soothe me, but with the nightmare still riding me, I get up, overwhelmed by a need to go walkabout with Priss.

Within quarter of an hour we're out on Carlos's land. Shadows flecked by the light of the moon hover about us. They flicker and form, then seconds later, obliterated by a swirling cloak of darkness, they glint on blades of grass and the leaves of trees. It's three o'clock in the morning and the dream's steering me, even though I'm straddled bareback on Taj Mahal, with Cobra behind me. Overhead, Priss, an inky smudge of movement in the sky, is on the lookout for her next kill.

I barely mumble: 'This time the dream was different, Cobra.'

'How was it different?'

Walkabout isn't walkabout when there's someone else with me. Cobra insisted on coming 'cause my distress when he woke me frightened him. I kept muttering Scarlett's name, telling her to hold on to me, never let me go. His fingers cool on my feverish brow, Cobra calmed me. But the moment my trembling ceased, the future lurched into view. In those few seconds between action and reflection, the dream coiled around me, and a lump of dread heavy as granite, settled in my gut.

A dream's just a dream, I know, but some of 'em talk to me, warn me when something bad is about to happen.

All the same, I don't want to talk to Cobra about it, 'cause when I'm as jittery as I am today, words confuse me. While instinct, sharp and strong as Priss's beak, I know I can trust. If I were rambling alone with Taj and Priss, I reckon more likely than not, I'd tease out the true meaning of the dream, and what's about to happen, in a twinkling.

As it is, that lump of dread trails me like a bloodhound puppy. Snuffles around Taj's ankles, jumps up, tries to lick my hand. Won't let me go, no matter how sternly I point a finger at it and say: 'Down, dog! Stay!' Might as well jab a finger at the wind and tell it to stop blowing.

I jump down from Taj, nuzzle my nose against his, and Priss, gliding on the crest of a breeze, flexes her wings. An owl hoots from a juniper tree. Priss hisses in reply and I pause to listen to their banter.

The owl calls; Priss responds and then disappears in the darkling sky.

'How was the dream different?' Cobra asks again. He slides down, walks beside me, and I wish I were bold and canny enough to shake him off without hurting his feelings.

'Dream was about Scarlett,' I tell him. 'Same boat as always, but this time Scarlett was trapped. Tried to save her but in the end I realised that only one of us would survive.'

'Figures,' Cobra replies. 'Girl's as unpredictable as a firecracker and every bit as dangerous, but Cat and you can't seem to get enough of her.'

I nod, caught in a dilemma of what my head wants me to do and what my heart's telling me is true. Head, heart, then there's Cobra.

'You know I'm right, Sante. That girl's got inside you, same as she's got inside Cat. Most probably did the same with Miguel, but bit off more gristle than she could chew.'

'That's where you're wrong, Cobra. As far as Scarlett's concerned, being right isn't what matters.'

A warm southerly breeze ruffles the grassland beyond Carlos's meadow as we stride through it. I paddle my fingers in clumps of wild rosemary and thyme, brush my legs against 'em, and a sharp, tangy scent hits my nostrils. I keep walking till my head begins to clear, and my eyes adjust.

I take a deep breath of rosemary-spiked air, then cluck and call Priss. Talons dangling, she swoops to the gauntlet on my hand.

'Priss,' I say. 'Priss, you're going to stay here today, you hear? You're to stay with Taj and Midget Man. You're not to come looking for me, not to follow me 'cause I'll be back before nightfall.'

I talk to my bird and that bloodhound pup *yap*, *yap*, *yaps*.

Priss spreads her wings, steadies me, while Cobra says: 'After everything I said last night, you're still going to go through with it?'

I try to dazzle him with a daredevil grin. But instead of pandering to me, his greens root out every morsel of uncertainty within my dream-soaked self. Cobra weighs me up, and the granite in my gut grows heavier and heavier, till I can't help but close my eyes to hide the quivering inside me.

Soon as I'm able to look at him again, I touch his shoulder: 'You don't have to come with us, Cobra. I can ride Redwood's bike and with luck on our side, we'll be back before the Old Ones miss us.'

Cobra curses under his breath, then says loud and clear, so even the most stubbornly stupid soul such as mine can hear: 'Your dream just told you what you know already, Sante. Scarlett could be the death of you, and you're still going?'

'I don't have a choice,' I tell him.

'Of course you do! It's your life! You can do whatever you want!'

I shake my head. If there's one thing I've learned since opening my sea-chest cradle, it's that those who saved my life did so for a reason. They have a stake in me now and they're claiming what's due to them.

'I don't have choice, Cobra,' I tell him again. And it's then, as I stiffen my back and brush my tears away, that he decides to ride with me.

26

The restless dead never stop talking. For years they've held me captive with dreams that bleed into my waking hours. And for as long as I can remember, even when I didn't fully grasp what was going on, they've whispered to me. Now, true as the sea is blue and salt is white, they're guiding me. I feel the tug of gold on my wrist and rub it for luck. Bangle tingles and I begin to appreciate what I didn't before: my father foresaw the dangers ahead of me and my feelings today – powerless, fragile as a snail without its shell.

I raise his gift to my mouth and as soon as it grazes my lips, I hear my mother's voice saying: *'Walk good, Asantewaa! Walk in step with our ancestors.'* My heartbeat quickens.

Once this is over, I swear on Priss's feathers and everything I hold dear, that I shall lay the unquiet dead to rest. I shall cover my ears to their cries, seal their lips with a final goodbye, and make them leave me for ever. But how? That's the question.

These are my thoughts as we hurtle back to Cádiz the way we came; Cobra and me in the lead on Redwood's motorbike, Cat and Scarlett on the pizza-delivery scooter. I think to clear my head, keep the yapping puppy at bay. Think; then focus on what lies in front of me. When I've exhausted every combination of what could possibly go wrong, and there's not much left to be anxious about, I let go and enjoy the ride.

After last night's storm there's a twinge of autumn in the air, a faint chill that makes me hold Cobra closer. My head against his back, the swell and sweep of the landscape drains the last dregs of tension from me and scatters it to the wind. I notice, to my relief, as an osprey flaunts its wings in the pearly grey sky, that there's not a flicker of Priss in sight – not a hiss or a whimper – just the noisy chatter of a dawn chorus.

We weave through lanes, up the steep incline of craggy hills, until wending downhill we hit the motorway to the city. The sun brightens, and as dawn somersaults into day, Redwood's motor, wheels spinning, propels us along the fast lane to Cádiz.

I meet Isaka in the café where Cobra and I first approached him. Introduce him to Cat and Scarlett, and a spark of recognition twinkles in his eyes. He takes Scarlett's hands. Holds 'em between his palms and says:

'I never thought I'd see you again. I tell all of you to run for your lives. And yet you – the one he wanted most – have stayed? Is that wise, my dear?'

'The least I can do,' Scarlett replies, 'is help the others escape.'

'Then be vigilant, my child, because Miguel and his men are still looking for you. And when you take that off – ' Isaka indicates the black beret covering Scarlett's hair – 'you stand out like a beacon of light at night.'

Scarlett readjusts the beret to make sure that not a single red curl is exposed while Isaka plucks at a loose thread on his robe. Plucks it and says: 'They warned me you were coming. Even so...' Then, disregarding what he was about to say, his lips jerk into what resembles a smile. Behind his bland exterior, he's as wound up as I am.

'Are you ready for what you must do?' he asks Scarlett. 'Are your wits steady enough?'

Scarlett nods.

'Then come this way.'

Isaka guides us to the back entrance of the café. When he's sure no one's watching, he darts down an alleyway, his robe fluttering behind him. We follow, walking quickly through the shadows of the old city, past the ramparts, down to a beach in the bay of Cádiz. And as we walk, Cobra and Cat either side of me, Scarlett hidden behind Isaka, I mull over what I've just heard.

First off, seems that before we met her, Isaka helped Scarlett get out from under Miguel. Seems he's helped others as well. Perhaps that's why he stays with the scumbags he works for: to help Young Ones escape. Then it comes to me, the same sensation that overwhelmed me in the stable yard. Call it intuition or a simple hunch. Whatever it is, it rises from the marrow of my bones to my head in a blaze of absolute certainty. Isaka said: 'They warned me you were coming.' Of course, I knew it already. Every cell in my body sizzles as I realise that since the upheaval of my last visit, Isaka has been hand in glove with the restless dead. The truth seizes me, shakes me by the throat and I begin to grasp how long they must have waited for this moment. Fourteen years. Five thousand two hundred and eighty-nine days and nights. My whole life they've been watching me, anticipating my every move, to bring me here today.

'Don't worry,' Isaka says, reading my mind. 'It'll be over soon.'

Easy enough to say, but then why do I feel as if forces beyond my control are pushing me to the edge of a precipice? I stop in my tracks. Dig in my heels. Cobra links his fingers in mine, gives me a tug, and we continue walking.

My feet drag, and I almost stumble as I wonder what Isaka meant when he said to Scarlett: 'Are you ready for what you must do? Are your wits steady enough?' Does he know how dangerously flaky she can be at times? How disturbed and erratic?

Isaka checks, once again, that no one's tailing us. Cobra's fingers in mine tighten. I hold my breath until Isaka, satisfied we're alone, shepherds us into the Caleta – a huge pleasure-dome pier made of wood and concrete. Its legs, straddled on the beach, paddle in the sea at high tide. Right now the tide is out and banked on a crest of the shore are rowing boats. The pleasure dome, newly painted, resembles a curved cluster of gigantic blowflies relaxing in the sand; their wings, open windows, shimmer in the sun.

Isaka releases the door of the Caleta restaurant. Inside, waiters in white gloves are laying tables. Silver knives and forks are placed precisely on starched linen while huge vases of roses are carried in. Above the tables, hanging from the restaurant's cavernous ceiling, are three trapezes. We look at 'em and Isaka explains what he wants us to do:

'The Captain will eat here with his friends when the time comes. The maestro will give me a signal, I'll nod, and you three will jump through the trap-doors on to those swings. All you have to do is create a diversion with your act and the spirits will do the rest, understood?'

Cobra and Cat nod, then I say: 'Might be better if we're up there right from the start, Isaka. Trap-doors can be dicey.'

Isaka shrugs and Cobra adds: 'We need to test those trapezes as well. Make sure they're safe.'

'Do what you need to,' Isaka replies. 'But I repeat. Wait for my signal before you begin your act.'

His instructions are vague, but then again, every once in a while we've had to improvise on less. So what if we haven't practised on the trapeze for ages, and my hands are too soft to withstand friction burns easily? It's like Redwood and computers: once you know how, you never forget. In any case, we're members of Mama Rose's Family Circus and no matter the circumstances, our aim is always to entertain.

'What about the present for the Captain?' I remind Isaka.

Isaka brings out a brown paper parcel from the pocket of his robe. 'The ceremonial dagger that belonged to my family before I gave it to you, Asantewaa,' he says, 'I now give to Scarlett. When you see my signal,' he tells her, 'give this to the Captain. That's all you have to do. Place it in his hands and the dagger will do the rest.'

Scarlett puts the parcel in the leather satchel that she takes everywhere. Pats it shut as we shadow Isaka to our final destination: a cramped dressing room for artists and helpers who are taking part in the Captain's birthday celebration.

'Have you got everything you need?' Isaka asks before he leaves us.

He's given us costumes to wear, masks to hide our faces and food to snack on while we wait. He's showed us how to get up to the ceiling, and then on to the trapezes. Gone over what he wants us to do once the Captain settles down in his seat of honour in a few hours. We're to hold the audience captive while Scarlett delivers the parcel. And when we're done and what he describes as 'the fireworks' are over, we're to skedaddle. There'll be no questions asked, no debriefing. The police, Isaka assures us, will sort out everyone left behind. So, unless we want to be taken into custody, we'd better get out of there fast.

'Understood?' Isaka says, once again.

I nod at the same time as Cobra and Cat, while Scarlett stares vacantly at Isaka, which is most probably why he declares with as much authority as he can muster: 'This time, my dear, when I say go away, I mean it. Go far away, because no good will come to you if you linger here.'

'Of course!' Scarlett replies and I wince. She's using that voice again: condescending, chin raised in such a way that I'm convinced she has every intention of doing exactly as she pleases. Not what I'd call a team player, Scarlett. Not today at any rate. All the more reason to watch her closely.

Cobra, catching my drift, gives a triumphant told-you-so-Sante grin. He's too canny to say anything out loud, but there's a glint of grim satisfaction in his greens.

Cat and I stare him down. Stare so hard we wipe the smirk clean off his face.

Isaka bows, takes his leave of us, and we start to get ready.

Mama Rose is forever saying that once you've taken a shine to it, the lustre of show business never rubs off. What we do, day after day, when we're covering ourselves in clover, lights up my soul and puts a smile on my face. That lump of granite may still be stuck in my gut, and the pup still grizzling at my feet, but by dressing up in a costume – any costume, any time of day or night – my heart spins higher than Priss reeling in the sky. And with luck, more often than not, I'm rewarded for enjoying myself.

Today's performance is altogether different. Don't need that grizzling pup to remind me, or my innards twisting and turning. I know in my heart, and the baggage of last night's dream that's still weighing on me, that whatever I do in the next couple of hours is much more than a calculated risk. It's downright dangerous and could be the end of me. Even so, I pull gossamer mesh over my arms and legs. Heave myself into a bird costume with golden feathers across my chest and bum. Accentuate my eyes with a dash of kohl, then, once I've fastened a diamanté mask over my eyes and nose, and covered my locks with a blonde wig, I'm more or less done. Arms, legs and belly are topaz yellow, while the diamanté glitter of my mask turns my face purple, blue and black.

'Not bad,' Cat says about my outfit.

'Not bad yourself.'

Cat, striped like a Bengal tiger, clips a feline disguise over her face, then buckles a knife around her waist.

'You planning on killing someone today?' asks Cobra, zipping himself up in a leotard. Leotard flickers emerald with his every move, a snake splashing in light.

Cat straps a second knife on the inside of her thigh. 'You never know!' she says, and begins helping Scarlett on with her costume – that of a serving girl.

According to Isaka, identical butterfly masks will hide the faces of all of the Captain's Young Ones. What's more, the girls will be dressed in the same outfit as Scarlett: a blue corset over a white blouse, an itsy-bitsy skirt over a flouncy underlay of lace. Boys will be in britches, girls in snatches of netting. They like to see our legs, the Captain and his friends. Like to look at their merchandise before they sample it.

'This is the sort of look Miguel likes,' Scarlett says, teasing on a pair of black net stockings.

'Kind of slutty,' Cat sniffs.

Scarlett twists her hair in a ponytail bun, covers it

with a mop hat, and then eases a butterfly mask over her face: 'Do I look tasty or not?'

'Slutty but tasty!' Cat confirms.

I chuckle nervously in case that skimpy outfit inflames flirty Scarlett and she jumps out and scorches us again.

'With that ridiculous mask over your face,' says Cobra, 'you look more like a demented insect on legs than a human being.'

Scarlett flicks her tongue out at him. 'A bit like you!' she replies. And he does too, 'cause he's disguised in a mask identical to hers.

We laugh and from the outside looking in, it seems that Scary Scarlett is buttoned up as tightly as that corset.

A little later, after we've eaten our snacks and Cobra, Cat and I have worked out a routine on paper to perform on the trapeze, the dressing room is hijacked by long-limbed dancers. Men and women, all of 'em a good deal older than us, some with slithers of grey in their hair. Flamenco dancers, I reckon, 'cause as soon as they come in, they start to limber up by playing castanets and tapping their feet.

One of 'em is Carlos's sister, Imma. Of course I don't know that to begin with. We're sitting on stools in a corner, our backs to the door, when a woman practising her moves behind us, pauses. Feet stop strumming the floor, and in the silence that follows, I turn.

Head cocked to one side, left hand rigid from palm to elbow, her right hand twitches mid-air as she stares at us, Scarlett, in particular. Dark eyes clamour with questions. Then, the woman rushes up to Scarlett and says: 'Are you crazy? Are you looking for trouble?'

Scarlett's mask with its exaggerated butterfly eyes hasn't fooled Imma. Infuriated her more like it, for she goes on to say: 'Does my brother know you're here? Do the others?'

Scarlett sitting on a stool, plays dumb. Bad move, 'cause Imma grabs her, hauls her up in the air and shakes her not once but twice. Scarlett pushes her away. Pulls down her corset, and says in that high and mighty voice of hers:

'Why do you Spaniards have to be so exhausting? Why don't you just die and leave me alone?'

Imma steps back as if she's been punched in the chest. You'd think they'd never met each other before; that Imma never offered us refuge at Carlos's farm. She's about to turn away when Cat winks at her. Puts a finger to her lips. Imma nods. Nods a second time, crumples at a dressing table, and flicks a switch.

Make-up lights glare at the creases on her brow, the crow's feet around her eyes. Meticulously, she rearranges her rumpled features with grease-paint: beige base, foundation, powder. Her eyes and lashes coated dusky blue, Imma pauses. She looks at Scarlett once again, baulks at her sleazy get-up, and takes a phone from her bag. Talks rapidly to someone at the other end.

She's speaking to Carlos. Why else would my innards knot? If Carlos knows, the Old Ones will find out as well. Where we are. What we're up to. I reckon Imma's telling her brother that we're digging a grave big enough to bury ourselves in, or words to that effect, 'cause she sighs, is about to confront Scarlett again, when – of all the scumbags in the world that I'd rather not see – Barrel Man barges in. On his right is Concha.

My heart falters, almost seizes as Barrel Man's presence sucks all the air in the room.

There's no better method to test out a disguise than to flaunt it in front of the person you aim to hide from. This I know and yet what I'm feeling is altogether different. If I could, I'd disappear in a puff of smoke. I take a deep breath, and begin to stretch. Stretch my gossamer gold arms and legs; tease out a knot of tension in my shoulder as Barrel Man's eyes flit over the room.

There's no light in those eyes, only the dull, milky sheen of a dead fish, which the moment it brushes me, raises the hairs on the back of my neck. Hackles bristle, pulse quickens, and then, as Barrel Man's gaze settles on Scarlett, I get ready to jump him or run.

Cat, to my left, touches the middle of her forehead, our signal for 'Steady. Hold your ground.'

Not an easy task when my armpits, already wet with sweat, grow clammier by the second. The bloodhound pup scrambles over my feet, jumps up at my chest, and I breathe slowly to stay calm.

'You,' Barrel Man says at last to Scarlett. 'What are you doing here?' Instead of waiting for a reply, he bellows: 'You should be in the kitchen with the others going through the drill.'

Scarlett hurries out of the dressing room with her satchel.

I continue stretching. Swing my arms, twist my torso. Extend my thigh muscles. Cobra and Cat, following my example, expand arms and chests. Barrel Man stares at us, is on the verge of inching closer, when Concha says: 'We've the others to sort out before the Captain arrives. Come along now.'

27

'All right, Sante?'

I nod. Cobra and I are sitting side by side on a trapeze. A second trapeze, adjacent to ours, is lower down, as is the third. We've tested all three of 'em to make sure they're secure. They are. Our problem is they're static trapezes, and Mama Rose and Redwood trained us on the flying variety: whizz-through-the-sky-leap-and-catch, better-have-a-safety-net-or-you're-likely-to-die trapezes!

Our challenge is to create an act that uses our skills and brings us together. As it is, though we can move from side to side and up and down, we can't dazzle spectators by swinging from one trapeze to another. Nonetheless, we can leap and jump and create momentum. We can synchronise our moves, and try out a few tricks.

There's a mighty turbulence racing through my

heart, a crazy tension sparking my nerves, 'cause as soon as I start to dwell on what might happen next, I start to feel wobbly. We create a distraction and then what? The restless dead have waited a long time to bring me here, and even though I've had to trust them to come this far, I haven't a clue what they're planning to do, or what they really want.

There's one thing I do know: if that ceremonial dagger they gave me is going to be part of the mix, folks are likely to freak out Big Time. In an hour or so, there's going to be mayhem down there.

The restaurant, already filling with the Captain's friends, bustles with the chatter of middle-aged men and women, a few old folks and young ones as well; all of 'em smiling and joking, kissing cheeks and hugging. Laughing toddlers in buggies, babies in prams, little ones cradled in their mother's arms. Dressed in pale summer suits, splashes of colour here and there – a red pocket-handkerchief, a blue silk cravat, men nod and wink at each other; while women in light linen dresses, scarves fluttering, hair swept back, fiddle with heavy gold bangles sunflower-bright.

A few Old Ones enter with a swagger; confident, a touch overbearing. Used to being waited on. Used to giving orders, 'cause when the head waiter ushers 'em to their seats, most of 'em can't be bothered to thank him, let alone look him in the eye. Not all of 'em are rich, though. There are poorer folk among the Captain's family and friends: black-clad in ill-fitting suits and loose clothing. Ruddy-faced relatives, hands calloused from working on the land. Reckon it takes all sorts to know the Captain and be invited to celebrate his special day.

Even Barrel Man's family are here. I recognise 'em from the photos on his phone: wife pinched, daughters pigtailed and plump. Barrel Man sits 'em down at a table, then clicks his fingers. Five of Miguel's gang scuttle up. He tells 'em what to do and they do it. A man in every corner of the restaurant, while Barrel Man and another hulk position themselves either end of a top table.

Not a single one of the guests, or Miguel's crew for that matter, has any idea what's in store for them; but then neither do I. And if something were to go wrong? If that dagger was to whizz through the air and plunge into someone? If that someone got hurt, badly hurt, would I be to blame?

Cobra covers my hand with his on the trapeze: 'Come on, Sante, let's do this!'

We manoeuvre ourselves into place: Cobra at the top, Cat at the bottom, me sandwiched in-between. Cobra nods, the three of us point our toes, and with hands on the ropes of the trapezes, swing our legs.

More guests take their seats. Waiters fill glasses with sparkling water and teams of serving girls, dressed in the same ridiculous costume as Scarlett, carry buckets of Cava to each table.

I search for Scarlett among 'em, but can't make her out, 'cause every one of those corseted girls is disguised in masks that make it impossible to recognise their features. Hair's completely hidden as well and there isn't a twizzle of maple-red, brown, black or blonde in sight.

Bottles pop open. Froth spills into glasses and is gulped down. *Pop!* Amid joyous sprays of laughter. *Pop! Pop! Pop!*

The insistent explosion of corks jars, reminding me of a dark undertow beneath the smiles and laughter. Human cargo trafficked, held captive; human cargo destroyed in a strafe of bullets.

I think the thought, and straightaway the forbidding tide of my dream drags me to its shore. *Pop! Pop! Pop!* And I'm back there, once again, as the Captain's grey vessel, a trail of carnage in its wake, surges forwards with a splutter of gunfire. Bullets splinter the deck, ripping it open as the trawler erupts in flames.

But this time, in a way I don't fully understand, Cobra and Cat are above and below me and the three of us are moving as one, removes the sting that flips my dream into a nightmare. I remain calm on the outside, while inside that bloodhound pup claws open my heart. Then, from one moment to the next, a tsunami of emotion sweeps me into a world in which I see them.

Around and about me; amid the laughter of revellers and outpouring of Cava, they're everywhere. And for the first time I begin to appreciate what they're truly capable of. Blowing out candles was nothing. A dagger levitating and drilling into a wall was simple compared to this. Might as well ask a bear to dance before it mauls you, or tell Priss to cease flying and stop dipping her talons in blood, before she rips the head off her prey.

The unquiet dead whisper and murmur with intent. They hover and glide – little more than faint wisps of smoke. Smoke that gathers, thickens, whirls and quickens.

A blot darkens the sky. Clouds form and a wind ripples the smooth surface of the sea beyond. Ripples turn into waves that crash on the beach, while inside a hush of expectation descends. I hear the *tap tap tap* of that golden-topped cane, the shift and shuffle of his laboured tread. He sounds weaker than he was before, desiccated.

I look up. Cobra hears it too. Sees terror in my eyes, and gestures: 'Stay calm.' Then he mouths: 'We're almost there, Sante. Hold on.'

The Captain's footfall outside the restaurant door pauses as he gathers strength for his entrance. A clatter of feet assembles around him.

I swallow my fear and continue doing what I'm doing: swing back and forth, in time with Cobra and Cat, who're blind as bats to what I'm seeing.

Those whirls of smoke coil up to the ceiling. As I

fix my gaze on them in anticipation of the Captain's arrival, the smoke blooms into a throng of dark moths that flit about the room. They move as one, ballooning, stretching, fluttering up, down, in a tumultuous swarm until they congregate above the restaurant door.

A drumroll announces the Captain. The doors swing open, and male dancers in black rush in. Hands clapping, fingers clicking, their feet tap to a beat of sharp advances and quick retreats as they progress, three abreast, to the top table. Behind them is Isaka and behind him, either side of the Captain, are Grey Eyes and Miguel.

It's the Captain I keep my eyes on; the Captain and those moths. Soon as he enters the restaurant – *whoosh!* – they swoop from the ceiling and hang over him, like a vibrating blanket of wings.

Last time I saw the Captain he didn't look too hot; but this? His hair's still the same: dyed black, combed over to hide a bald patch. Still has the same gold-topped ebony cane, but that's about it.

The man shuffling slowly towards the top table, the old man with a troupe of noisy dancers bustling in his wake, can hardly place one foot in front of the other. Supported at the elbow by Miguel and Grey Eyes, the stain of evil on his face has leeched deep into his bones. Man's got the shakes as well, and with every step he takes, twitches like a fish plucked from the sea, gasping for breath.

While Isaka strides ahead in a robe emblazoned

with silver embroidery that highlights the blue-black beauty of his face and skin, the Captain limps and falters. Stops to catch his breath, and the moths cluster in a black cloud above his head.

I've heard talk from Mimi and Midget Man of folk on their last legs. Heard 'em whisper late at night that when the bony finger of death prods someone, they're like a dead man walking. Never seen it before today, but now I have: the Captain hasn't much time left in this world, because the restless dead are intent on dragging him into theirs.

28

Turns out it's Isaka who opens the proceedings, Isaka who gets everyone to cheer the Captain, and then tells 'em to tuck in to the birthday feast. Isaka claps his hands and serving girls bring out salvers laden with the bounty of land and sea: huge hunks of cured ham, barbecued chicken, gigantic lobsters garlanded with oysters and shrimps. Boys in britches – all in masks – wield vast trays of paella and peppered potatoes. Heavy platters held aloft, then placed carefully on tables. Never seen so much food in the whole of my life; never smelled anything so delicious.

Guests pile food on their plates and eat. Eat till bellies full, the urge to sweeten their mouths tickles 'em into slicing ripe figs. They devour the figs with almond cake, strawberries and ice cream. Swill it down, and bit by bit, one fig after another, slices of cake on top of spoonfuls of ice cream, they gorge themselves.

And as their cheeks bloat and their stomachs bulge, the moths teeming above the Captain's head become fat as bats. Eyes protruding, they flick out their tongues, steadily multiplying until, as the meal draws to a close, not only are they above the Captain's head, they've covered the entire ceiling of the restaurant as well. From where I am, swaying on the trapeze, it doesn't look good. Not at all.

A half-smile flits over Isaka's mouth. A gleam of triumph surfaces on his face. Stands up, and as he does so, glances at the ceiling. A single, satisfied smirk that's all it takes; a look of recognition that convinces me that I'm not the only one present who sees 'em.

Isaka rearranges his features, taps a glass with a knife.

Grey Eyes, on the Captain's right, leans back and lights a cigar. Miguel, on the left, takes a swig of wine. The restaurant rustles and then quietens down.

'We've come here, ladies and gentlemen,' says Isaka, 'to celebrate the Captain's birthday. We're here to thank him for all he's done for us. Indeed, if he hadn't shown mercy on me many years ago, I wouldn't be with you today. You know my story well. This man here –' Isaka, a smile greasing his lips, turns to face the Captain – 'this man plucked me from a tempestuous sea. He saved my life when the boat I was in, a boat full of migrants and refugees, capsized.'

Isaka closes his eyes, bows, and hand on heart, salutes the Captain: 'My dearest friend, I thank you for everything you've done for me. Accept this gift as a token of my deep appreciation.'

Isaka waves at a figure at the entrance of the restaurant, and beckons.

It's a girl who I believe is Scarlett. Should be, even though she's replaced the clothes she was wearing with a blue evening gown that trails behind her. A butterfly mask still hides her face and covering her head is a long, black mantilla. In her outstretched hands is a brown paper parcel. She *must* be Scarlett. If it is her, every trace of playfulness in her walk has disappeared. Any hint of the teasing laughter she displayed earlier has evaporated, replaced by stiff, solemn majesty.

And with every move she makes, I sense that there's something wrong. Terribly wrong. I know there is. There has to be, for the closer she gets to the Captain, the faster some moths peel away from the main colony and cluster over her head.

Then I feel it again – that taste of mango on my tongue – followed by a blast of emotion that stirs my senses with Scarlett's and binds us together. I'm in Scarlett and Scarlett's in me, yet I can't stop her, or make her do what she was supposed to. I knew it!

I try to shout: 'No, Scarlett! No!' But my throat gags as her fury seizes me with an intensity that makes it impossible to decide which one of us is angrier: Scarlett or me.

'Please, Scarlett! No!' I want to scream. The storm

inside her throttles my voice and the only noise that comes out of me is a whimper.

Can't believe what I'm seeing – those huge moths dividing and multiplying as the violence deep in Scarlett's soul feeds 'em and helps 'em breed.

She stops in front of Miguel.

He looks at her puzzled.

She pulls the butterfly mask off her face, flings it at him, and he jumps back.

'You are so dead!' she cries, and ripping off the mantilla, brandishes her curls like a freedom flag as she shreds open the parcel.

Barrel Man and Grey Eyes see what's inside before anyone else. See it and leap at her, to topple her over, while Miguel lurches back, an arm raised to protect his face. But once the dagger's in Scarlett's hands, no one can overpower her. No one, not even me, 'cause whatever's riding her is a million times bigger than the two of us together. There's a whole world in her that, seething in its restlessness, is pumped up tight, about to strike.

Scarlett wields the dagger high and plunges it down.

'No!' Cat shrieks.

Cobra echoes Cat. And while I sit stunned, the two of 'em swing and somersault to the ground.

At that very moment, as Isaka nods to signal that we should begin our act, a glimmer of gold shimmers at the edge of my vision. It glows and fills my eyes.

If Isaka wanted a distraction, he's got one now.

'It's that bird again,' someone shouts. 'If it's here those gypsies are as well! Catch it! Kill it. Find them!'

Barrel Man clutches the neck of an empty bottle and flings it at Priss.

Misses.

'See to Miguel first, you idiots!' cries Grey Eyes. 'Get help.'

'Miguel. Miguelito! My son! My son!' the Captain cries.

The screams of a frightened old man shift in an instant, from baffled surprise to the keening of a parent on his knees, the blood of his child on his hands. 'Miguelito! What has she done to you? What have they done?'

'Priss!' I cry.

Too late. Priss, retracting her talons, drops on Barrel Man and takes a chunk out of his cheek.

'Leave, Priss! Leave!'

She flies over the Captain, over Scarlett, her golden wings batting aside the moths. They scatter, regroup, then descend in a haze of vengeful black wings.

This time the Captain sees 'em. I know he does, 'cause he gapes, shakes his head, and then shrieks as moths flap about his face and ears. Tries to bat 'em away, but they zoom into his eyes and open mouth.

His terror electrifies the restaurant. So much so, that the veil that hides this world from the next and conceals the seen from the unseen is torn asunder. And now everyone sees 'em. And everyone runs: old folk, young ones, men and women. Chairs crash to the ground, tables topple. People collide, screaming, waving arms, hands, napkins, bags – anything to keep the moths away.

I tumble from the trapeze on to a chair. Cat, way ahead of me, leaps from one table to the next till she reaches the top table. I follow, Cobra alongside me.

'Leave her alone!' Cat yells as Scarlett, in the clutches of one of Miguel's thugs, kicks him on the shin. Man staggers, falls over.

Scarlett thrusts the ceremonial dagger a second time. No one, it seems, can subdue her while she's unleashing the pent-up rage of a cargo of lost souls.

Cat propels herself forwards. Jumps once. Twice. Is about to reach Scarlett, when a bevy of moths flutter over her face and drive her back.

'Priss!' I scream. 'Priss! Help Cat.'

Priss, perched on a chandelier, stares at me, feathers quivering. Talons skitter on the domed surface of the chandelier. Crystal tinkles and Priss glides on to the window ledge and peers at me.

'It's me, Priss,' I say. 'It's me, Sante-girl.'

Bird jerks her head, her eyes flash and quiz me and I realise what's upsetting her.

I pull the blonde wig off my head. Take off my mask. Stretch out my hand and say: 'Priss, help me.'

A bottle smashes on the window ledge, and she flies away.

I know, before I turn to face him, that Barrel Man threw the bottle. And I know it's him behind me, his breath hot on my neck.

I swivel and then slowly back away from eyes wild with hate. His cheek gushes blood.

'Yes, I've got you, girl. Look at me! Look what you've done.'

I tread on someone behind me, someone cowering on the floor, head covered with a napkin. Stumble and Barrel Man lunges. Shakes me. Then – *boom!* – a tornado of moths attacks him, blackening his face with their wings.

'Help,' Barrel Man roars. 'Someone! Help me!'

Moths swarm around his mouth, down his gullet. Snuff the breath out of him till he's gasping for air. No one comes to his aid, 'cause everyone – including Concha, his wife and kids – is tangled up in the stampede to get out of there.

'Sante, here!' Cobra sweeps plates and flowers from the top table, bowls of figs and grapes, cutlery and glasses. I run to help him and whip out the tablecloths underneath. Throw one to Cobra, the other to Cat. The third I use to cover Barrel Man snivelling on the floor. I clear moth wings from his eyes, help him spit 'em out of his mouth.

Soon as I lay him down again, the thick, breathless

air becomes even more cloying and impenetrable. Only now the moths glimmer green and blue, their wings luminescent. And like exotic creatures of the deep, they dart up and down in shoals of light, prompted by invisible currents. The moths glow, and as their ghostly radiance brings an early gloaming to the room, the wind stirs outside and the sea at high tide smashes against pillars undergirding the Caleta.

Waves rush beneath the floor and Cat, her voice soft and low as a warm breeze in summer, tries to soothe Scarlett: 'Give me the dagger,' she urges. 'If you want, you can take this one instead.' Cat offers the knife strapped on the inside of her thigh.

Rage churning her up, Scarlett shakes her head and snarls. A bitter taste of bile floods my mouth and tugging at my heart, reels me ever closer to her.

So close, I can almost touch her, when Cobra cries: 'Sante, grab a napkin. Quick, Sante!' Cobra, kneeling over Miguel, presses napkins to his bloodied chest.

Miguel stirs. Groans. And Scarlett, the ceremonial dagger in her hand, shakes her head. 'Leave him! I'm warning you,' she says. 'Let him die!'

I look from Cobra to Scarlett as she hisses at me and I feel the wildness in her, unfurling in me.

'Sante! Now!' Cobra cries, and tearing my eyes away from Scarlett, I slip beside him on to my knees.

My right hand glides over Cobra's and as he places another napkin on Miguel's chest, I press on it, struggling to talk down a gathering dread that this splintering of one world into another is due to me: Scarlett, the moths, everything. Try to talk myself down, yet I can't stop fear chatting back to me. No, sir!

Never knew a body could weep so much blood and still be breathing.

Seen birds and beasts lose less and drop dead: a blackbird chick batted by a wild cat; rabbits stunned by Priss.

Never seen such a thing or heard the stuttering of a man's breath as life turns its back and tiptoes away from him.

I see it, hear it, and before any memories I have of Miguel overrule my inclination, my heart heaves, and instinct kicks in. 'Hold on, Miguel,' I say.

Scarlett lashes out. Cobra ducks, and the dagger almost slices my cheek. 'Take your hands off him! He's mine!'

'He's no good to you dead, Scarlett! Isaka! Where's Isaka?'

'He left with Grey Eyes,' Cobra tells me. 'Went to fetch help.'

Man orders us to skedaddle as soon as the fireworks begin, but then skedaddles himself, leaving us to clear up. The breath of a dying man is on my face, his blood on my hands while a whole world is turned inside out.

Then it comes to me: I've got to talk to Scarlett. 'It may not seem like it now,' I say, 'but you and me,

Scarlett – we're much better than this. Better than Miguel and his crew. Better than the Captain and the bad things he did.'

Scarlett laughs at me, intoxicated. A wild laugh that makes her a thousand times scarier than she ever was before. Laughs and her howls attract moths to her; moths that congregate, lighting up her ashen face and skin, the veins in the hand brandishing the dagger that glitters dangerously in the half-light. Scarlett glows incandescent with malice. And when the winged ghosts dive into her hair, my heart capsizes at the tumult inside her.

Cobra passes me another napkin. I place it on top of one already soaked with blood.

Miguel's breathing dips and, weak as a kitten, the fingers of his left hand clasp my wrist.

'Don't make me do it, Sante,' says Scarlett. 'If you don't get away from that man right now, I swear, I'll do you in as well.'

She threatens me and her eyes begin to lose their lustre. Blinks, unable to focus on what's right in front of her. She twitches, distracted, then cocks her head as if tuning in to a scene only she can see.

I gauge the pulse and flow of her and register what she's hearing: a faint *tap, tap, tap* that slowly becomes louder. The Captain's ebony cane.

I look behind me. The Captain, crumpled on the floor, open mouth crammed with the crushed abdomens of moths, raises a hand to where his eyes used to be: hollows blackened with discarded wings and antennae. What's left of him twitches one last time as he steps slow as a parson on the highway to hell.

'Drop the knife, Scarlett,' says Cat. 'Please, for my sake, drop it.'

Scarlett closes her eyes. The dagger tilts. When Scarlett looks out at the world again, her pupils contract into pinpricks of anguish. She stares at me a second time. But now, she reminds me of my dream last night. Trapped, floundering, unsure where she is, she gives the distinct impression of never having seen me before.

The moths surrounding her flicker and dim. And as their light fades, I sense their hold over Scarlett waning.

'Scarlett,' I say. 'Let's finish what we started.'

A vacant, sealed expression steals over her face and I try to reach her once again. 'It wasn't supposed to end like this, Scarlett. This isn't about you. It's a day of reckoning for those who drowned to save me, a day to put things right. Put the dagger down and let's be done with 'em.'

Scarlett gazes perplexed at the weapon in her hand. Then, at last, she drops it.

The moment the dagger clatters to the ground, the room convulses with light. The gloaming brightens, searing our eyes with the brilliance of a noonday sun. As dusk returns and gradually lightens into day, the moths wither, sparkle, dwindle, disappear. Until there's nothing left of them or the dagger but patches of black ash on the restaurant floor.

29

If I've said it once, I've said it a thousand times. I shall never understand the reasoning of Old Ones. They tell us they're outlaws one day, yet by the afternoon of the next, they do something that rocks us even more: the one thing they've warned us against time and time again.

'Don't talk to black-boots! Don't go anywhere near 'em!'

They drummed it into me from when I was a toddler able to string words together, but wise enough to admit – despite Priss's prompting – that I'm a creature that will never fly.

So, imagine my surprise when, just as I'm beginning to think that Miguel's definitely a goner, they thunder into the Caleta restaurant with a battalion of black-boots led by Federico Angel de Menendez.

'*You* again,' he says and my heart sings, for skulking

behind the black-boots, trying to manoeuvre around 'em to get to us, is my circus family: Mama Rose in the lead, Redwood and Lizzie behind her, and beside them, Midget Man, Mimi and Carlos. Families! They may look different on the outside, but once you've adopted one, like I've done mine, you learn to take the rough with the smooth, the good with the bad. Tears of relief dribble down my cheeks and gratitude overwhelms me. Not only have the Old Ones come for us, they've brought help as well.

First off, while Mama Rose hugs us up and makes sure we're OK, a team of paramedics take Miguel away. Black-boots help Barrel Man to stand and escort him out for questioning. Then they seal off the restaurant. Say it's a crime scene and we're not to touch anything.

'Can't I wash my hands?' I ask.

'Hold on,' Menendez replies.

Can't say for sure that I'll be able to. Now the commotion is over, the adrenalin rush firing me up stalls and exhaustion settles in my bones. Weaker than a gnat, I resist the temptation to nestle in Mama Rose's arms. I'm too old for that now. Nonetheless, sensing my inclination, Mama Rose hugs me up again.

We're herded into the dressing room as a team in white overalls arrives and start snapping a whole heap of photographs. They take photographs of the Captain's body and gold-topped cane, followed by snaps of tipped over tables and chairs. Snaps of food strewn on the floor. Then they focus on the patches of black ash and scoop up samples for testing.

After that's done, Menendez decides that it's high time he talked to us. That's when Mama Rose freaks out Big Time. Says she won't allow us to be part of any interrogation that coerces us into giving false statements. Indeed, she makes what's about to happen sound every bit as menacing as interrogation techniques Redwood once told us about. 'Torture by another name,' he called it.

'But, *senora*,' Menendez says to Mama Rose. 'You will be present throughout the interviews, I assure you. You may call a lawyer now if you wish.'

Mama Rose replies in a voice that puts her way up on a throne with the high and mighty: 'We alerted you to what was happening here today, officer, because we believed our children's lives were in danger. Concerned for their safety, we tipped you off. So remember, my children have done *nothing* wrong. If anything, they're the victims not the perpetrators here.'

Menendez hears the clenched fist in Mama Rose's English and takes in the strength of her generous frame, the fire in those dark pebbled eyes. About to reply, Carlos intervenes. Rubs Menendez's arm and rattles at him in rapid Spanish. Speaks fast, so fast, I can't make out what he's saying. What I do know is there aren't any bad words in his utterances: no name-calling, no mention of black gypsy scum.

Truth be told, I wouldn't mind having a conversation to figure out what happened back there. Wouldn't say no to a chance to get my head around what I saw. There's no hope of that happening. Not while Mama Rose is clucking around us like a mother hen with her chicks. From the glances and nods we've exchanged since the black-boots turned up – the three of us – Cobra, Cat and me – have agreed, with some eye-balling encouragement from the Old Ones, that when pressed, we're to shred our story to the bare bones.

Menendez nods at Carlos, apparently agreeing with him. Then his eyes drift in Scarlett's direction. She may be wearing a blue evening dress – a dress splashed with blood – but the tangle of red curls about her face is seared in his memory. The girl who almost drowned herself.

Scarlett, still trembling, is clutching at Cat like a sinking child to a lifebuoy while Cat whispers. Looks as if they're sharing secrets, but I know better. In much the same way that I murmur to Taj Mahal when he's skittish, Cat's soothing Scarlett. Keeping her voice low and steady, she rubs Scarlett's forearm, her back. Strokes her. Pets her. Urges her to breathe long and deep to ease her shaking.

'Is she one of yours?' Menendez asks Mama Rose.

'She's a friend of my daughter's.'

'I shall have to talk to her and your children before I let them go,' Menendez replies.

Easier said than done, I reckon, 'cause the way Scarlett's behaving right now, I don't imagine she'll talk to anyone but Cat for some time. Won't let Cat out of her sight, in fact. Even so, unless I try to shape it first, the truth will out in the end. Can't hide the stink of a dead mouse with the best perfume in the world. Better jump in before the black-boot sniffs it: 'I don't mind talking to you,' I say to Menendez.

Mama Rose rolls her eyes at me: a signal to stop talking and sit tight, to desist from foolishness this instant! Redwood and Bizzie Lizzie glare at me as well. All of 'em do, except for Midget Man, who most probably has an inkling of Scarlett's china-cup fragility. Touch her clumsily and she'll shatter. Prod her too much and she'll break.

'Be careful, Sante,' Midget Man whispers, before Carlos intervenes once again.

'Why not interview them all together,' he says. 'We have a long journey ahead of us.'

Perhaps he sees what I'm sensing: Scarlett inching ever closer to a precipice of No Return.

Menendez and his black-boots *um* and *ah* at Carlos's suggestion. Once they've agreed, the Old Ones deliberate and Mama Rose finally gives her consent. Then we drag the stools we sat on not so long ago to a chair by a window of the dressing room.

It's late afternoon. Sunlight dapples a silver-grey sea. Cormorants, wings outstretched, dry their feathers in the last of the sun's rays. In the distance a flash of gold whizzes through the sky. Priss, by the look of it.

Menendez sits, pulls out a notebook and asks the question he's been mulling over since he arrived: 'My friends, what transpired in there?'

Cobra and Cat turn to me, as if they're so shook up, I'm the only one present who knows her left from her right, her up from her down. And if I don't, that's too bad, 'cause they've decided – since I put my hand up for it – that I shall do the talking for them. Truth is, there're more questions than answers scurrying through my head. Questions such as, where's the ceremonial dagger? What happened to it? Can objects move from one world to another? I twizzle the golden bangle on my wrist and decide, yes, they can. Then I promise myself that once this ordeal is over, I'll go walkabout to the sea that cradled me. Only this time I'll ask Cobra to accompany me.

I think my thoughts and after due consideration reply to Menendez: 'Mister, I'd love to answer your question but I'd be lying if I said that I knew what happened. It started this way: a man who saw us perform the other day, Isaka, invited us to entertain the Captain and his friends on the trapeze. We were entertaining them when the others came.'

'What others?'

We've agreed to stick to plain facts stripped of any speculation; the reason being, a simple tale is the easiest to tell, and the easiest to repeat a thousand times over.

'Looked like moths to me. Isn't that so, Cobra?'

Cobra nods. Cat would too if she wasn't busy with Scarlett. Girl's likely to collapse if she doesn't calm down quickly.

'Moths?' Menendez asks.

'Yes, moths! Moths as big as my fist, that's how big they were. As soon as everyone saw them, they ran out of there faster than bats through the gates of hell.'

'Then what?'

'I can't say, mister. It was wild in there with people running everywhere. And those moths.'

'Did you see what happened to the Captain?'

'No, sir!' I reply. 'But I reckon the moths did that.'

'And the same moths stabbed his son?'

I pause. It's never a good idea to rattle off a lie quickly. Best to prepare the ground before laying a falsehood down. 'I didn't see a thing, mister. I was up on the trapeze, like I said. We all were.'

Cobra and Cat nod, while Scarlett's uncontrolled shaking escalates to heartwrenching sobbing.

'This interview has to stop,' Redwood says. 'The poor girl is in no fit state to be here. She's traumatised.'

Menendez turns to Scarlett, and with his voice low and confiding, asks: 'Did you see anything, *senorita*?'

Wracked by weeping, unable to answer, Scarlett

simply quivers while every single one of us, except the black-boots, silently will her to reply: 'No.'

'Please, Scarlett. Please,' I plead mutely. 'Go on. Do it. Say it.'

She shakes her head. Which is just as well, 'cause from the throb and thrust of her, I don't think she remembers what she did. Won't most probably for a long time. And when she does remember, she'll have to decide how much was down to her and what was due to the others: the spirits of the dead. She may never fully know.

When her sobbing eases, Cat retrieves a phone from a pouch on her lap: 'This may help you understand what's been going on,' she says. 'I got it from one of the Captain's men. That barrel of a man that your men led away just now. Took it from him when he was laid low.'

'Thank you,' says Menendez. He doesn't look at the contents of Barrel Man's phone, just pushes it aside.

It's then, and only then, when he's rustling through the possibilities in his mind, that I'm tempted to tell him more. Like an itch on my tongue, I'm minded to tell him about the others. Tell him there's a whole heap of them out there without a home for the night. Tell about the Captain's party and what I saw with my own two eyes. I bite my tongue to keep the words inside, 'cause with Carlos's friends on the case, and the pictures in Barrel Man's phone, the truth will come out eventually. I keep my tongue tied, and sure enough Menendez stops probing.

He says to Carlos: '*Hombre*, you may take them home now. If I need to speak to them again, I'll get in touch with these witnesses through you. Understood?'

Carlos smiles. He knows as well as I do that the Captain's got a better chance of resurrecting from the dead than we have of sticking around to answer more questions from black-boots.

Next morning I return to the Caleta beach with Priss and Cobra. Priss flies away to hunt for food while Cobra stays beside me.

In my left hand is Mamadou's flute, in my right, a small boat. Cobra helped me make it after supper at Carlos's last night. A meandering meal peppered with queries from the Old Ones. They wanted proper responses to the questions posed earlier by Menendez, and a good deal more besides. Such as: why hadn't we told them of our plans to entertain at the Captain's party? Did we appreciate how worried they'd been when they woke up and discovered us gone?

Mama Rose wiped tears from her eyes. 'It's a basic

courtesy,' she said. 'Always keep us informed.'

Mimi moaned. Then Bizzie Lizzie said: 'Don't ever do that again, Sante-girl, you hear?

'Yeah,' Redwood said. 'We expected better from you, son. Don't ever hightail it out of here without letting us know, understood?'

I nodded. Cobra did too. No chance of Cat complying, 'cause she was already up in the pigeonnier helping Scarlett clean up.

The Old Ones exchanged nods and glances and then chose that moment, of all the moments in the world – when we were exhausted, battered and bruised – to unload a barrelful of botheration on us. What really happened in the restaurant? How did the Captain die? What part, if any, did Scarlett play in Miguel's stabbing? Moths? What on earth was I talking about when I mentioned moths? Families! When you want them out of your hair, they stick to you meaner than an infestation of nits.

Between us, Cobra and I told 'em what we could. I did most of the talking as usual, but when I think about it, it's only right that I should. Told 'em about the unquiet dead, their day of reckoning, and the forces unleashed at the Captain's celebration. And no, I had no idea of the whereabouts of Grey Eyes and Isaka. They disappeared with everyone else in the commotion, so how was I supposed to know where they were?

Once the Old Ones had finished probing and were digesting what I'd said, I mentioned what I was thinking of doing next day.

'Makes sense,' Midget Man replied, caressing his beard. Tends his beard as carefully as a rose bush he does – as tenderly as Mimi brushes her hair at the end of every evening. 'Saying goodbye is never easy, Sante,' he added. 'And it doesn't necessarily mean those ghosts won't want to talk to you again. Still, it's worth a try.'

Mimi, running an ivory comb through peppered grey locks, agreed. They all did. Even Mama Rose who, at first, was reluctant to let me return to Cádiz. But I did. She couldn't stop me.

The tide's low again today and the sea calm. A mysterious grey haze swirls over the water. One of those shadowy sea-hazes, which makes it impossible to tell from a distance where the shoreline ends and sea begins, but creates a blurring of time and space. Seagulls strut and call on boats beached on the shore as Cobra and I step through the mist to the water's edge.

As soon as I've done what I'm here to do, our plan is to leave Spain. Travel to France and catch a ferry to England. The next hurdle will be to find out if Scarlett will go back to her parents. I'm not sure if I'd want to if I were her, but you can never tell. As it is, if Cat gets her way, Scarlett will stay.

They depend on each other, those two. Scarlett may still be splashing in the deep end of crazy, but she's winkled herself deep into Cat's heart. Whatever happens between 'em, we've decided that Mama Rose's Family Circus is heading to Wales to meet what's left of the Williams clan. According to Mama Rose, they live in a big country house close to Brecon. Deer's Leap, it's called: an ancient manor house with space enough for all of us, not to mention fields for Taj Mahal and wide-open sky for Priss to roam in. Imagine! We're to live in a house with a roof over our heads and stay put for three months at least. Even Mama Rose and Redwood think it's a good idea to hole up for a while. Lie low over winter, so that by the time spring arrives in a froth of green shoots, we'll have an idea what to do next.

But first I have to finish this.

The boat in my hand is made of rectangular pieces of wood, a cork keel and an oilcloth sail. After we'd glued it together, Cobra helped me paint it red, yellow and green. On the hull is a black star in memory of the restless dead here and everywhere, lost souls who drowned in the cold, dark grave of the sea.

I explain what I intend to do and Cobra stares at me with that puzzled frown he's been giving me lately: raised eyebrow, greens dark with concern.

'Sante-girl,' he says. 'I don't know how to tell you this, but you can't return a gift that doesn't exist. There's nothing there.' He lifts my arm.

The bangle slides to my elbow and I feel the delicate throb of its beauty. 'You can't see it?'

Cobra shakes his head.

'It's here,' I tell him. 'As real as your eyes in front of me now.'

Shakes his head a second time and I remember. No wonder he was spooked when I first showed him my bangle. No wonder he glances at me when I start playing with it.

Silence nestles between us while I listen in and begin to appreciate his predicament, mine as well. My special talent, as Mama Rose calls it, goes deeper than delving into the fizz and whirl of people's feelings. I may have had a knack for it before, but with the help of my bangle, I've seen beyond this world and glimpsed mysteries most people, Cobra included, have no indication of.

'Does it bother you', I ask him, at last, 'that you can't see it? Or d'you think that, like Scarlett, I'm a bit psycho?'

Cobra smiles and touches the wrist on which the bangle lies. 'I certainly don't like it when I notice you toying with something you believe in that I can't register.'

Pauses 'cause his tongue's tied. Unties it by caressing the crease of my palm until, suddenly, the love-shine in him beams from his face and licks mine. 'No, Sante,' he says. 'I don't think you're crazy. You're my best girl. I love you. I want you to be safe, that's all.'

'Then help me, Cobra. Help me do this properly.'

I sit cross-legged at the water's edge, close my eyes, and step into the ocean of feeling inside me. The ocean Cobra dredged up with our first kiss. His palm fondling my knee brings tears to my eyes, as every little bit of me – heart, head, body and soul – turns inwards to dwell on parents I never knew.

I recall the faces of my mother and father as they appeared to me in my dreams: the curve of my mother's cheek, the gentle slant of her eyes, my father's strength and laughter. I brood over every single thing that I remember, every glance and every gesture; and sensing the breath of their presence around me, I feel a twinge of anxiety. Once the *pit-patter* of my pulse steadies, I open my eyes, and say their names out loud:

'Kofi Prempeh and Amma Serwah, I wish I'd got to know you better. That isn't possible now, and yet true as my blood is red, I shan't forget what you've revealed of yourselves. I'd like to believe that, somehow, wherever I go, you'll be with me. Don't know exactly how that's going to happen. But Cobra here told me not so long ago that you are inside me, same as his parents are in him. Isn't that so, Cobra?'

Cobra nods and his hand on my knee tightens.

'You see,' I say to my parents. 'A part of you will always be with me. And yet, to be present in this time and place, to occupy the space you created for me, I've got to let you go. Walk good! Travel well.'

Eyes moist with the salt-tang of the sea, my tears fall.

Cobra lights a candle. He drips wax on the boat's bow and fixes the candle in place. When I'm ready, and I'm no longer blubbing like a lost child; when the ache in my heaving chest has eased, I take the bangle from my wrist and fasten it to the sail. Then I push the boat out to sea.

As the tide carries it away, I hear one of the melodies Mamadou performed through me. Hear it drifting on the dawn mist. I reach for the flute and begin to play.

The tune that emerges conjures images from my dreams: a lush, magical forest glade and in it a golden mango tree; beyond that, as the crow flies, a flat savannah landscape dotted with giant baobabs. The music paints pictures of magnificent cities with buildings that seem to touch the sky, gigantic pyramids appear, and beside them, caravans of camels travelling over dunes scorched by the glare of the sun. Buoyant and joyful, as generous as the ocean inside me, the melody is laced with high notes that set my toes tapping while my heart soars. Then, out of nowhere, a sad song in a minor key takes hold of my fingers.

The boat sails into the deep as I thank my parents and the cargo of souls who died with them. I thank them through Mamadou's tune. Even so, the moment the boat disappears my heart lurches, and suddenly I smell 'em: the fragrance of cedarwood on my father's skin, mango on my mother's breath. I want them to come back to me. I want them to stay. And if they don't, I shall get up and follow them into the sea.

I manage to keep playing the only way I can: by imagining my father's hand on my shoulder, my mother running her fingers through my hair. Then, as Priss swoops from the sky and settles at my feet, their presence grows stronger still. My mother's nose nuzzles against mine; my father pats my shoulder. My mother kisses my cheek. She kisses me again and again and each time she kisses me, I believe that I shall never let her go. Never. Until through my tears, I realise that it's Cobra kissing my cheek, Cobra's hand on my shoulder.

I continue playing for a good while longer. I play till Cobra takes my hand and pulling me up, says: 'I think we should go, Sante. We've a long journey ahead of us.'

'Yes,' I say to him. 'It's time to go home.' Time to return to my circus family and walk good.

Acknowledgements

Thanks to my fabulous editor at Zephyr, Fiona Kennedy, who encouraged me to have another crack at this story and our mutual friend, Jinny Johnson, who introduced us. To Maya, Cam and Colin for reading earlier drafts of *A Jigsaw of Fire and Stars* and being unstintingly generous. And finally to my remarkable parents, Emeritus Professor Emmanuel Augustus Badoe and Mercy Fadoa Badoe, who gave me time and space to pursue what I love best in the world. Thank you!

Yaba Badoe
London,
May 2017

Wolf-light

by Yaba Badoe

Three young women, Zula, Adoma and Linet,
are sisters of the secret order of the heart. Born in
wolf-light, the magical dusk, in Mongolia, Ghana and
Cornwall, they are custodians of the sacred sites
of their homelands.

When copper miners plunder Zula's desert home
in Gobi Altai, and Adoma's forest and river are
polluted by gold prospectors, it is only a matter
of time before the lake Linet guards with her life
is also in jeopardy. How far will Zula, Adoma and
Linet go to defend the wellbeing of their homes?
And when all else fails, will they have the courage
to summon the ancient power of their order, to
make the landscape speak in a way that
everyone will hear?

Coming in 2019

At Zephyr we are proud to publish books you can read and re-read time and time again because they tell a brilliant story and because they entertain you.

That's why we've launched the Zephyr Review Crew. We'd like to hear about the things you love in our books and what you think we could do better.

Join our review crew and be the first to read the very best new books. Members will receive exclusive author content and chances to win signed books. Just drop us a line at hello@headofzeus.com

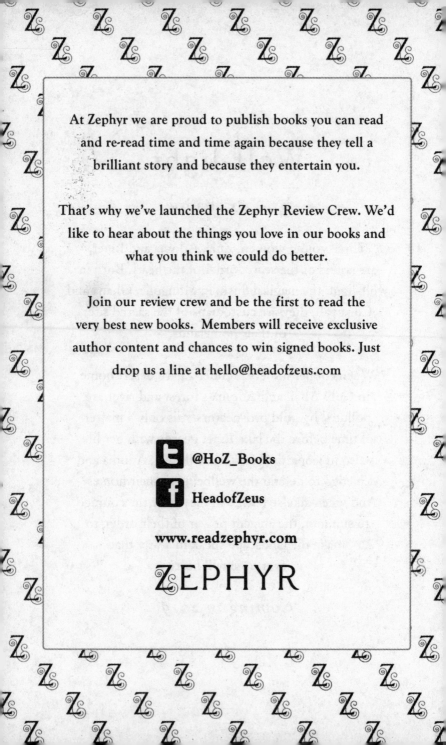 @HoZ_Books

HeadofZeus

www.readzephyr.com

ZEPHYR